Liz Byrski is a novelist, non-fiction writer, former journalist and ABC broadcaster, with more than fifty years' experience in the British and Australian media. She is the author of eleven bestselling novels, including *Gang of Four* and *A Month of Sundays*, as well as more than a dozen non-fiction books. She lives close to Fremantle in Western Australia, with Gazza, her three-year-old rescue dog who is in charge of exercise, household security and chasing cats. She has two sons and twin grandsons.

www.lizbyrski.com

Also by Liz Byrski

Fiction
Gang of Four
Food, Sex & Money
Belly Dancing for Beginners
Trip of a Lifetime
Bad Behaviour
Last Chance Café
In the Company of Strangers
Family Secrets
The Woman Next Door
A Month of Sundays

Non-fiction
Remember Me
Getting On: Some Thoughts on Women and Ageing
In Love and War: Nursing Heroes

LIZ BYRSKI

At the End of the Day

MACMILLAN
Pan Macmillan Australia

Pan Macmillan acknowledges the Traditional Custodians of country throughout Australia and their connections to lands, waters and communities. We pay our respect to Elders past and present and extend that respect to all Aboriginal and Torres Strait Islander peoples today. We honour more than sixty thousand years of storytelling, art and culture.

The characters in this book are fictitious and any resemblance to real persons, living or dead, is purely coincidental.

First published 2021 in Macmillan by Pan Macmillan Australia Pty Ltd
1 Market Street, Sydney, New South Wales, Australia, 2000

A catalogue record for this book is available from the National Library of Australia

Typeset in 12/17 pt Palatino Roman by Post Pre-press Group

Printed by IVE

Aboriginal and Torres Strait Islander people should be aware that this book may contain images or names of people now deceased.

The paper in this book is FSC® certified. FSC® promotes environmentally responsible, socially beneficial and economically viable management of the world's forests.

Chapter One

On the day she is due to fly home to Australia, Miriam Squires is sitting at a table in the hotel restaurant, sipping her second cup of coffee and staring at the English Channel, which is so still it looks more like a lake than the sea. It's the end of her annual visit to the UK, always a month or six weeks with her sister Alice in Oxford, followed by a few days of nostalgia here in Brighton, where they had grown up. The town, with its stony beach and two piers, one thriving, the other now a wreck, always lures her back. But now – at seventy-five, with painful mobility problems – the prospect of long queues, struggles with baggage and hours in the air is daunting. Today, she thinks, is probably the last time she will see the place where she was born. It's not just the misery of the journey itself, but her increasing disenchantment with England. Beautiful villages have become ugly towns bordered by industrial estates; unique country pubs have been swallowed up by hospitality chains, and those shops that can't withstand the shift to online shopping are disappearing, leaving high streets sadly diminished.

'Even Marks and Spencer's is fading away,' Alice had told her. 'Imagine no M and S knickers or bras! And then there's Brexit. England's a basket case – it'll be a disaster if we leave the EU. You're so lucky with that Jacinda Ardern.'

'She's the prime minister of New Zealand,' Mim had said, 'but I do think you'd love Australia. You should come and stay with me, Al.' She has issued the invitation many times over the years.

'I'll think about it,' Alice had said. 'I really will.'

That's what she always said.

Back in her room, Mim finishes her packing and checks her watch. It's almost time to head to the airport. Before leaving Brighton, she had planned to visit the old hospital where she spent so long as a child, but she has run out of time. She always promises herself she'll go, but here she is, decades later, and she still hasn't done it. *So that's it*, she thinks. *I'll never go back there now, and what would be the point of it anyway?*

Relieved to have avoided the hospital once again, she wanders over to the glass door and steps out onto the balcony. The weather is surprisingly warm, and the beach is packed with holidaymakers; even the sea seems crowded. The Palace Pier is heaving with people queueing for the fairground rides. Mim turns westwards towards the skeletal remains of the abandoned West Pier. Now totally cut off from the shore, its bare, iron bones seem etched in charcoal against the stunning blues of the sea and sky. The pier and its changing life have always fascinated her. As a child she had known it as a working pier and a piece of history, a dignified reminder of Victorian Brighton, but over the years it has been battered by the ferocity of the elements and twice attacked by arsonists. It's just an old wreck now, but to Mim it is dignified and haunting. She has taken its life story rather personally.

She turns away from the pier and goes back into her room, zips up her suitcase and takes a final look around. Satisfied that she has left nothing behind, she takes out her phone and dials Jodie.

It's Kirra who answers. 'Jodie's with a patient at the moment,' the vet nurse says. 'A labrador. She's cleaning his anal glands.'

'Yuck! Well, don't disturb her then. Could you just tell her that I'm leaving for Gatwick Airport now? I'll call again from Doha.'

'Of course, I'll tell her as soon as she's free. I know she has the details in the diary to pick you up at the airport. You have a good trip home.'

Mim chucks her phone into her bag, thankful that she chose a job in which she only has to clean up old books rather than dogs' anal glands.

Ten minutes later, she pulls out of the hotel car park and, with a final glance at the old pier, drives along the seafront. There is just one more thing she has to do . . .

A couple of minutes later, she turns into a side road and draws up outside a small second-hand bookshop. Both her legs are aching badly this morning and she is careful to steady herself as she gets out of the car. Sometimes she uses a stick but, to her own disgust, she's twice managed to trip herself up with it.

The bookshop seems dark as she steps inside out of the sunlight. The walls are packed from floor to ceiling with books, and the narrow staircase on one side leads up to another floor which she knows is just the same. She'd spent more than an hour here yesterday and bought so many books that she had to ask the owner to post them home for her. Even so, she'd forgotten to buy what she had actually gone there for in the first place, and now she heads straight towards the shelves.

The owner recognises her immediately. 'Back for more?'

'I got so carried away yesterday I forgot what I originally came for!'

'Ah well, you can never have too many books,' he says.

'I couldn't agree more,' Mim replies. 'I have a second-hand bookshop of my own back home in Australia.'

'Is it as chaotic as mine?'

She laughs. 'Not quite,' she says, 'but close.' She is lying, because her shop is neat and well organised. It has to be, or she'd always be falling over things or losing them.

She pays for the books and heads back to her car, and minutes later she is on the road, heading to the motorway.

'No!' she says aloud as she passes the exit which leads to the hospital. 'Goodbye, Harold House – I don't need to see you again. Goodbye, England – I won't be coming back.' And she straightens her shoulders, puts her foot down and moves out into the fast lane towards the airport.

Chapter Two

*M*athias Vander wanders through the business lounge of Doha Airport, looking for a quiet spot in which to spend the next three hours. The flight from Brussels always seems endless, and he thinks he should have a shower, but that feels like a bit of a hassle. What he needs is a cup of coffee, and something sweet and delicious that he can eat in private without strangers watching him.

'What is it with you?' his daughter had asked him recently. 'Do you think you're so famous now that people will stop and stare? *Oh, look there's that writer – Mathias something or other – and he's dropping crumbs down the front of his suit!*'

Mathias had laughed. 'Not quite, but there is an element of that, I suppose.' What he doesn't say is that he is fine about being seen eating if he's among other people who are eating but eating alone in a public place makes him feel vulnerable, something that stems back to the time when, as a teenager, he had spent a lot of time hiding from all but his closest friend. But he has no desire to discuss his early life in post-war Belgium, not even with the one remaining member of his family.

Hearing the faint sound of water, Mathias remembers that the last time he stopped in Doha on his way home to Australia he had found a seat by a large shallow pool with a fountain playing gently in the middle of it. He abandons all thoughts of a shower, deciding that it would be far more pleasant to sit near water than to actually get into it, and heads off in what he thinks is the right direction. To his satisfaction, the area is just as he remembers it. There is a small bar with tea and coffee, wines and spirits, cakes and sandwiches at the far end of the pool, and the few people who have settled nearby are reading or sleeping rather than talking. It is invitingly peaceful. Mathias makes for a seat in a far corner where there are two pairs of armchairs with high backs facing each other. All four seats are empty. He puts his coat on one and his cabin bag alongside it, delighted to have so much space to himself. He dreads having to make conversation with strangers. The prospect of boarding the aircraft and finding himself in close proximity to someone who wants to talk brings him out in a sweat. He collects a cup of coffee, a smoked salmon sandwich on rye bread and two miniature chocolate eclairs, and sits down with a sigh of relief. As usual he had not eaten and barely slept on the flight from Brussels. His anxiety about being in the city takes a long time to dissipate once he has left. Old memories of the fear he had experienced there as a teenager overwhelm him. He'd been to London first, where he'd spoken at an international conference and caught up with his European publisher, and from there flew to Brussels, where he picked up a car and went straight to Bruges. He stayed for a couple of days in a small hotel near the canals, close to the place where he'd lived as a child, and where he and Therese had lived when they were first married.

Sitting at a pavement table, sipping a cup of coffee, he had watched the slow movement of the water and recalled riding his bike along the cobbled streets when he was young, stopping to talk to the nuns and to the lace-makers who sat on little stools in their doorways, black velvet cushions in their laps, spinning their bobbins at mesmerising speed. He'd loved this place, but his nostalgia was mixed with pain; in the late 1950s he and his mother had fled Bruges, seeking refuge with Mathias's maternal grandparents in the Ardennes, where he spent much of his teenage years. This year he had, once again, returned to the Ardennes, driving there from Bruges to visit his oldest friend, Luc, whom he had met on his first day at the new school there. After all these years, and despite the vast physical distance that now separates them, their friend-ship retains a special significance. It is unlikely they will be able to meet again. Luc has only a few months left at best, and this knowledge weighed heavily on them. They had taken slow walks in the woods, done some fishing in a nearby stream, sat beneath the trees drinking good red wine, and talking – of their youth, adulthood and the state of the world. Luc's wife, Patrice, had plied them with their favourite meals. Fifteen years younger than her husband, she was lovingly firm with him about his medications, his diet and exercise. Watching them together, Mathias could see that his own future would be different, without a partner. Therese, the love of his life, had died eighteen years earlier, so the care, if he needs it, will be institutional, delivered with professional efficiency and, hopefully, some compassion, but certainly not love. He is determined that he will not be a burden on his daughter, though Carla has already told him she will fight him on this.

After two weeks with Luc, Mathias drove from the Ardennes back to Brussels. He will have to learn to live without Luc, just as he has slowly learned to live without Therese. Mathias had always been a shy boy and he grew into a shy, anxious teenager. But in his twenties, when he had returned to Bruges to teach part time at the College of Europe, he met and married Therese, who worked there as a secretary, and his life began to expand. Unlike Mathias, Therese did not see life as a hazardous journey along a pathway scattered with dangerous potholes and grenades that could explode at any time. She was practical, strong-willed and sufficiently confident to risk marriage to an as yet unpublished writer. Mathias had written a series of six books for children called *Adventures with Capo*, as well as an adult novel, some short stories and essays. But everything he sent out came back to him accompanied by rejection slips. It was only when Therese discovered she was pregnant that they agreed he would have to put his writing aside for a while and ask the college for more work. Three weeks later, on the afternoon of the day he was offered a full-time position as a lecturer, he arrived home to find a letter from a publisher to whom he had sent *Adventures with Capo* seven months earlier. They were offering him a contract with a surprisingly large advance. Mathias took the job at the College of Europe, but once the first *Capo* book was published a novel for adults was contracted by the same publishing house. He resigned from teaching to write full time, and his work became better, stronger, more innovative. Slowly he was recognised in other European countries and eventually in America and England. *Adventures with Capo* continued to thrive and became a success as an animated television series in several countries and, later, a feature film by Disney. Now his novels and non-fiction books are widely published, going straight to the bestseller lists in his home, Australia, and many other countries as well. Money is no longer an issue.

Mathias wakes with a jolt to find that he has been asleep for more than an hour. His back hurts, his coffee is cold and, to his irritation, a young man in uniform is pushing a woman in a wheelchair straight towards his quiet space. He picks up his book and pretends to be reading.

The attendant stops the chair, and the woman gets out, gathers her things and settles into a facing seat.

'Please, madam, you stay here?' the attendant says. 'I can know that I find you here when I come to take you to your flight to Perth.'

'I'll be here,' she assures him. She looks across at Mathias. 'Don't worry, I promise not to talk to you.'

Mathias blushes and takes off his glasses. 'I'm sorry – was I so transparent?'

'You were! But only because you looked like I feel when I've found a nice quiet spot and someone else intrudes.'

He gets to his feet. 'I'm going to get myself a fresh cup of coffee. Can I redeem myself by fetching something for you?'

'Thank you, that would be lovely. White tea, please, no sugar.'

Mathias fetches the tea and more mini eclairs.

'These are very good,' he says, putting them down in front of her.

'They look delicious.' She pulls a book out of her bag, puts it on the low table and gets out her phone. 'I have just one phone call to make,' she says apologetically. 'I'll keep my voice down and after that I shall be as quiet as a dead snake.'

He laughs. 'I shall not try to listen.'

'It will be very mundane,' she says. 'I'm sure your book is far more interesting.'

Mathias is not so certain. His book was a farewell gift from Luc's personal library.

'All my life I've been recommending books to you, and you have usually enjoyed them,' Luc had told him. 'This is my last recommendation – a final request from a dying man so you will feel obliged to read it. When you have read it, call me, and we will talk about it.'

'This book is about Expo!' Mathias said, so shocked that his hands began to shake. 'You know I never want to hear or see –'

'Yes, I do know!' Luc interrupted. 'Of course, I know that. The very thought of that time is like the Berlin Wall: insurmountable – except that it wasn't. People broke down the wall and claimed their freedom. Now *you* need to break down *your* wall. There is no longer anything to fear, realistically you must know that. I am your oldest, closest friend and I know things that you feel you cannot share with others. But soon I will be gone, and there will be no one left to help you bear that load. I would prefer to die knowing that you have banished the demons.'

Mathias looked down at the book. 'Perhaps I could read it the next time we are together?'

Luc had looked him in the eye. 'Mathias, we both know that there is no next time. Do this for me, and for yourself. You won't regret it.'

Even though the last thing he wanted to do was read about 1958 and the Brussels Exhibition, of course Mathias had agreed to do as his friend wished. He had started the novel on the flight from Brussels but didn't make it past the first page, even though it is by Jonathan Coe, his favourite author.

When I get home, he tells himself now, glancing at the book on his lap. His secluded house in the Dandenong Ranges outside Melbourne is the place in the world that he finds most conducive to reading and writing. Instead, by the calm of the pool, he takes a deep breath and picks up a newspaper.

Chapter Three

Jodie is almost asleep when the phone rings.

'Hello?' she mumbles, her eyes still closed.

'It's just me,' Mim says. 'What time is it in Fremantle? You're not out delivering a calf or anything, are you?'

'I was just dropping off to sleep, actually.' Jodie yawns and sits up against the pillows. 'Though chances are I'll be called out in the middle of the night to deliver a foal down at the riding stables. Jim Strong's mare is due. Where are you?'

'Doha Airport. They'll be calling the flight quite soon. Sorry I woke you.'

'It's okay, but Brenda doesn't look too happy about it.' She glances at the retriever curled up at the bottom of the bed.

'Oh, is she sleeping with you? You *are* good to her.'

'I think she's been missing you.'

'What's the weather like?'

'Cold,' Jodie says, 'and wet. It's bucketing down.'

'Sounds like a lovely night to hang out in a stable! Mind you take care driving in that weather. Do you still think you'll be able to meet my flight?'

'Of course – I plan to take the whole day off to annoy you.'

'Wonderful, I will bore you silly. I'm going to ring off now to let you get some sleep. I'll see you soon.'

The bedroom is freezing and Jodie, now wide awake, decides to make a cup of tea. She pulls on her slippers and reaches for her dressing-gown while Brenda wriggles awkwardly into the warm spot that she has just vacated. Jodie loves Brenda as if she were her own, but she would prefer it if Mim's retriever slept downstairs with the other dogs.

Down in the kitchen, Fred, the beagle, looks up sleepily from his basket then closes his eyes again, but Hoonoze leaps up in delight and bounds towards her.

'Okay, okay, shush, calm down,' Jodie says, crouching down to cuddle him. 'Be a good boy and you can have a biscuit.'

Hoonoze rolls over on his back on the thick rug in front of the wood stove, letting out little yelps of delight as she rubs his tummy. Five months ago, she had found him dumped on the doorstep of her surgery. He was in a sack, half-starved and terrified, and she'd fed him by hand and cleaned him up.

'So, you're obviously going to keep him,' Mim had said a week later.

'Well . . . I should really try to rehome him, but Fred's taken to him and so have I. How could anyone dump such an adorable little dog!'

'Well at least they brought him to your doorstep.'

'Thank goodness for that. I still can't work out what breed or breeds he is. Maybe schnauzer with something else, maybe several other somethings . . . who knows?' And thus the dog had acquired its name.

Jodie fills the kettle, switches it on, gets the milk from the fridge, a teabag from the cannister, and opens the biscuit tin. She breaks a digestive biscuit in two and gives half to Hoonoze. Then she leans against the benchtop, eating the other half and waiting for the kettle, thinking about Mim. She'd sounded a bit tense on the phone. But she hates flying, Jodie reminds herself; she was probably feeling a bit on edge at the prospect of the long flight to Perth. Jodie is relieved that Mim is on her way home; despite the fact that she often gets grumpy with her when she is home, she really misses her. Jodie is fiercely independent, and some-times she feels that Mim behaves like a de facto mother to her: advising her on her life choices, trying to help out to an extent that Jodie sometimes finds intrusive. This friendship, which they both value greatly, feels as close as a family connection and is both cherished and resented in much the same way.

She takes her cup of tea and, with a last glance at the dogs (Fred is snoring again and Hoonoze is back in his bed, though still staring longingly at the biscuit tin), she goes back upstairs to bed, nudging Brenda over to make room for herself. For a while she sits upright, drinking her tea and thinking about Mim – who, she realises, would say that tea is the last thing you should drink at night, because it's a stimulant. They've been friends for years, ever since Jodie bought the vet practice on the edge of Fremantle. Mim was one of her first clients; her seventeen-year-old retriever was dying and eventually Jodie was called to her house on a Sunday afternoon to administer the final injection. Seeing that Mim was alone and very upset, she stayed on to have a cup of tea and listened to the story of the beloved dog's life. As Mim finally got control of her grief, they started to talk of other things. Mim said she would never have another dog. Jodie suggested that she might feel differently in a few months' time. Mim insisted she wouldn't.

A few months later they met by chance on the beach at Cottesloe, where they had both gone to see the Sculpture by the Sea exhibition. It was a very hot day; they stood there talking for a while until Mim suggested they go to a cafe for ice cream.

'I've been hoping we'd meet again since the day . . . well, the day I cried all over you.'

Despite the difference in their ages – Jodie being almost thirty years younger – they found that in addition to a love of dogs they had much in common. It was several years, though, before Mim agreed to adopt a nine-month-old retriever whose elderly owner had died three weeks earlier.

'Her name's Brenda, and she needs a good home,' Jodie said. 'She's a real darling and I want her to go to someone special, so I thought of you. It's about time you had another dog.'

Within half an hour, Brenda had moved in with Mim.

Jodie puts her empty mug on the bedside table and slides down into the bed, turning off the light and nudging Brenda away from the middle. She lies in the darkness, thinking again about the edge in Mim's voice. Had she actually gone back to visit the hospital where she'd been as a child, perhaps? For years she has insisted that she would go there on her next visit, but she always seemed to find some reason not to. She sighs and turns over, closing her eyes, and starts to drift slowly into sleep.

It is four in the morning when the phone rings again.

'Sorry about this, Jo,' Jim Strong says. 'It's a terrible night to ask you to come out but she's in a very bad way. Could you come, please?'

'I'll be there in ten, Jim. Just try to keep her calm.'

Jodie gets up, drags on her jeans and a jumper, and runs downstairs. This time the dogs ignore her. She picks up her coat and vet bag, goes out to the car and heads off to the riding school in the pouring rain.

Chapter Four

*T*wo hours out of Doha, Mathias is almost asleep. Having declined the meal, he is dozing in the half-light as the crew clear away the last few dinner trays. He is roused when a flight attendant hurries past him, an anxious expression on her face. Moments later, another follows. A storm, perhaps? Mathias moves his seat upright and tightens his seatbelt in anticipation of an announcement. Mathias hates surprises. He likes things to go as planned: transport to run on time, people to arrive punctually for appointments and the weather to be just what the forecasters have predicted. Now he senses something unexpected is happening, something over which he has no control.

Another flight attendant – the senior one, he thinks – is heading for the intercom.

'Apologies for disturbing you, ladies and gentlemen. Unfortunately, one of our passengers has been taken ill. If there is a doctor on board, could you please make yourself known to one of the attendants? Thank you.'

Mathias relaxes. It's an emergency, but not one that requires his participation.

Two rows ahead of him, a woman gets to her feet and waves at the attendant, who steers her off into economy, thanking her profusely. Meanwhile, passengers disturbed by the announcement are getting comfortable again. Mathias glances across the aisle to where the woman from the lounge is apparently asleep. Once again, they had found themselves seated across from each other. She has completely missed the action and Mathias envies what he imagines is the calm and peace of mind that lets her sleep. He loosens his seatbelt, leans back again and closes his eyes.

Fifteen minutes or so later the intercom comes to life again and this time it's the captain. The passenger's condition is critical, he informs them, and requires urgent surgery that cannot be done in the air. It has been agreed with air traffic control that they will turn back to Doha, from where the patient will be transported by ambulance to the nearest hospital. The captain apologises in advance for the inevitable long delays that will inconvenience the other passengers and assures them that arrangements will be made for them in Doha until their flight can be rescheduled. Meanwhile, the cabin crew will be serving drinks and hot beverages. He thanks the passengers for their understanding and cooperation. He is, of course, unable to hear the sighs and groans that are washing through the cabin.

Mathias is not irritable now that he knows what's happening. On the contrary, he is shocked that some people are grumbling about the delay when a human life is at stake.

The woman from the airport has woken up and leans across to speak to him. 'Did he say we're turning back?' she asks anxiously. 'I was still half asleep. Is there something wrong with the plane?'

'No, no. Someone's been taken ill; we're going back to Doha so she or he can be taken to hospital.'

'Oh dear, how awful. I can't think of anything worse than getting really ill on a plane.' She sits up straighter and looks around. 'People seem a bit riled by it, don't they? But of course, we have to turn back.'

'I expect they're concerned about how long it will all take,' Mathias says. 'By the time we get back to Doha the crew may be out of flying hours, meaning they can't just turn the plane around.'

'You mean we might have to wait until tomorrow to resume our journey?'

'Possibly. My guess is that they'll reschedule the flight and we'll be back in Doha for the night and probably most of the morning.'

'Oh well,' the woman says, 'the delay itself is not a problem for me, as I'm not in a rush to get home – but I loathe flying, and this means more hours in the air.'

Mathias nods, undoes his seatbelt and stands up. 'There's no point trying to sleep now,' he says. 'I'm going to the bar for a drink. Would you care to join me?'

As they rise from their seats, Mathias wonders why he made the suggestion. He's not a sociable person and tends to avoid encounters with strangers as much as possible. But the change has addled him; he needs to move, needs to pretend that things are normal – and this is one of those odd situations where it can be pleasant to have someone to talk to.

The woman walks ahead of him down the aisle, and Mathias notices that she is wearing a brace on her left leg, and she has a noticeable limp. Strangely, he finds this makes him feel better, lessening his social anxiety. There is something comfortably ordinary about her, something reassuring.

He orders two brandies and they settle on the curved purple leather sofa. There are only two other people in the bar, both men sitting on stools. They smile and nod, and one rolls his eyes in a 'we're all in this together' look.

'I'm Mim, by the way,' the woman says. 'Short for Miriam.' And she extends her hand.

'Mathias,' he says, shaking it, then he leans back on the purple couch, watching as she shifts her position to accommodate her obviously painful leg.

Now that he has set up this situation, he doesn't know what to do with it, what to say, how to start the conversation. He knows he could write dialogue for a character in a novel, but in real life he feels gauche and awkward; he is so much more at home inside a book. Then he remembers that she had been reading through the stopover in Doha.

'In the airport I saw you were reading a book about Brighton,' he says. 'Do you have a special interest in it?'

Mim smiles. 'I do,' she says. 'And you were reading about the Brussels Exhibition. Do you have a special interest in that?'

'Not especially,' Mathias lies. 'Tell me about Brighton.'

Chapter Five

*C*arla turns up at the cafe in Applecross during the lull between the pre-work coffee crowd and the daily invasion of yummy mummies with their rambunctious toddlers. There are two men in cycling gear at one of the outside tables – last night's rain is a distant memory – and an elderly couple inside at the corner table. Behind the counter, Nick, the owner, seems to be dismantling the coffee machine.

'Before you completely destroy that, could I have a long macchiato topped up?' Carla asks him.

'Probably!' he says with a grin. 'I think I may just have performed a miracle on it. Let's see . . .' He steps back lifts a lever and it hisses into life.

'Aha! I'm a genius! But you knew that, didn't you?'

'If I didn't before, I'm convinced now. And I'll have an almond croissant, too, please.'

'You're late this morning,' he says. 'Skiving off?'

'That's the advantage of being self-employed. I'm granting myself a bit of leave.'

'Of course, your dad's coming to stay – I forgot. Hope you'll bring him in for coffee. I like Mathias and so does Paolo. Tell him I now have excellent coffee eclairs here, on his recommendation. They're very popular.'

'I'll let him know,' Carla says. 'If he ever gets here. The flight was turned back because someone had to go to hospital, so the last I heard he was stuck in Doha. Not sure yet what time he'll arrive.'

'Are you okay? You look a bit down in the dumps. Are you worried about Mathias?'

'No, it's not that. I'm just feeling . . . well . . . no – I'm okay, thanks, Nick.'

He raises his eyebrows but doesn't pursue the matter as she taps her card to pay then walks out to the pavement. She has just settled at a table with a view of the river when her phone rings.

'It's me!' Tracey says. 'I'm still in Port Hedland – looks like I won't get away until this afternoon.'

'Really?'

'Yep. I probably won't make it home until late afternoon – early evening, perhaps.'

'That's extraordinary,' Carla says. 'You must have superpowers, because I just saw you here, in Applecross, sitting outside Dome, eating breakfast with Mandy. The same Mandy with pink-and-black-striped hair that you photographed for *The Sunday Times* and whose picture was all over the weekend supplement a few weeks ago.'

There is a long silence. 'Well,' Tracey begins, 'I think

you may have got the wrong end of the stick . . .'

'Oh? I don't think so. No! No stick, no wrong end, no Port Hedland. You may be a good photographer, but you're a useless liar. So, since you're just around the corner from where I'm sitting, I'd like you to go back to my place right now and start packing your stuff. I'll meet you there in an hour. I want you gone before my father arrives.'

'Isn't he here already?' Tracey asks.

'His flight's been delayed.' Carla's head is throbbing, and she rubs her eyes so hard it hurts.

'But, Carla, I don't *want* to go! I like being there with you.'

'Do you really? I think you'll be happier with stripy Mandy. You've been spending a lot of time with her lately. So, do me a favour and just fuck off.'

'But I love you,' Tracey whines, and Carla can hear that she sounds affronted rather than upset.

Things between them have not been good recently; Tracey has been withdrawing from her for several months. At times she's seemed remote, sometimes even hostile: criticising Carla's clothes, telling her she should try to look younger and more stylish, buy tight-fitting jeans, wear them with stilettoes, put some colour in her hair. Carla realises this is partly down to the age gap. She is forty-nine, Tracey approaching thirty-three. She'd always known that at some stage this could be a problem, but she hadn't expected it so soon. There is something of the bossy, flirty, over-confident teenager about Tracey, who refuses to act her age.

'The only person you love is yourself,' Carla says

sharply. 'I've warned you before. Now get over to the house and start packing.'

'But where will I go?' Tracey whines. 'Where will I live, Carlie?'

'Don't call me that! You know I hate it. You can move in with Mandy. Or have you forgotten that you are a well-paid photographer with your own studio, and there's a flat above it which is empty because you're too lazy to get a tenant? I suggest you try going there. Be at my place at ten thirty with your stuff packed or I'll chuck it all in the bin.'

'But . . .'

'No, Tracey, no buts – just go. And make sure you take the white pills and the foils of coke that I found in your underwear drawer. I told you if you started doing that shit again it would be over between us.'

She hangs up immediately and switches off her phone in case Tracey tries to call back. It feels like a huge relief. She's been building up to it for weeks but had decided to wait until after Mathias's visit to ask Tracey to leave. At least now she can just tell her father that it's over. He'd never really liked Tracey, she suspected, so he'd probably be relieved too.

'Mind if I join you?' Nick says, setting her coffee and croissant on the table and clutching his own mug. 'You okay? I was coming out with the coffee a couple of minutes ago, but you sounded like you were telling someone to fuck off, so I waited for a more propitious moment.'

Carla raises her eyebrows. 'Hark at you – propitious, eh?!'

'Just don't ask me to spell it. So, what's happening?'

She takes a deep breath, feeling the relief turn to something less solid, more wobbly.

'I just split up with Tracey over the phone.'

'Ah!' Nick reaches across the table to take her hand. 'Paolo and I were wondering . . . We've seen her out a couple of times with someone else.'

Carla nods. 'Pink-and-black-striped hair?'

'That's the one. We saw them again on Saturday night; we were having a meal in Northbridge and they walked past. Tracey was looking a bit . . . you know . . .'

'Yes, she's back on the drugs. I'd suspected it for a while, but now I'm sure of it.'

'I'm so sorry, mate,' Nick says. 'We wondered if you knew. Paolo said we should tell you anyway.'

Carla sighs. 'I've known for a while that it was over; I just didn't want to face up to it. Well, at least it's sorted before Papa arrives.' She pats away her tears with a tissue. 'Sorry, Nick, it just swept over me.'

'Don't be daft,' he says, taking a folded white handkerchief from his pocket. 'Here – use this.'

'Oh my god! You use real handkerchiefs and they're ironed! I don't know anyone who does that these days.'

Nick rolls his eyes. 'You're obviously mixing with the wrong sort of people.'

'Too right,' she says, managing a smile. 'I'll try to do better next time . . . if there is a next time.'

'C'mon, of course there'll be a next time,' Nick says. 'I was forty-eight when I met Paolo. Remember me then? I was hopeless, and helpless, sure I'd never meet anyone. That was six years ago and look at us now.'

Carla nods. 'I suppose so . . . but perhaps I'm doomed to make bad choices. I had a partner when I was working in Melbourne; she wasn't like Tracey but there were similarities. Then, when I moved here, I met Olivia. Remember her?'

'Oh, I do! I liked Olivia, we both did, and I was really surprised when you said it was over. But back then I didn't know you well enough to ask why.'

'You were being discreet? How unlike you!'

'Yes, and it was a bore – so tell me what happened.'

Carla hesitates then says, 'Olivia is a lovely person; we still meet occasionally and it's nice but . . . awkward. You see, she fell in love with someone else.'

'Bummer,' Nick says. 'But it happens to the best of us, I suppose.'

'Mmm.' Carla sips her coffee, watching as a four-wheel drive pulls into the car park to disgorge an attractive woman in activewear and a small screaming child. 'But this was particularly hard because the person she fell in love with was a man. To be fair, he's a really nice man, but it left me feeling doubly rejected.'

'Oh, shit, Carls, I'm so sorry. That must have been horrible.'

'It was. Sometimes I think I'm not over it yet, and that was about eight years ago. Anyway, you don't have time to sit here.' She nods towards the car park, where four more SUVs are lined up. 'It's the invasion of the yummy mummies.'

'Oh no, what have I done to deserve this? These women drive me bonkers.' Nick rolls his eyes. 'Sorry, darling, but

Paolo will kill me if I don't go back inside. Are you going to be okay?'

Carla nods. 'Don't worry, I'll be fine.'

'Look, why don't you and Mathias come to us for dinner on Saturday?'

She grips his hand. 'Thanks, that would be lovely. Papa would really enjoy it. He always asks after you two.'

'Saturday, seven o'clock then.' He kisses her on the cheek. 'You deserve better,' he says softly. 'Don't take any shit from Tracey. If there's a problem, you know where we are.'

As the women from the car park descend on the cafe in a flurry of small children and large prams, Carla drains her coffee, gets up from the table and walks down the slope to the jetty. Several pelicans cruise past peacefully in the morning sunlight. She stands there for a long time, gazing out across the river to the city skyline, caught in a mix of emotions: hurt, disappointment and a lot of anger. She thinks again of life with Tracey; it had never really felt right, always had a temporary air about it. Now she admits to herself that she should have ended it ages ago. She imagines Tracey climbing into stripy Mandy's car and whining about her. Part of her feels relieved to know that Tracey and her possessions will soon be gone from the house. But Carla is reminded yet again of the number of times she has fallen for women who are totally wrong for her. Perhaps she should try a dating agency, she thinks. They couldn't make worse decisions for her than the ones she has made for herself.

*

Half an hour later, Carla closes the front door and leans back against it, listening for the sound of Tracey's car starting up. It's over. Tracey has gone and the house is pleasantly still; all the time she had lived with Tracey it felt as though something was about to happen, something unexpected, some disruption, whether good or bad. It had never felt quite like her own place as long as Tracey shared it. Carla is sociable, loves seeing friends and having them over, but her work requires concentration, silence. Now, as the sound of Tracey's car recedes in the distance, she feels a familiar and welcome sense of peace. She can do what she wants, when she wants. No more putting up with Tracey's friends, who are party people, often big drinkers and, although Carla had strictly forbidden it in her house, heavy users of recreational drugs. She remembers now that once, when her father came to stay, he'd said that the house felt different since Tracey moved in.

'That must be nice for you,' he'd said. 'More company.'

'Yes, it's lovely,' she'd replied, adding that it worked well because Tracey was often away for two or three days at a time, so she had time for herself, too. Even then, she knew he could read her like a book and would probably detect a lack of conviction in her tone. I doubt he'll be surprised, she thinks now. Her life for the last three years has been so different to the sort of life she enjoys. And the more she thinks about it, the more she is aware of all the adjustments she has made, all the things she put up with to avoid an argument and to satisfy Tracey, who was needy and demanding. Tracey had never seemed to understand that when Carla disappeared into her studio to paint or illustrate, she was actually working.

Carla wanders around the house now, moving ornaments, pictures and furniture to suit herself. The scent of Tracey's perfume still floats on the air and she opens all the doors and windows, wanting it to drift away. Then she goes upstairs and collects sheets and pillowcases from the linen cupboard to make up the spare room for Mathias.

When she is done, she returns downstairs to flop on the sofa, closing her eyes and breathing deeply to relax herself, unwinding limb by limb, releasing the tension in her neck and shoulders and finally feeling the tightness in her face and chest soften.

An hour later she is woken suddenly by an ambulance siren a few streets away, and her first thought is that maybe she will never have another relationship, never love or be loved again. *Perhaps I'm just meant to be single*, she thinks. *I haven't managed to get it right yet.* And she wonders whether being an only child has made her this way. She had grown up the sole child of parents who loved each other and her. It hadn't always been easy; when Carla was fifteen, the family had moved from their home in Bruges to Melbourne, and Carla had been forced to master a new language, but she'd worked hard at her private girls' school and managed to achieve great results. She wonders sometimes if her childhood and education had failed to prepare her for the emotional upheaval and setbacks.

After she'd broken up with her partner back in Melbourne and decided to move across the country to Perth, Mathias had seemed to understand her need to move on, but Carla knows how much he misses her. Her mother has been gone for a long time now and as far as Carla knows he has never had another relationship.

Perhaps this is just who I am, she thinks now. *Better on my own, just like Papa. We're both introverts, and we both hold back, put up our barriers, and we shy away from conflict.*

Therese had always eased the way for her husband and daughter with others; she was sociable, warm-hearted and more open to meeting new people than they were.

'Did you and Mama ever have rows?' she'd once asked Mathias.

'Not rows as such, no. We often disagreed, but your mother always quoted the apostle Paul: *Never let the sun go down on your anger*. She even had it inserted in our wedding vows. And we stuck to it, she better than I. It wasn't always easy, but it was always worth it.'

Her parents had been so close; Carla knows that he wants her to find equal fulfilment in a relationship. But she seemed destined not to find a love to match that of Mathias and Therese. Now Carla thinks of how to break the news about Tracey in a way that will prevent her father from worrying about her.

Chapter Six

*M*im has completely lost track of the time zones: she'd only slept for about half an hour before the turnback was announced, and not at all after that. Then there was disembarkation and a trek to the lounge (fortunately in a wheelchair), before they were taken to their hotel rooms. Exhaustion and anxiety have left her feeling jittery, her leg is a constant throbbing pain, her back aches, and her hips feel as though they have been dismantled and put back together in the wrong places.

She wonders what Mathias is doing now. When she'd first met him at the airport in Doha, she'd thought he looked vaguely familiar, but it was only much later, as they left the bar, that she realised he was a well-known writer. He was behind her in the aisle as they walked back to their seats, and she stopped so suddenly that he bumped into her and apologised profusely.

'No, no, I'm the one who should be apologising,' Mim

said, turning. 'I just realised who you are! You're Mathias Vander, aren't you?'

The light was low, but she still saw him blush.

'I am,' he said, 'but quite often I pretend I'm not.'

'Oh!' Mim had said. 'I'm sorry. How thoughtless of me to have blown your cover. I guess you're sick of being recognised and having to be polite to strangers.'

'Not on this particular occasion, but it can sometimes be intrusive.'

They both had to move then, to make way for a passenger coming out of the toilets.

'I'm so sorry,' Mim said again.

'Please,' Mathias said. 'Don't be. I enjoyed our conversation in the bar. I was going to suggest that we might meet up again in Perth. I'd like to introduce you to my daughter.'

'I'd love that,' she said. 'And look, I'll just say this once: I love your books and I think I've read all of them. *A Patient Woman* is my favourite novel ever. I have a second-hand bookshop back home and the Capo books come in and out on an almost daily basis. Children just love them. But you know that already. There, that's it. I've had my say. Now I'm going to be that dead snake again.'

And when Mim was back in her seat in the darkened cabin, she'd felt as she had when, at the age of fifteen, she was Christmas shopping in Selfridges and the man in front of her in the queue at the jewellery counter quite suddenly stepped back and bumped into her.

'Oops, sorry, love. Did I hurt you?'

Mim was so surprised to find herself face to face with

him that she almost lost her balance. He took her arm to steady her.

'You all right, love?'

'Yes,' she gulped. 'Yes. Oh my god, you're . . . you're John, aren't you? You're John Lennon!'

'I am, but let's not tell anyone else, eh? I'm doing me Christmas shopping and I haven't got a lot o' time.' He had a black cap pulled down over his forehead and it was only because she was so close to him that she'd recognised him.

'Could I get . . .'

'Autograph?' he cut in, raising his eyebrows.

She'd nodded, rummaging in her bag for something to write on. 'Please . . . yes . . .'

He slipped his hand inside his coat and pulled out a black-and-white photograph of himself. 'Here you are – got a pen?'

Speechless, she handed him an old biro from her bag.

'What's your name, love?'

'Mim,' she said, 'just Mim.'

'Here you are then, Mim,' he said, handing it to her, the signature scrawled across the bottom half of the photograph.

She took the card, gasping, 'Thank you, I love you so much, John, I really love you.' And lurching forward she wrapped her arms around him, hugging him fiercely.

He'd gently detached her arms. 'Thanks very much, Mim,' he said. 'Keep playing the music.'

And then he was gone, swallowed up by the crowd, and she'd just stood there. It had all happened so quickly it seemed unreal. She remembers it clearly: how naive and awe-struck she'd been back then, how young she'd seemed for her age. She considers it now, in this hotel room, in what feels like the middle of nowhere, neutral, untethered to anything else. *And I was naive and awe-struck again today,* she thinks, *all these years later.*

The time she'd spent in the polio hospital had set her back in so many ways. It had taken her a long time to catch up on what she'd missed, both at school and outside it. For so long she was in a class for younger children and some of them knew a lot more than she did. It was Alice who had got her through; she had been devoted to helping Mim fill in the gaps, cheering her up with stupid jokes and teasing her gently, while everyone else treated her as though she were fragile. Mim realises that she has never told her sister how much that had meant to her. How important it had been to her recovery.

She wanders into the hotel room's ensuite, which is a triumph of cold white tiles and cold white light, designed to reveal every wrinkle, every lone and previously unnoticed facial hair or sunspot. She tries to remember how she'd looked at fifteen. Thin, pale and freckled, her red hair tied back in a ponytail, wearing a dark green duffel coat, the wretched brace on her leg and a pair of ugly leather surgical boots.

Bloody polio, she thinks now, peering at her tired, washed-out face in the mirror. In her sixties she had developed post-polio syndrome, a late life legacy of the disease, and it is taking its toll now. The effort of getting from home to the bookshop and back seems a trial. *I'm not sure how long I can go on like this*, she thinks. *Maybe I'll talk to Jodie about it, see what she thinks.*

It reminds her that she should call Jodie and let her know about the flight delay, but she's too tired to work out the time in Perth. Leaving the bathroom, she rummages in her handbag for her phone and sends a text explaining what's happened, saying she'll call again when she has an arrival time. Then she eases herself onto the bed, relieved to take the weight off her aching leg. She might have once again avoided a visit to the hospital, but it seems memories from those years weren't very far from the surface. She's surprised by how vividly she recalled how she felt at fifteen.

How complicated life is, she thinks. *I thought I was a completely different person now, but I reacted to Mathias just as I did when I met John Lennon. Oh well, I suppose I should be thankful that at least this time I didn't declare my undying love.*

*

Mathias, refreshed after a decent, albeit short, sleep, has made his way to the hotel pool and is swimming lengths with a vigour that surprises him. With every stroke he realises how stiff and tight he feels after the long flight from Brussels and then the upheaval of the aborted flight to Perth. He stretches his arms, relishing the sense of pulling himself through the water and working his legs. The pool is empty except for another man from the same flight, doing much the same. Having at first ignored each other, they are now on smiling terms.

As he settles into a rhythmic stroke, he ponders the strange muddled dream he had about his daughter. Over the last few years, since Carla had settled in Perth and found a partner there, he's wondered if he might move there himself; not too close, but somewhere that would make it easier to meet more often. He thinks their relationship might work more naturally, that they would be more at ease, if they could see each other more often. Some years ago, when she and Olivia broke up, Carla had talked about coming back to Melbourne. But once she had dealt with her grief, she decided to stay in Perth. If he wanted to forge a closer relationship with her, it would be up to him to take the next step – and, really, there is nothing keeping him in Melbourne. In recent years, most of his friends have died or moved away. He gets on well with his neighbours but most of them are young families. Mathias is not lonely, but he does feel his aloneness, and while maintaining his independence is important to him, he also feels he needs something more. He wants to share this later stage of ageing with others his own age, and he wants to be closer to his daughter.

He had mentioned this to Mim, when they had started to talk about getting old, how you change in ways you had never imagined and can barely explain.

'I don't have a friend to talk to about getting old,' Mathias had said at one point. 'I used to talk about it with Luc – my oldest friend, who lives in the Ardennes – but the process of ageing is over for him. He is dying and that's his world now; it informs everything. He's let go of so much. I know that in some way he's already left me behind. It's very sad.'

'I'm sure it is,' Mim had said. 'I've felt that too, the desire to talk to someone about how things change, how so much keeps slipping away, leaving infuriating blanks in your memory – stuff you still vaguely know but just can't articulate. Being old is different from just ageing. And it's hard to explain that to someone in their fifties or even their sixties. It makes me want to laugh out loud when I hear people in their forties talk about getting old. They just don't have a clue, and I know I used to be like that at their age. Now I sit and listen feeling like some ancient sage, thinking, *Just you wait!*'

They'd also talked about how strange it was for both of them to be speaking so openly with a stranger.

'Evidently we're both loners,' Mathias had said, 'but here we are discussing our lives as if we've known each other for years.'

Mathias stops swimming and leans against the pool steps, thinking of that conversation and how he wants to continue it. Mim has articulated what he had felt. There is no right way to be old, he thinks. It just has to be your own way. He had seen that when he visited Luc. He had entered that unique stage of life when you are free to be selfish with your time and energy, reveal your most irritating habits, speak without wondering whether you're offending someone. It is time to do exactly what he wants – which is not much at all, except to be able to see his daughter often, take an afternoon rest without feeling guilty, have endless time to read and listen to music, and keep walking and swimming regularly . . . and, of course, to write.

The other swimmer has also stopped for a rest now and is flexing his shoulders two lanes away.

'Great pool,' the man calls out. 'Consolation for the delay.'

'Indeed,' Mathias says. 'Have you heard what happened to the patient?'

'Doing well apparently. She was taken straight into surgery – heart–lung problem, I believe, and they were just in time.'

'A life saved,' Mathias says. 'That makes it worthwhile.'

The man nods. 'Absolutely. Well, I'll get another few laps under my belt.' And he lunges forward, cleaving his way through the water at an enviable speed.

Mathias glances up at the clock. He has arranged to meet Mim. A couple of hours ago his new boarding pass had been delivered to his room along with a revised flight schedule. He'd called Mim to see if she might be interested in a swim, but she had declined, suggesting they meet at the hotel restaurant for breakfast instead.

He hauls himself up onto the side of the pool with some difficulty, aware that before too long his arms and shoulders will not support this, and the steps will be essential. He picks up his towel and dries his face, and his hair which is grey now but still thick. Then he pulls on the white towelling robe supplied by the hotel and heads to the changing room for a shower. He is more than ready for breakfast with Mim.

*

Mim texts Jodie with the revised flight arrival time of 4.45 a.m. She keeps getting confused over which day it is, and as she sits in the hotel restaurant waiting for Mathias to finish his swim she finds she doesn't really care. Long ago, in her late teens and twenties, when she had regained some strength and mobility after the long stay in hospital, she'd loved to swim in the sea or a pool; being in the water took the pressure off her legs and the exertion was good for her lungs. These days, she can usually cope with getting in and out of the pool, although sometimes she finds the steps pretty challenging. The beach is an even greater challenge. The return of the polio symptoms makes it painful to walk on soft sand, and she doesn't have the strength to battle big waves. She's more inclined to just sit and watch unless she has someone else with her.

She orders a pot of coffee and glances at the rack of thick glossy magazines close to the buffet. They are mainly business or finance publications, the advertising featuring luxury cars or haute couture fashion, prestige jewellery and watches. But there's one title that seems slightly more interesting than the rest; it's called *Ravishing Resorts*. Mim is not a ravishing resort sort of person, and while she's visited lots of places which were truly ravishing – from lakes to small villages, beaches and woodlands – there was never a resort in sight. But the magazine cover features a resort in the English countryside: some cows grazing, a man in a flat cap with a dog beside him walking out of the picture, a couple of small cottages in the distance and, beyond them, a hazy glimpse of a church spire rising behind the trees. Mim feels the familiar tug of nostalgia. *Ah, Sussex*, she thinks, forgetting her recent, less favourable observations. There's a shout line in white print that screams: MAR-A-LARGO IN SUSSEX! FROM STATELY HOME TO LUXURY RESORT.

'Stone the crows,' Mim murmurs. 'Just what Sussex

doesn't need.' And she opens the magazine and flicks through the pages to find out where the resort actually is.

The first page of the feature is a shot of three men on a vast golf course. On the facing page there are smaller pictures: a large indoor swimming pool and another outside; people playing tennis; an elegant restaurant; and a luxurious-looking bedroom with a king-size bed. Turning another page, she begins to read:

> Welcome to Harold House – a stunning new venue with a varied and fascinating history. Built in 1803 as a family home, this grand building was later a private school for boys, then an isolation hospital for tuberculosis sufferers in the First World War before being reinvented as a live-in haven for children with polio. Magnificently restored, Harold Hall now provides luxurious accommodation, gourmet dining in its five-star restaurants and a world-class course for golfers as well as indoor and outdoor pools, four tennis courts, two billiard rooms and an archery park.

Mim feels a chill run through her. 'A haven?' she growls under her breath. 'Prison more like.'

Glancing up, she sees Mathias heading towards the table. She closes the magazine but keeps it in front of her, thinking that she will read it later. She's freezing now, the air conditioning makes her shiver, and she pulls her woollen jacket from the back of her chair and puts it on just as Mathias arrives at the table.

'Oh, have you eaten already, Mim?' he asks, standing beside her chair. 'I'm sorry I'm late.'

'No, I'm not leaving, and you're not late. I just felt rather cold all of a sudden.'

Mathias takes a seat and they both peruse the menu. When they have ordered, he peers across the table at the magazine in front of her. 'You seemed totally engrossed in that magazine,' he says. 'What is it? Oh! I wouldn't have thought *Ravishing Resorts* was your sort of thing.'

'It's not,' she says. 'I helped myself to it from the rack, but there's a long article in there I now want to read. Do you think you could smuggle it into your sports bag for me? It's too big for my handbag.'

He leans forward across the table. Lowering his voice, he says, 'Are you asking me to steal it for you?'

'I am.'

'It would be a pleasure,' Mathias says and, glancing around, he picks up the magazine, drops it into his open bag and closes the zip. 'Am I now a mole?'

'A mole?'

'Like a drug mole.'

Mim laughs out loud. 'That's a mule – a drug mule. That's the first time I've heard you make a mistake; your English is perfect.'

'Ah, but there are always things that catch me out,' he says. 'The mule is like a donkey and now I feel like one. It's not a word I've needed! A mole, I think, is small, black and furry, isn't it? I have made this mistake before. But in this instance it was a good mistake, because it made you laugh. You were looking disturbed when I came in. Has something happened to upset you?'

'Not exactly,' she says. 'It's just something I saw in

that magazine. Silly, really, but that's why I want to finish reading it.'

'Do you want to talk about it?'

She sighs. 'Not yet. It's complicated. Perhaps I'll tell you about it later.'

He nods, picks up the pot of coffee that the waitress has just delivered and pours some into a cup. 'You look as though you need this,' he says, passing it to her. 'And here comes our food.'

With the magazine safely out of sight in Mathias's bag, Mim has no trouble allowing a plate of scrambled eggs and bacon to command her attention.

They have been in the air for some time and the cabin lights are being turned down when Mim remembers the magazine. *I'll read it at home*, she thinks. *There's no rush.* The shock of seeing Harold House has eased. She turns out her light and, in the semi-darkness of the cabin, she ponders why its fate even matters to her, why she was so shocked by its latest reincarnation. *It all happened so many years ago – I should just get over it, leave it behind me. Whatever it is now has nothing to do with me.*

There is a moment of satisfaction in taking this position and she briefly relishes it, but her equanimity evaporates in the time it takes her to recline her seat. There is no really comfortable position for her, even in the latest business-class seats. Her hips, her knees, her back all conspire against her, so lying down is not an option. She raises the seat back again and then lowers it more slowly, trying to find a level that will both support her back and raise her legs at the knees. Across the aisle Mathias is apparently asleep, with the book given to him by his friend clutched closed against his chest. She stares at him for a moment, and almost as though he has sensed her watching him, he opens his eyes, looks across at her and smiles.

*

They are still a couple of hours from Perth when Mathias wakes up. The cabin staff are preparing breakfast and at any moment the lights will come on. He shifts his position and looks around, and a passing flight attendant offers him some tea. He raises his seat and looks across at Mim, who is still fast asleep. She is an enigma, he thinks; a physically small and slight woman, with fair skin and thick curly hair that she had told him was once a dark red but which has now been overtaken by a liberal amount of grey. He admires her breadth of knowledge, her robust opinions and sense of humour, and is intrigued by the caution with which she moves – such a contrast to her feisty person-ality. He's sure she would be a formidable adversary in any difference of opinion. He thinks she and Carla would get on well and wants to introduce them, preferably when Tracey is not around. Though he has always tried to be courteous, Mathias has never much liked Tracey. She is just not right for Carla, he thinks, but he would never say that to his daughter. He wonders if fathers always think that their daughters' partners are not good enough, not worthy. Therese's father had known him as a boy and had welcomed him into the family. But what had he actually felt? Did he just bite his tongue and put on a brave face, or had he really meant it when he spoke so warmly of Mathias at their wedding?

It's still dark and raining heavily when they touch down in Perth, but Mathias is happy to have arrived finally and is looking forward to seeing his daughter. Mim, too, seems cheerful and happy to be close to home.

With an airport attendant pushing Mim in a wheelchair, they pass through passport control together and make their way to baggage collection and customs.

'I'll get your suitcase,' Mathias offers. 'Purple, isn't it, with a lime green label?' And he ducks through the crowd and returns quite soon with her case, and then his own.

'Could I take the wheelchair now?' he asks the attendant. 'And maybe you wouldn't mind bringing the two suitcases.'

The attendant smiles and shrugs. 'Of course.' He changes places with Mathias and they head out through the automatic doors towards the waiting crowd.

Chapter Seven

The flight had landed exactly on time and Carla, who arrived early, is at the front of the barrier. When the doors slide open and she sees her father, he waves to her and his face tells her how happy he is to see her. To her surprise he is pushing a wheelchair in which is a woman of about his own age. Carla watches as he points her out to the woman, who smiles and waves at her too. Carla chides herself for the sudden and unreasonable flash of jealousy she feels at seeing him taking care of a total stranger. Right now, she needs all the care and concern he has to offer, and she has no desire to share that with anyone else.

'My darling!' he says when he reaches her, and he hugs her for a long time as she fights back tears. Eventually Mathias releases his hold on her and turns to the woman in the chair. 'Mim, this is my daughter Carla. Carla, this is Miriam, whom I met in Doha and who has kept me sane for the last however many hours it's been.'

Carla, surprised that he has connected so quickly with someone whom he seems to like very much, shakes the woman's hand. 'Hello, Miriam, nice to meet you. Papa doesn't usually talk to strangers.' Immediately she realises how weird that must sound and she wishes she'd said something warmer.

But Miriam – Mim – is smiling. 'Nor do I,' she says, 'but we have had some good conversations and some equally good silences. It's lovely to meet you, Carla.'

A man in a uniform bearing the airport's logo is standing behind them with their luggage on a trolley. He clears his throat. 'Excuse me, ma'am,' he says to Mim, 'will you be needing the wheelchair any longer or may I return it?'

'Oh no,' Mim says, getting up from the chair. 'I'll be fine now. Thank you so much for your help.'

'Have a happy homecoming,' he says, and he wheels the chair away.

'My friend Jo is meeting me here,' Mim says, looking around.

'We'll wait with you until she gets here,' Mathias offers. Grasping the handle of the baggage trolley, he says, 'Why don't we go over there to that seat near the door? It's not as crowded and your friend will be able to see us as soon as she comes in.'

'Could she be waiting outside?' Carla asks, as they reach the seat.

'It's unlikely, but I'll call her.' Mim rummages for her phone and dials the number.

Mathias touches Carla's arm. 'I don't want to leave her

here alone,' he says softly, turning away from Mim to avoid being overheard.

'No, of course not. We can drop her home if her friend doesn't come. Where does she live?'

'Fremantle, I think.'

'So, how long have you been chatting up women in airports?' Carla asks, smiling. Her moment of resentment has passed.

Before he can answer, Mim says, 'This is strange.' She is putting her phone back in her bag. 'She's not answering. Usually she's so reliable; if something had happened to stop her coming, she would have let me know. But she hasn't even replied to the texts I sent from Doha.'

'She could still be on her way,' Mathias says. 'Maybe there's a traffic hold-up.'

Mim nods, but she is obviously anxious. 'Even so, she would call from the car . . . Oh! That young woman over there waving – that's Jodie's vet nurse, Kirra.' And she waves back to the woman who is heading towards them.

'I'm so sorry,' Kirra says breathlessly. 'I slept through the alarm. Are you all right, Mim?' She leans over to hug the older woman.

'Of course, I am,' Mim says, and she introduces Mathias and Carla. 'There was no need to rush. I suppose Jodie got tied up with some emergency?'

Kirra's eyes slide away and Carla sees that the vet nurse is not just breathless from the rush; she is also agitated.

She hugs Mim again. 'I'm sorry, so sorry to be late, and, um . . . look, there's no easy way to say this: Jo was in an accident. She went out in the storm to deliver a foal and the car skidded off the road and rolled into a deep ditch. She's in hospital.'

*

Mathias puts his suitcase into the boot of Carla's car and climbs in the front seat beside her. He wishes he could have taken Mim home in a taxi or even got Carla to drive her. He didn't like the idea of her going back to her house and being alone there, when she'd had such bad news. The young woman who'd come to get her did seem nice and helpful, though, and apparently she'd already taken Mim's dog back to the house ready to greet her.

'So, off we go at last,' Carla says, starting the engine. 'That was all rather dramatic wasn't it? Poor Miriam – she was very upset. I hope she'll be okay.'

'Me too,' Mathias replies. 'When I was telling her about you she told me that Jodie is like a daughter to her.'

'Does she have children of her own?'

He shakes his head. 'No. I'm not sure if she's ever been married.'

'But that doesn't necessarily mean . . .'

'She has no children, Carla,' he says irritably. He doesn't like the fact that Mim has gone off in the early hours of the morning and he's not with her. 'And if you're thinking she is lonely and helpless, she is certainly not,' he says abruptly. 'She has her own business, and she has plenty of friends – but Jodie is special to her.'

'It's okay, Papa, I wasn't suggesting anything at all – I was just asking. I liked her, and I like that you were so friendly with her. You don't do enough of that.'

'Meaning?' he snaps.

'Meaning getting to know people, allowing them to get to know you!'

They lapse into silence for a while, and then Mathias shifts his position and takes a deep breath.

'Sorry,' he says in his normal tone. 'That was completely unnecessary. I was feeling so upset for her that I . . . well . . . I'm sorry. I'm not used to . . . oh, never mind.' He's embarrassed and awkward now and attempts to change the subject. 'Tell me about you. And how's Tracey? Is she at home or is she away taking photographs?'

Carla takes a deep breath as she draws up at the traffic lights.

'Well, actually . . .' And now she is the one who looks uncomfortable. 'Actually, Tracey and I have split up and she's moved out.'

Mathias's first reaction is to feel relief, but he manages to hide it. 'Darling, I'm so sorry. Are you all right?'

Carla turns towards him. 'Not really,' she says, 'although I feel better now that you're here.'

'But . . . I thought you were very happy together. What happened?'

Carla sighs. 'It was a number of things really. We were wrong for each other from the start. I expect you'd already worked that out.'

'My opinion doesn't matter,' Mathias says. 'You loved her, I thought, and she you. When did you break up?'

Carla gives him a weak smile and pulls away as the lights change. 'Yesterday.'

'It wasn't about me coming to stay, was it?' Mathias asks, alarmed.

'No, of course not. We'd been building up to it for months; it's just a coincidence that it should happen now. Actually, it was overdue.'

Mathias has no idea how to respond, and again he has the feeling that if he were writing this he would know what his characters should do and say; but this is real life, Carla is his daughter, and he hasn't a clue how to help her.

'Carla, are you sure you're okay?' he asks, ashamed of his emotional incompetence.

'Well, I feel awful at the moment,' she says, 'but it's the right thing and it was my decision. Can we talk about this when we get home?' He hears a catch in her voice and realises she is close to tears. 'I'll tell you about it then – I just can't do it while I'm driving.'

'Of course,' Mathias says, wondering what Mim would think if she saw how awkward he was.

Carla starts to talk instead about her friends Nick and Paolo, whom he likes very much, and he answers sensibly, but he can't dispel his anxiety – for Carla, and for Mim, going home to an empty house in the dark cold hours of the early morning, worrying about her friend. He tries to get a grip on himself, to put things in perspective so that he can be useful and comforting. *Carla has to come first*, he tells himself. *She needs my attention and support; I have to focus on her, help her through this.* He wants to tell her that Tracey was never good enough for her, but perhaps that's not what she wants to hear. And what about Mim? They had been briefly bound together, and it had felt good, close, as though they understood each other very well. Now he has the strange feeling of having been robbed of something special. *I'll call Mim first thing in the morning,* he decides, *to see if she needs anything. And I'll try to arrange a time to meet.* And as Carla talks he tries hard to listen and respond, even as his thoughts constantly slip back to Mim.

Chapter Eight

lice is watering the vegetables she had put in over the weekend, encouraged by a short burst of warm dry weather. It's late May and she can tell already it's going to be a very hot summer. The roses are also looking encouraging. She swings the hose across the path to her favourite icebergs, their densely packed, white petals curled into tight greenish-white buds, almost luminous in the evening light.

Since Mim left, Alice has been thinking seriously about visiting her in Australia. Mim had suggested, as she always does, that Alice should come and spend some time with her, but this time Alice detected something different in her tone. It sounded as though Mim was really asking for her own sake, as well as for Alice. She talked about the things they would do together, the places they'd go, how she wanted to introduce her sister to her friends. She'd reminded Alice that when Colin was alive, he too had urged her to go. Alice's husband had hated flying and couldn't face so many hours in the air, but he'd encouraged Alice to visit her sister in Australia. Alice had considered it occasionally but never got around to doing anything about it. But now Colin has been dead for more than three years, and she is still here in this big house in Oxford, where she's lived for most of her adult life – doing all the housework and tending the garden all on her own.

'You could move somewhere smaller and easier to manage,' Mim had suggested. 'I bet Michael would be in here like a shot. But come to stay with me first. I think you'd love Fremantle.'

Colin's family has owned the house in Oxford since 1901, and while it's her home now, it would pass to Colin's son Michael on her death.

Michael had been twelve when Alice married his father. His own mother had left five years earlier, and he'd resented the arrival of a stepmother. Relations between them had never been easy. *I need to have a chat with Stuart*, Alice thinks now. *Get my head around what the arrangements are and exactly what I'm worth.* Colin's solicitor had explained it all to her after the reading of the will, but Alice, stricken with grief, had barely taken any of it in. All she knew was that the house and income from Colin's investments were hers for the rest of her life. Alice turns off the tap and starts to wind the hose back into place. *Mim's right*, she thinks. *I need to start preparing for the next phase of my life.*

Alice was in her early twenties and completing her PhD when she and Colin met. Her childhood had been lived in the shadow of Mim's polio. Early attempts to develop a vaccine had proved fruitless and by the 1950s the disease was reaching epidemic proportions, resisting the control of contemporary medicine and reviving old suspicions that there was something essentially wrong with the affected families. They were cursed or had 'bad blood'; some even believed that it ran in families and was a punishment from God. Lack of cleanliness and criminal behaviour were also rumoured to play a part. Often, if one child in a family was afflicted with the disease, their siblings bore the social stigma.

As a child Alice had never really understood the burden she carried and it wasn't until she met Colin that she could actually speak to someone about it. Marrying him had changed her, given her confidence, helped her to separate herself from Mim's illness. Aside from various ructions caused by Michael, they had had a peaceful life, both working in the same university. Colin was the elder by fourteen years, and when he retired Alice had stayed on for a couple of years. Later, she too had retired, but she still often reviews books for *The Times*, *The London Review of Books* and occasionally *The Atlantic*. But losing her husband had changed her. She had lost not only the person she loved most in the world, but also the physical and mental energy which he had helped her to discover and develop. His death seemed to have sucked the life out of her. She had been a serious woman who also loved to have fun, involved herself in local events and had a significant role in the community. But since Colin's death she had retreated, spending most of her time alone, often declining invitations. As she coils the hose around the tap, she decides that it is time she took herself in hand. No more moping, she chides herself.

Back inside, she stares at her face in the bedroom mirror, seeing herself as she thinks Stuart, the solicitor, might see her: an old woman stuck in a rut. Her hair looks dull and lank, her face is pale. *I look like a woman who is tired of doing nothing*, she thinks. *Colin would be shocked if he saw me now. No, not shocked – he'd be sad and disappointed.* Turning away from the mirror, she picks up her phone and calls Stuart's office to make an appointment and then dials her hairdresser.

Chapter Nine

Jodie is drifting in and out of sleep. She has lost track of what time it is, and what day of the week, but the light outside tells her it's daytime, and she vaguely remembers being woken earlier to swallow pills and have her blood pressure checked. A trolley rattles to a halt outside and she realises it's the first time she's actually felt hungry since she's been here, and she thinks that must be a good sign. She wonders if she can move and then remembers the switch that puts the back of the bed up. Reaching out, she presses it and feels herself lifted halfway to upright, which seems to be quite enough for the time being.

There is a woman in a pink overall standing in the doorway holding a tray. When she sees that Jodie is awake her face breaks into a smile.

'Hello,' she says. 'You're looking a lot better. You slept through breakfast; this is lunch. But I guess you may not be ready for cottage pie?'

Jodie shakes her head. 'Not really, but I could murder a cup of tea and piece of toast!'

She pushes the switch again and the bed moves her into a sitting position, which makes her feel slightly dizzy.

'Anything else?' the nurse's aide asks. 'Eggs, sausages, bacon, avocado . . .'

'Oh no,' Jodie says, squeamish at the thought of so much food. 'Just the toast, thanks.'

As the woman hurries to arrange this, a nurse walks in.

'You're sitting up! Well, that's excellent. Did you manage it yourself?'

Jodie nods. 'I needed to see more than the ceiling. But my ribs don't like it much.'

'No, they won't, but just take it slowly.' And she quickly takes Jodie's temperature, gives her some tablets in a small plastic cup and hands her a glass of water.

Jodie leans back against the pillows and closes her eyes, thinking about Mim, wondering if she's home yet. She vaguely remembers Kirra visiting yesterday and assuring her that she would meet Mim at the airport. And then she remembers Jim Strong and the foal she'd failed to deliver and looks around for her phone, intending to call him. But the phone is just out of reach. If she could reach it, she could call Jim and also try Mim's number, but stretching for the phone is too painful and she closes her eyes again, listening to real life going on in the corridor – people talking, lunch trolleys being wheeled along the corridor, a doctor being paged – as she waits for the painkiller the nurse had given her to kick in.

*

Mim sits in the waiting room outside the ward where Jodie is a patient, anxious to get some definitive information from someone who knows what they're talking about. She yawns – a yawn so wide that it seems to crack her face in half. It was almost 6 a.m. when they'd got back to the house, and Brenda's ecstatic welcome had certainly helped to lift her spirits. Kirra had put the heating on when she'd left Brenda there earlier, but even so the place had the dead feeling of a house that's been empty for some time. Brenda was ecstatic and ran around the room in excited circles, barking in a most uncharacteristic way. When Mim sat down on the couch Brenda leapt up beside her, half sitting on her knee to stare into her face.

'Yes, Brenny, it's really me,' Mim had assured her.

'I hope it was all right that I used Jo's key to come in,' Kirra said as she set about making tea. 'And I've put some stuff in the fridge for you.'

'That's wonderful, Kirra, thank you so much,' Mim said. 'Can you tell me again how Jo is? I was in a bit of shock at the airport and couldn't quite take it in.'

'Well, she's got a broken leg,' Kirra said, 'and she's cracked a couple of ribs. The doctor will be able to tell you more; Jodie has you listed as her next of kin so they're keen to talk to you.'

Mim had decided to grab a couple of hours sleep before going to the hospital and ended up sleeping until midday. She'd dragged herself out of bed and into the shower, then got dressed. She longed to crawl back into bed, but she was also determined to visit Jodie in the hospital.

Three-quarters of an hour later, Mim is waiting outside

the ward. She had arrived fifteen minutes earlier but was prevented from going in to see Jodie as a nurse was with her, checking Jodie's pulse and blood pressure and so on. But when the curtains around Jodie's bed were opened, instead of a nurse emerging two doctors strode in and the curtains were closed again. One of the doctors, a woman, looked vaguely familiar, but Mim can't remember where she's seen her before. She leans her head back against the wall and closes her eyes. She imagines Mathias catching up with his daughter and feels a pang, wishing he was here waiting with her, assuring her that everything would be all right. She misses the way she had felt while she was with him: confident, at ease, supported.

Now she has crashed to earth and it's a shock. Even getting the car out of the garage and driving to the hospital seemed to require enormous effort and concentration. A matter of hours ago she had been happy at the prospect of getting home and back to her normal life and spending some time with Mathias. But normal life has been turned upside down by her friend's accident. She's decided that Jodie should stay with her when she's released from hospital, so she will need to prepare for that – and of course there are her bags to unpack, which means washing and ironing, and she has to do some shopping. And she needs to go and sort things out at the bookshop as soon as possible. Doug, a long-term employee whom Mim considers her second-in-command, has always run the shop when Mim is away; she will call him later today and go in tomorrow to sort out a plan for the next few weeks. It all seems overwhelming, like falling into a black hole of work and responsibilities. *I am too old for this,* she tells herself. *Too old and too tired.*

'Ms Squires? Miriam?'

The voice startles her and she opens her eyes and sits up straighter.

'Sorry to disturb you,' the woman says, 'but I'm Rosemary Parks, the doctor looking after Jodie here at the hospital. Jo and I are also friends. We've known each other for years.' And she sits down on the seat next to Mim, who is struggling to remember her. 'Actually, we met some time ago, on Jo's birthday,' Rosemary reminds her.

Mim feels as though she's been dragged out of a very deep sleep, though she can only have dropped off for a few minutes. 'Of course,' she says, attempting to look and sound normal. 'I do remember.' She smothers a yawn. 'Sorry,' she adds. 'I'm a bit jet-lagged. I just flew in from the UK early this morning.'

'Oh, jet-lag's horrible,' Rosemary says with a sympathetic grimace. 'I always feel as though I'm doing everything in slow motion while the world spins around me very fast. Look, I'm sorry for pouncing on you when you must be desperate to see Jo, but I thought we might have a quick word first.'

Mim sits up straighter, trying to focus.

'Jo has a complex fracture of the right tibia,' the doctor begins. 'So obviously she won't be walking out of here.'

'The tibia?' Mim echoes, trying to remember where the bone is.

'The shinbone,' Rosemary says. 'She also has two cracked ribs, and her left ankle has sustained some severe damage – we're still considering how best to deal with it. Otherwise, apart from cuts and bruises and a nasty knock on the head, she was pretty fortunate; it could have been a lot worse. She's going to be here with us for a while, and then she'll need care. She won't be able to look after herself for some time.'

Mim pulls herself together. 'Okay, I can start to get things organised for her at home. I think it would be best if she stayed with me.'

Rosemary puts her hand on Mim's arm. 'She'll need to go to rehab for a while when she's discharged from here.'

'That won't be necessary,' Mim says. 'I can look after her. She'll be able to have the dogs with her – she'll like that. We'll be fine.'

Rosemary's grip on Mim's arm tightens a fraction. 'Let's talk about this later, when we see how she's progressing. But right now, I'll just check the contact details we have for you are up to date, and then you can go in and see her.'

*

'It's so good to see you, Mim,' Jodie says, pushing herself up a bit in the bed and holding out her arms, hiding her shock that Mim looks so pale and haggard. 'I've been thinking about you so much.'

Mim bends down to hug her, then slips into the chair beside the bed.

'Aren't I lucky to end up with my oldest schoolfriend as my doctor?' Jo asks.

'You certainly are,' Mim says. 'She's a very nice woman. So how are you feeling?'

'Better than yesterday,' Jodie says cautiously. 'But pretty sore all over. My right leg is quite painful, and the left ankle too. And I'm up to the eyebrows in various drugs that make me feel really weird.'

'You'll need to take it very slowly when you're discharged,' Mim warns her.

'Enough about me,' says Jodie. 'Tell me about your holiday. How was England? And Alice – how's she doing?' Jodie listens as Mim describes her weeks in Oxford with her sister, finishing with the days she'd spent in Brighton.

'And did you go to the old hospital?' Jodie asks, feeling pretty confident that the answer will be in the negative.

Mim blushes, shakes her head. 'I chickened out at the last minute,' she says. 'But I found out the most extraordinary thing. I came across a magazine article about it. It's been turned into a sort of luxury resort.' She shakes her head in disbelief. 'Anyway, I've only had a quick glance at the article – I'll tell you more when I've finished reading it. Now, back to you: I've told Rosemary that of course you will stay with me when you're released from the hospital.'

Jodie stiffens; she had known this would happen. 'I have to go to rehab, Mim.'

'I know that's what Rosemary thinks, but I'm not really convinced that rehab is essential,' Mim says quite briskly. 'Anyway, we're going to talk about it later. For now, you just have to get well again.'

'And you need to go home, unpack and relax,' Jo says. 'I'm fine here, very comfortable and well looked after.'

Mim gets to her feet, leans over the bed and kisses her. 'Good. Okay, I'll head off now, but I'll come again tomorrow.'

Jodie watches as Mim walks away, turning at the door to wave and blow a kiss. She'd been surprised by how exhausted Mim looked. *Perhaps it's just jet-lag*, she thinks. *It's an exhausting trip at any time, and the post-polio makes everything harder, I suppose.* This is one more reason why she should go to rehab; she worries that the strain of looking after an invalid will be too much for her friend.

When Rosemary stops by the ward to see her later, Jo asks her what she thinks. 'Mim is determined that I should go straight to her place from the hospital,' she says.

'Yes, she said something similar to me,' Rosemary replies. 'But there's no question you will have to go to rehab for a while after the injuries you've sustained. The issue is where you should go *after* rehab. There's no way Mim could manage it, I'm afraid.'

Jodie nods. 'That's what I suspected. I love her to bits, and I want to try to manage this without upsetting her, but I just don't think me staying with her while I recover is a good idea. In the last couple of years she's slowed down a fair bit, and she's in quite a lot of pain herself. But she insists on looking after me, when really I think she's worried about needing more help herself . . .'

'Ah!' said Rosemary. 'Yes, I see. I wonder if she's transferring her own need for help to you, to convince herself that you need her when really it's the other way around.'

'Do you really think it could be that?'

'I'm not a psychologist, but it seems logical to me. Anyway, don't you worry about it – we'll sort it out in the most sensitive way possible. Now she's seen you for herself, and we've both reassured her that you are going to be okay, she'll probably back off.'

'You reckon?' Jodie says. 'I'm not so sure. I'd take a bet that Mim's been planning how to get me sorted from the moment Kirra told her what had happened – and when she's over her jet-lag, she'll be a force to be reckoned with!'

Chapter Ten

When Mathias first walks into Carla's house, he thinks Tracey must have come back. Her perfume still hangs in the air, and he has the uneasy feeling that at any minute a door might open, and she will walk out and greet him in that chirpy voice he'd found so annoying. He'll go out later and buy some scented candles, he thinks – lemon maybe, or lavender, to diffuse the cloying sweetness. It was not a subtle perfume, but then nothing about Tracey was subtle, and he knows that the impact of the break-up on Carla will last a great deal longer than the wretched perfume.

He takes his bags up to his room which, fortunately, the perfume has failed to reach. He showers, unpacks – putting aside Mim's magazine, chuckling at the idea of himself as a 'mole' – and goes back downstairs to find Carla in the kitchen warming croissants and pushing the plunger down into a large pot of coffee. 'There you are,' she says.

'Just in time for breakfast.' She seems more relaxed than on the drive home from the airport; she gives him a big hug, tells him how happy she is to see him . . . and then bursts into tears.

Eventually, when she is calmer, she starts to tell him about Tracey: the lies, the secrets, the drugs and, finally, the devastating admission that she knew Tracey had always been wrong for her, but her longing to be in a relationship had driven her to give it a go.

'But why, sweetheart?' he asks. 'Why are you so desperate? You're a beautiful woman – a beautiful person – and anyone with half a brain in their head –'

'No, Papa,' she interrupts. 'It's not like that. People don't fall in love with me. They don't ask me out or even make passes at me. I'm not . . . well, I'm not one of those people whom others find desirable. One of Tracey's friends said I was *forbidding*! There's something about me that puts people off. They like me as a friend, as a colleague, but no one falls in love with me. After Olivia there was no one until Tracey, and that never really felt absolutely right.'

Mathias is left floundering; he has no idea how to respond, so he says nothing, patting Carla's shoulder awkwardly as she wipes her eyes with a tissue. Finally, feeling that a response really is called for, he begins, 'But, darling, you're –'

'Don't,' Carla cuts in. 'Please don't say anything. I know you're trying to help, but you're my father. You can't see me as others see me. Please just try to understand how it is, how it feels for me.'

'Of course,' he says. 'Of course. And if there's anything I *can* do to help, if you need anything, you will tell me?'

'I will,' Carla replies. 'And you know what? You're doing the best possible thing right now, just being here with me, being normal. That's what I want most: to feel normal. And I know you only planned to stay a week or two, but if you could stay longer, I'd like that very much. Having you around would be a great comfort.'

They both lapse into silence for a few minutes, then, recalling Carla's insistence that she wants to feel normal, Mathias asks about her work, her friends. She in turn asks about the book he's working on, and about Luc and Patrice. The conversation turns then to the news: the Brexit shambles and their shared horror at, and fascination with, the chaos of Trump.

By the time the coffee plunger has been drained and the croissants reduced to crumbs, Carla seems to have regained her equilibrium. When Mathias offers to do the breakfast dishes, she shoos him from the kitchen. 'The best thing after a long flight is sunlight,' she insists. 'Well, daylight,' she amends, after a glance out the window. 'It looks like rain again. But you should definitely get some fresh air to clear your head.'

As always, Mathias feels trapped in a cloud of disorientation and confusion that haunts him after long flights. He would have liked a swim, but while the nearest indoor pool is not far away, he can't muster the energy to get there. Instead, he walks down to the jetty and watches the gulls swooping and diving back and forth above the ruffled grey water of the Swan River as the rain starts to fall. A couple of people walking their dogs greet him and comment on the dreadful weather. Otherwise, he is alone with that particular sense of solitude created by the wind swirling around him, cutting him off from everything except his own thoughts. He replays his conversation with Carla and realises how arrogant it had been of him to tell her that she was wrong about herself. She was right to tell him that it was how she felt about herself that was important. And he begins to wonder what he has missed over the years, how she'd gone from being a girl bursting with self-confidence to a woman who is undoubtedly strong, but who seems blind to her own obvious qualities. Carla was fifteen when they'd moved from Belgium to Australia, to the house in Monbulk, in the Dandenongs, where he still lives. She had done well at school and worked exceptionally hard at languages and she began to create some interesting artwork. She was popular, soon made friends and those friendships had lasted. She'd had various boyfriends, but nothing serious, and finally she had confided in Therese that she was attracted to women. Mathias had been relieved then; it felt right, as though it really defined for him who she was. But where did her confidence go? Mathias asks himself now. She had always seemed to have her mother's vivacious outgoing nature. When was it that she became so inward? So . . . so closed off – not really secretive but reserved.

When he walks back into the house, Carla is taking a cake out of the oven.

'Oh, that smells wonderful,' Mathias says. 'It also smells quite familiar.'

Carla straightens up from the oven and puts the cake on a tray. 'It's Mama's recipe, that's why – it's the chocolate cake she always made.'

She puts down the oven mitt and walks over to him. 'Sorry to have been so grumpy earlier. I'm so glad you're here. We should try to do some fun things together. Why don't you give Mim a call, ask her for dinner or lunch sometime? I'd like to get to know her.'

Chapter Eleven

Alice is trying to decide on something to wear for her appointment with Stuart. She tries on a couple of loose floral dresses but decides they are not smart enough for a solicitor whose office is filled with precious antiques and mahogany furniture. She needs to look like an upper-class woman of substance, imposing but approachable. She has aimed for this most of her life since she married Colin. She struggled to look appropriate for him, and to Alice 'appropriate' means substantial, but because she was physically rather more substantial than she would like to be she always felt she'd failed. Something was always too tight: blouses strained at their buttons, skirts and trousers at their zips and seams, and bulges of flesh peeked out around the armholes of dresses. From day one Colin had said that he loved the 'generosity' of her body, but Alice thought her body was far too generous. She often saw women much larger than her carrying their weight with confidence, wearing tight-fitting clothes that seemed to celebrate their lumps and bumps and bulges, their spare tyres and their plump thighs. Alice had never managed to capture the confidence that might have given her a sparkle in her eye, a swagger in her walk, a swing to her hips.

She had never been really slim. The sixties were a nightmareish time for her, especially when Twiggy appeared on the scene. There she was on the cover of seemingly every magazine, wearing tiny, close-fitting dresses so short they barely covered her bum. And then one day, while searching for something to wear to a friend's twenty-first birthday party, Alice found a dress that she loved. She remembers that dress now: fine, creamy white cheesecloth, trimmed discreetly at hem, neck and shoulders with scarlet stitching, a pattern of tiny red and white beads across the bodice. She piled up her hair on top of her head in loose curls and fixed it in place with scarlet combs, some tendrils escaping around her face. It was August 1967, a mild evening. She was twenty and for the first time in her life she felt beautiful in the softly lit garden, where people were dancing to Scott McKenzie singing 'San Francisco'. All evening Alice had felt Tim Helpmann's eyes on her. They'd started university at the same time, and that night Tim had looked super cool, dressed in black, his blond hair bleached to a silvery white and a black stud in one ear. He smiled, pinched out the tip of his joint and tucked the remains into his pocket.

'You look amazing, Al,' he said. Grasping her hand, he pulled her to him on the dance floor, his grassy breath drifting across her face. But as he wrapped his arm around her waist, Alice saw his face change as he encountered the roll of fat where her waist should be.

'Get rid of that spare tyre, babe,' he said, 'and then you'll really be something!'

Alice froze, her face flushed a deep red, and she pulled away, turning her back on him to hide her tears. When she had regained her composure and turned to face him again, he was gone, weaving his way through the crowd of dancers, leaving her standing alone.

'D'you really want to go on letting a moment with that moron define you?' Mim has asked her, more than once. 'You're beautiful, Alice. Colin saw it; he adored you. He said you were Rubenesque.'

'And we all know what that means,' Alice always replied.

Any sliver of confidence in herself and her body had vanished that night, despite the evidence that other men had found her attractive. But Alice has never been the right shape for fashion. And now even her 'crowning glory', as her father had called her reddish gold hair, is heavily streaked with grey. She sighs and continues her inspection of her wardrobe.

She settles on a simple blue wool dress that flares out gently from the shoulders, conveniently hiding what lies beneath. It has a round neck and three-quarter sleeves. She clips on the double string of pearls that had been Colin's wedding present to her, and completes the ensemble with low-heeled shoes in blue leather. To anyone else she would look like a discreetly well-dressed woman in her early seventies; to herself she looks like a blue elephant. She sighs. *Plus ça change* . . . she murmurs, and she picks up her handbag and calls an Uber to take her to Stuart's office.

The law firm of Burton, Waters & Manstone occupies the first two floors of one of Oxford's oldest buildings. When Alice pushes open the heavy door and steps inside, she inhales a combination of polished wooden floors and the scent of a lemon tree in a huge pot lodged on a stone plinth in the centre of the entrance hall. She makes her way up the wide, carpeted staircase to the reception area, where the receptionist greets her with a smile and leads her through to Stuart's office.

'Alice, how lovely to see you,' Stuart says. He gets to his feet and walks around the desk to kiss her on both cheeks. 'It's been such a long time!'

The receptionist takes her coat and hangs it on the coat stand in a corner of the room, and Stuart asks her to bring them some coffee.

'So, what can I do for you, Alice?' he asks when he is sitting behind his desk once more, and Alice is in a seat facing him.

'I'm considering a trip to Australia to stay with my sister – a longish stay, three months or maybe longer – but I wanted to check the conditions of Colin's will before I make any definite plans. When you first read it, I was still a bit of mess . . .'

'You were, quite naturally, grieving.'

'Exactly. And I know that it said the house was mine for life and then it goes to Michael. But I think there was something else . . . something about having to occupy it?'

Stuart's eyes narrowed. 'I think you're right about that, but I'll have to double-check. We have all the documents online now, so it won't take a minute . . .' He types something into his computer and waits. 'As far as I remember, it was something that he added in case you had to move out to go into some form of care. In that circumstance, Michael could take over the house, but there's financial provision for the cost of that. Aha! Here we are: *Last Will and Testament of Colin James Wilson.*' He turns the computer so that Alice can see the screen. 'Down here.' He points to the clause in question. 'Yes, if you are no longer able to live in the property or no longer want to, then it reverts to Michael. But it certainly doesn't mean you can't go away for a few months. Then there's the part about the allocation of funds for your alternative accommodation should you choose to move elsewhere or have to move into care. Such a move would be financed by Colin's estate and managed by whomever you have listed as your next of kin. You could buy a place of your own or pay for care and accommodation. There is plenty of money for all that. Your income from the family trust continues until your death. Have you looked at the capital that Colin bequeathed you personally?'

Alice shakes her head. 'No. This must sound ridiculous, but I've barely even thought about it. Isn't that pathetic? But the income is so generous, most of it just goes into my account and stays there. I spend very little.'

Stuart smiles. 'Well, you could easily manage a few months with your sister then. I'll have my secretary print all this out for you, highlighting the relevant sections.'

'Thank you,' Alice says. 'I'd appreciate that. So, there's

nothing to stop me staying in Australia for, say, three to six months?'

'Nothing at all. And we have a private security service for clients who are away from home. They do a drive past every day and go onto the property to inspect it once a week, checking for damage, that kind of thing. Would you like me to organise that for you?'

Twenty minutes later, Alice walks out of the building and straight into a taxi which is being vacated by its passenger. Once settled in the back seat she gets out her phone and checks the world clock to see what the time is in Western Australia. She's disappointed to see it's the middle of the night. For a moment she's tempted to call anyway, but instead she replaces her phone in her bag. She can't wait to tell Mim that she is finally planning a trip to Australia!

Chapter Twelve

Mathias is not accustomed to buses, but this one seems pretty good. It arrived on time, the fare was surprisingly cheap, and the air conditioning is very efficient. All that remains is his concern over whether he will recognise the bus stop where he is supposed to get off.

'Get off at the Fremantle War Memorial,' Mim had said. 'I'll be waiting by the corner.'

Mathias prefers his information clearly detailed to eliminate the possibility of ending up in the wrong place, but when he'd pressed for more information she had simply said not to worry, she would come to Carla's house to pick him up.

'No, no,' he'd said, feeling foolish. 'I'm sure I'll find you.'

When he'd called a few days ago to suggest lunch, Mim had said she'd love to see him, but she needed to go to her shop for a couple of days and sort some things out there, and she also needed to visit Jodie.

'You called her the day after you arrived,' Carla had pointed out. 'You've barely given her time to draw breath.'

Mathias had agreed – and he understood that Mim was busy – but he was frustrated by the delay. He needed to see Mim, to talk to her. The unexpected nature of their shared journey had made it seem almost unreal. When they were in Doha Airport for the second time, sitting once again in the armchairs by the pool, they had talked about their unlikely first meeting there and the fact that they now felt like old friends.

'I don't make friends easily,' Mathias had told her. 'I never have, and I've become more cautious than ever with age.'

'Me too. My friends are mostly people I've known for a long time. And there aren't many of them left now.' Mim had hesitated. 'I think I've got increasingly picky about the people I want to spend time with.'

But now he needs to know that they were talking not only about themselves but also acknowledging that this new friendship was significant. A private person by nature, he has spent much of his life avoiding casual connections with people who are intrigued by his public self as a writer. He wants to know that this new friendship is real, that it is solid, despite how little they really know about each other. He returns again to his conversations with Mim, trying, as he might with a book, to read her more closely, in the hope that as each page is turned it will deepen and strengthen the connection made on that disrupted journey.

As the bus rolls smoothly on, Mathias sees a memorial

ahead of him, and it's so obvious he knows he need not have worried about missing it. As the bus slows to a halt, he is the first to step down onto the pavement. Mim is standing near the corner under the shade of a huge tree, waving to him, and minutes later they are in her car heading for a cafe near the beach.

'You really should have let me pick you up,' she says. 'It's not far. Have you had breakfast? The place I'm thinking of has a great breakfast menu. And I thought that after that I could show you my bookshop, *Life Support*. What do you think?'

'I think that's a great idea,' he says, buoyed by her willingness to show him something of her life. 'And what an excellent name for a bookshop.' His awkwardness unwinds gently, and he feels again as he had felt in Doha and on the flight home; they have reconnected after the complicating silence of the last few days.

'I brought your magazine,' Mathias says, pointing to the carrier bag on the floor by his feet. *'Ravishing Resorts.'*

'Thank you,' Mim says. 'I think. I have rather mixed feelings about reading it.'

'Mixed feelings? After I went to all the trouble of stealing it for you?' Mathias teases.

Mim starts to laugh. 'Oh dear, that's true – I turned you into a mole!'

Mathias starts to laugh too, and he feels his shoulders loosening, his body slowly relaxing. 'You'll have to keep *Ravishing Resorts* forever as a reminder that I sacrificed my good character for you.'

*

Later, Mim insists on dropping Mathias home to his
daughter's house, then hurries back to the hospital to visit
Jodie. Searching for a space in the hospital car park is like
a particularly irritating board game, she thinks; one where
you are constantly bested by someone sharper or more
ruthless. Mim hates board games. Eventually she sees a
potential opportunity just ahead of her in the parallel lane.
A woman is leading an older man to a silver Toyota in one
of the disability bays. Mim accelerates rapidly to the top of
her lane and turns sharply into the adjacent one against
the direction of the traffic. As the silver Toyota backs out
and drives off, she swings into the empty space, cutting
off a man in a Subaru waiting at the head of the cars in the
correct lane for the vacant bay. He stops right behind her
and blasts his horn. In her rear-view mirror, she sees him
give her the finger. She stays inside the car until the rest of
the cars behind him start hooting and he is forced to move
on. Mim apologises to God, something she is still prone to
do when she knows she's behaved badly.

Is it actually a sin? she wonders. *Well, anyway, I'm sorry.*

She doubts that God actually accords her intermittent
requests, misdemeanours, apologies or thanks much attention, but she can't quite let go of this connection to Him.

With the angry driver now at a safe distance, she takes
a swig from her water bottle, grabs her bag and the books
she has brought for Jodie and gets out of the car.

As she walks into the hospital, Mim wonders what
Mathias would have thought of her thuggish behaviour
in the car park. She suspects he would have disapproved.
But she's pretty sure that God would approve of the

comprehensive plan she has made for Jodie, which she has brought with her. She's quite proud of it; she has gone to a lot of trouble to cover all possibilities, depending on how incapacitated Jodie might be. Trying to plan for every eventuality was pretty demanding, though, she admits to herself, and she's realised that caring for an invalid will likely prove much more difficult than she's imagined. The same was true of her last two days at the shop. She'd felt tired and confused, as though she couldn't slip back into the daily routine; Doug had had to help her out a few times and she'd come home exhausted. Had she not arranged to meet Mathias, she would have stayed in bed most of the day, but it had been lovely to catch up with him. It made her realise how much she had missed him.

*

Jodie is sitting in a wheelchair reading *Unexploded*, a book that Mim had brought her yesterday.

'Hello, Mim,' she says, 'you *are* good coming again. I hope you're not doing too much; you look pretty tired.'

'Jet-lag, I think,' Mim says. 'And I've spent the last couple of days at the shop. That was quite tiring. How are you going?'

'Okay, though time seems to move very slowly in here,' Jodie says. 'Luckily, this book is wonderful – I don't want to put it down. Did you buy it because it's about Brighton, or because you like the author's other books?'

'Both, really,' Mim says, settling herself into a chair. 'I've loved Alison MacLeod's other books, but I found this one particularly interesting because it's set in Brighton in the immediate post-war years, when I was a child there. It captures that time perfectly – it nudges memories that are so far back it's almost impossible to articulate them. I'm so glad you're enjoying it. I'm sure you could do with the distraction.'

'I have been worried about how they're coping at work,' Jodie confessed. 'The good news is that Steven has said that he can cover for me at the surgery for as long as I need.'

'Oh, that *is* good news,' Mim says. 'It must be a weight off your mind.'

Jodie nods. 'It really is.' She glances out of the window for a moment, dreading what she has to say next, then looks back at Mim. 'He's also organising an intercom connection between the house and the surgery, so I can call for help if I need it.'

'But if you come to me that won't be necessary,' Mim says. She reaches into her bag and pulls out a notebook, then slips on her reading glasses. 'I've made a plan, and I think you'll see that I've thought of everything.'

'I'm not staying with you Mim,' Jodie says, gently but firmly. 'We spoke about that the other day. I'm going to rehab and after that I can go back home. I want to be close to the practice, so I can keep up to date with what's going on. I want to be in my own place.'

Mim looks up from her plan and takes off her reading glasses. 'I have had a rethink about the rehab since we spoke,' she says. 'And you're probably right, it makes sense. If that's what Rosemary recommends, then you should do it. And I should have realised you'd want to be in your own place; I'm sure I'd want that too in your situation. So here's a new plan: when you're released from rehab I'll move into your downstairs bedroom. It's very pleasant, and it even has its own ensuite. It's ideal, in fact, because I really don't feel I can manage your stairs on a regular basis.'

There is an awkward silence. 'Well, the thing is,' Jodie says, 'I'll be in the downstairs bedroom myself, because obviously I won't be able to manage the stairs on crutches.'

Mim stares at Jodie who is holding her breath, trying not to get rattled by her friend's expression. It's an expression that seems to encompass disapproval, disappointment and wounded pride, just like the look Jodie's late mother wore when she was disappointed in her daughter.

'Of course, how silly of me. But you'll need someone to look after you, to prepare your meals and do your shopping, help you in the shower and . . . and everything else. Ah well – I'll have to get used to the stairs, I suppose.'

'It's lovely of you to offer, Mim,' Jodie says, 'but I've already arranged for Kirra to stay with me. She'll help with the cooking and shopping and showering and all that, and she'll still be able to do some work in the surgery. And I've arranged for a full-time temporary vet nurse to cover for her at the practice. It's someone Steven knows and has worked with before. I'm relieved that it's all fallen into place so well.'

Mim's face seems to have turned to stone and Jodie feels her throat go dry.

'I see,' Mim says after an awkward silence. 'When was all this organised?'

'Steven and Kirra came over early yesterday morning, and we talked it through with Rosemary.'

There is another long silence. Then Mim shrugs, puts her notebook back in her bag and gets up.

'Well, you obviously won't need me around, getting under everyone's feet,' she says. 'I really don't know why I bothered making a plan. What a waste of time that was! Clearly you can manage perfectly well without me, so I'll be off now. I have a lot to do at home and at the shop.'

'Mim,' Jodie says, 'please don't be upset. I *will* need you; of course I will. You're my dearest friend. I hoped you might make me lunch sometimes to give Kirra a break, maybe do some shopping, take me to medical appointments or out for coffee. More than anything, I'll want your company. We can spend time together, talk, watch movies – we could even have a game of chess, like we've been promising ourselves for ages . . .'

But Mim has picked up her bag and slung it over her shoulder. 'I'll think about it,' she says. 'Like I told you, I have a lot to do at the shop. I'll pop back in a few days, before you go to rehab. Call me if you need me.' And she leans over to kiss Jodie goodbye then walks briskly out of the door.

Jodie sighs. *Well, I really made a mess of that*, she tells herself. *But it had to be done.* She leans back against the pillows, reminding herself that there was no way that Mim could have managed everything. She imagines herself stuck in the shower on one of those chairs with wheels and Mim trying to get her out; Mim trying to do the shopping, cook the meals, do the laundry and the housework and going up and down the stairs. *I just wanted her to be my friend*, she tells herself. *Keep my spirits up, help me get through some of the boredom and get me out of the house from time to time. Just be my friend, Mim, that's all I want.* Her eyes start to fill with tears and she reaches over to the bedside table to grab some tissues.

She knows their friendship is as important to Mim as it is to her, despite the difference in their ages. For Jodie, the presence in her life of a wise and loving older woman is a gift. She had been nineteen and at university in Perth when her parents and Joel, her younger brother, went to visit a friend of her father in Kalgoorlie. The man had his own small plane and one afternoon he offered to fly them over to see another property he'd bought recently. As they approached home at dusk the aircraft engine abruptly lost power and the plane dropped out of the sky. The pilot, her parents and Joel died in the crash.

The family had moved from Ireland to Australia five years earlier and for several years, as she struggled with devastating loss, Jodie battled with the shocking reality of being alone in the world. She considered going back to Galway, but eventually decided to finish her degree and find an internship so she could go back to Ireland as a qualified vet. But by the time that happened, she'd made some good friends, acquired a lot more confidence, and Ireland no longer felt like home. She worked for several years at a practice in Geraldton and later in Port Hedland. Finally, she realised she wanted her own practice and she moved south again, staying with an old friend from uni and working in another vet's practice until she found what she wanted. A vet who owned a practice near Fremantle was retiring, and although the property was a bit rundown, there were plenty of clients and lots of scope for Jodie to renovate and expand. Having recently come out of a long-term relationship, the only thing missing in her life then had been a sense of family – until she met Mim. And Mim, like her, has experienced loss. She hardly ever mentions her brief marriage – Jodie only knows that her husband died very young – but she is aware that Mim hasn't had a significant relationship since and is determinedly self-sufficient.

Jodie sighs. She has always felt that she and Mim are very similar: fiercely independent, often to their own detriment, stubborn and quick to take offence. It's that similarity, she thinks, that keeps their friendship alive; despite their often-fierce disagreements, they do understand each other. She takes a deep breath now and picks up her book. *Mim and I are so alike*, she thinks. *Dangerously so. We both blow up easily and feel shame when we know we have to back off. We behave like family, which is what we want, but we lack the security of a blood relationship, so when we disagree, we panic that we are falling apart.*

*

Mim drives home, sitting rigidly upright, clutching the steering wheel in a firm grip, aware that her face is tight and pinched. Although she had tried to keep her face neutral, she is sure that Jodie had seen how upset she was about the plan for recovery in which there was no essential role for her. Realising that Jo was absolutely right had not made it any easier to bear. She felt stupid, embarrassed for assuming that she could simply take over. Making cups of tea was not what she'd imagined; it was insulting. She tries to focus on the traffic, but her mind constantly drifts away. As she reaches Monument Hill, where she had met Mathias that morning, she remembers how happy and enthusiastic she'd felt then. Now she feels useless, unwanted. There have been so many times in her life when she had felt like this: rejected, assumed incompetent because of her disability.

'A lot of that is just in your head,' Alice had told her recently. 'Mainly it's people trying to take the pressure off you because you want to take on too much. You've always done that, and you don't need to. You have nothing to prove, and it's really annoying, and it will wear you out.'

Mim had listened but, really, she was thinking instead of the netball and hockey teams from which she'd been excluded, the times when she was the only girl at the party who was never asked to dance. Even when she had become a librarian, she was frustrated by the tall library steps which someone else would have to climb for her. There was always somewhere she could not go, could not reach. It left her with a sense of shame and inadequacy. All her life she has had to put up with well-meaning but unconsciously demeaning comments from people who make assumptions about her ability. And while she might appear stoic, inside she burns with frustration.

'No one ever really understands this,' she had said to Alice recently. They had just finished breakfast at the long table in Alice's kitchen, and Alice had got up to clear away the dishes.

'Really, you are so exasperating!' Alice had retorted. 'You won't ever give in and ask for help, let alone accept it or even admit that you might need it. You bite the head off anyone who offers. Well, everyone needs help sometimes, Mim, and the older we get the more help we need. Sometimes you really piss me off. Grow up, will you? Just *grow up!*'

And Alice carried their plates to the sink and slammed them down so hard on the draining board that the bottom one cracked.

Later they'd laughed about it, and Mim has reflected on Alice's words a few times since. *But this is who I am*, she tells herself now. *I'm too old to change.*

Mim turns off the main road and heads through the backstreets towards East Fremantle, willing herself to stop thinking like this, to be more positive. She turns into her own street and then her own driveway, where she stops the engine and sits for a moment in the car. Then she gets out awkwardly, goes into the house and puts the kettle on. As she takes her tea out onto the verandah, her legs are aching relentlessly, and she suddenly remembers the carrier bag that Mathias had given her when they met this morning. She puts down her tea and goes back out to the car to find the bag and bring it inside. As she lifts *Ravishing Resorts* out of the bag, she sees a white cardboard box beneath it and pulls that out too. Mathias has scrawled something on the box, and she puts her glasses on to read it.

Mim – some canine friends to sweeten your reading. M x

The box contains six chocolate dogs in red and gold foil. Mim feels her tension softening, loosening, as she chooses a chocolate poodle and eats it slowly. Then she picks up the magazine and opens it to the story on Harold House.

*

Jodie is sitting in a wheelchair by the window when Rosemary arrives.

'Hi there!' the doctor calls, walking over to her. 'How are you going? I came by earlier but saw that Mim was with you, so I thought I wouldn't interrupt.' She sits down in the seat where Mim had sat earlier. 'You were both looking really serious.'

Jodie nods. 'I told Mim I'm not going to stay with her after I leave rehab. It didn't go down too well.'

'Mim is a very smart and competent person,' Rosemary says. 'I'm sure she's able to understand the limits of her abilities in this situation. She may well be upset, but she's not stupid. She's had a tough life and she's learned to live it with grace and dignity. My bet is that she'll do the same with this. Just give her time.'

Jodie shrugs. 'We'll see.'

Rosemary leans forward, lowers her voice. 'You lost your whole family, and I remember how devastating that was for you; no one else could get near you for a long time. I know how much Mim means to you, and I'm sure that she knows it too. She is not going to give up on you or disappear from your life, if that's what you're thinking.'

Jodie's throat feels thick with unshed tears as she says, 'I hope you're right, because despite my concern about her neediness in recent months, I would be absolutely lost without her.'

Chapter Thirteen

As Carla lets herself in to the house, she can smell something cooking, and she hurries through to the kitchen.

'Have you made *hutspot*?' she asks her father, lifting a saucepan lid and peering in. 'Oh my goodness, Papa, it smells divine.'

'It's not bad,' Mathias admits with a smile. 'Put the lid back, please, and no, you can't taste it; it still has a way to go. I have very good pork fillets to go with it.'

Carla takes off her coat, drops it over the back of a chair and gets a spoon from the cutlery drawer. Ignoring her father's chiding, she lifts the lid from the *hutspot* again and takes a spoonful. 'Ouch! It's really hot,' she says, covering her mouth with her hand.

'Darling, it's on the stove, on the *hotplate*, of course it's *hot*. And, as I said, it's not ready yet!'

'Mmm, but it's so delicious. I haven't had *hutspot* since

the last time I stayed with you. I'm so lazy about cooking when I'm on my own.'

Mathias gets another spoon and samples the mix of boiled and mashed potatoes, carrots and onions himself. 'Yes, pretty good, although I always suspected your mother had some secret ingredient, because hers was always better than mine. Perhaps she just had more patience.'

He pulls the cork from a bottle of Beaujolais that he had bought at the airport in Brussels and pours two glasses, handing one to her. 'Here, let's sit down and drink this. The *hutspot* needs to stand for a while, and there's something I want to discuss with you.'

Carla raises her eyebrows. 'Sounds serious.'

'It is,' Mathias says. 'I'm thinking of selling the house.'

'You're selling? Really? Why?'

Her father takes a deep breath. 'Because I want to move here to Perth. Not to this house,' he adds hurriedly, 'but around this area. I love it here, and I would like to be closer to you, to see you more often, in more natural circumstances. I've been thinking about it for a while and I think it is time I did something about it.'

'What's brought this on?' Carla asks, concerned. Mathias has always loved the house in the Dandenongs; she never imagined he might move. 'Are you okay? There's nothing wrong, is there?'

'No, nothing like that. It's just that as I grow older, I feel the sense of time running out. I talked it through with Luc. Seeing how he is now made me consider my own future. Not in a sad way, just a more practical one.'

'And is Miriam a factor in this decision?'

Mathias shrugs. 'Perhaps. Who knows? We've only just met. But it would be an added pleasure to have her continuing friendship. That's not what's motivating me, however. The most important thing is that I would be able to spend more time with you. What do you think?

Carla is touched. 'It would be lovely to have you here and be able to do things together. And it makes sense, too, because if the time comes when you need a bit of help, it will be easier for both of us to be living in the same city. If you are really sure it's what you want, you should do it.'

Mathias nods. 'I thought I might speak to a couple of local real estate agents, get an indication of what's available, prices and so on.'

'That sounds like a good place to start,' Carla agrees. 'Have you thought about where you might like to live? Are there any particular areas that you're interested in?'

'I don't know Perth well enough yet,' he says. 'I'm ashamed to say that although I've visited you here several times, I've learned very little about my surroundings. When I went to Fremantle today with Mim, I liked it very much. There are lots of shops and cafes; it had a very nice atmosphere. And we went to South Fremantle to see her shop.' He laughs. 'It's called Life Support!'

'Oh, I know it well!' Carla exclaims. 'I often go in there. In fact, when I first met Mim at the airport, I thought I knew her from somewhere. That must be it.'

'She does seem to love the shop, although it's obviously a lot of work. Of course, I couldn't leave a shop like that without wanting to buy the contents of several shelves, but I managed to restrict myself to a few, one of which is for you.' He gets to his feet to retrieve a bag he'd left near the door.

Carla watches him as he bends carefully to pick it up and then unpacks the books onto the end of the table. He selects one, and she sees him peering at the cover. She makes a mental note to suggest he has his eyes tested; he might need new glasses. As he turns back towards her, he is fleetingly unfamiliar: an old man who moves stiffly, with a certain amount of caution; a man who looks tired and strangely sad. Carla feels a lump in her throat. She has not seen him this way before, and she thinks Luc's deterioration must have made him more aware of his own age. He is, she realises, adjusting his expectations, planning how and where to be an old man. She feels a sudden rush of gratitude that he wants to spend his final years near her.

'Here it is,' he says, holding up a weathered paperback. 'Doris Lessing, *The Summer Before the Dark*.'

Carla smiles. 'Is it about a writer meeting a woman in an airport and falling in love with her by any chance?'

'I very much doubt it,' he says, laughing. 'But I haven't read it, so you'll have to tell me. All I know is that your mother, who was not much taken with Lessing's early writing, really loved this and often urged me to read it.' He holds it out to her.

Carla takes it from him and flicks through the pages. 'Thanks, Papa, I'll read it for both of us.' And she puts her arms around his neck and kisses him. 'Thanks for the book and thanks for being you. I'm so happy you're thinking of moving here. I really miss you.'

Chapter Fourteen

*I*t's seven o'clock in the evening and Mim is lying on her bed talking to Alice on the phone; that is, she is lying on one narrow section of the bed, as Brenda has taken possession of the centre and is sprawled horizontally across it, while Mim is perched uncomfortably close to the edge. She would normally have nudged Brenda out of the way, but she feels she's had the stuffing knocked out of her today and doesn't have the energy for a territorial battle. Emotionally she is a mess of anger, resentment, helplessness and, unusually for her, loneliness. It's as though all those things have come together in a great blurry cloud and landed on top of her.

'Perhaps it's just jet-lag,' Alice suggests when Mim describes her mood. 'You've only been home a week; it takes some people a couple of weeks to get over it. I hope I don't suffer too badly when I come over.'

Mim, who had been thrilled to hear that her sister was

finally planning a trip, rushes to reassure her. 'It doesn't usually bother me,' she says. 'I'm sure you'll be fine.' She sighs. 'It's not that.'

'So, what is it?' Alice asks.

Mim hesitates. 'Various things. Jodie, of course; I wish I could do more to help her. I really feel left out, although I understand the reasons. My legs, especially the right one, are exceptionally painful at the moment. And I'm finding the shop exhausting. I just hope I have more energy tomorrow; Mathias wants me to go with him to look at some houses. He's thinking of moving here.'

'Really?' Alice says. 'Is this to be near you?'

'No, of course not; he's not a person to do something like that on a whim. His daughter lives here, and I think he's a bit lonely where he lives now.'

'No, I think it's you. I think he's fallen in love with you and wants to be near you,' Alice teases. 'Poor Mathias – he met this sweet old lady at the airport and has no idea what a cantankerous old bat she can be.'

Mim laughs. 'Only a sister could be so cruel.' Then she grows more sombre. 'I think my current mood has something to do with Harold House.' And she tells Alice about the article in *Ravishing Resorts*.

'So, someone's making a lot of money out of that place now,' Alice says. 'But it's nothing to do with you. That was years ago, Mim – decades. Last century. I do try to understand how polio affected your life and still does, but I don't know why that place continues to upset you so much.'

Mim sighs. She knows it's hard for Alice to understand the fear and loathing that still haunts her. 'There were a number of black-and-white photographs in the article from the old days,' she says. 'There were pictures of us.'

'Who?'

'Us children.' She swallows. 'Me. In one of the pictures I'm sitting up in my bed, one of a long line of beds out on the terrace. They used to push our beds out onto the terrace in summer to get the fresh air.'

'That must have been nice,' Alice says.

'No, Alice, it was not nice. Nothing about that place could be called nice, *nothing*, except perhaps a couple of the nurses. The caption under that photo – well, I'll read it to you. She pulls the magazine towards her and begins to read: *'Children with polio enjoyed sunbathing on the terrace. How fortunate they were to be in this glorious location, surrounded by fields, making friends with local farmers and playing with the animals.'*

'Animals?' Alice says. 'I didn't know you had animals there.'

'We didn't! I assume the moron who wrote this is referring to the cows that belonged to the farm nearby. We could sometimes see them from the terrace. And we certainly weren't making friends with the farmers – it was an isolation hospital. This article is complete rubbish. Sorry, Al, you know all this, but seeing the photographs, all those children packed in their beds or the iron lungs. Most of us couldn't get out of bed for ages – weeks, months; we couldn't move, couldn't breathe. There are several other photos taken during the time I was there. In one of them a little girl lying in one of a line of iron lungs has been turned on her side and a nurse has opened a flap on the lung and is reaching inside to wash the girl's bottom. The indignity of it! That little girl was *me*, Al.'

'Are you sure the nurse wasn't just straightening a blanket or something?' Alice asks.

'No, Alice, no!' Mim shouts down the phone. 'She was washing my bottom, I tell you! And I am clearly identifiable. How could they do that, publish these pictures of sick children to advertise a new resort? The shame of it!' She slams down the phone.

For several minutes she just lies there, breathing heavily, overcome with rage, sadness, humiliation . . . Eventually, she picks up the phone and dials Alice's number.

'I'm sorry,' she says. 'I shouldn't have yelled at you.'

'No,' Alice says. 'I'm the one who should apologise, Mim, and I do. I didn't realise . . . the thing is, I don't have any idea what you went through there. In all these years, you've never wanted to talk about it. Mum and Dad never said much either.'

'I know. That's my fault. I just wanted to forget about it, put it behind me, but of course I never have. It's always been there, festering inside me. Not just the place itself, but what it was like to come home after all that time. The way people treated us, the rejection. It wasn't easy to be different back then. For years people thought we might infect them, or they treated us as though polio was dirty, or even a mental illness.' She stopped for breath. 'Sorry, I'm going on about it again.'

'Mim, I think you need to talk about that time. If you want to talk to me, that would be good for both of us. Or perhaps you should get some professional help.'

'Professional help?' Mim is affronted. 'See a psychologist you mean?'

'Why not?'

'No way,' Mim replies. 'I don't want some stranger analysing me.'

'You could start writing it down then,' Alice suggests, 'just for yourself. Getting it out of your head onto paper might help.'

After they hang up, Mim thinks over their conversation. She knows she was horrible and rude and that she shouted, but she had been shocked by the fact that her sister seemed to know little or nothing about the hospital. But of course, Alice was right: when Mim was back home with her family she refused to talk about what she'd been through. Any questions about what it was like in the hospital were met with a blank stare. Has she ever told her sister anything? Had her parents not told Alice anything, or . . . Suddenly she sat bolt upright. Could it be, could it possibly be, that they didn't even know? She had been in the iron lung at Harold House for months. It had seemed endless. No visitors, not even parents, were allowed into that area. Later, when she was moved to a normal ward, it was still closed to visitors, to protect the children from infection.

'Wave to Mummy and Daddy through the window,' the nurses would tell them, and one at a time the parents' faces would appear at the small oval window in the door to the ward.

Mim remembers her mother's face, wet with tears, blowing her kisses, trying so hard to smile, and her father's eyes glistening as he waved.

People came and went; new children were admitted as others left to go home. Days dragged on and nothing changed. If the days seemed long, the nights seemed longer, alone in the dark. The sound of a nurse's footsteps on the wooden floors, the cries of other children. It wasn't until a month before she was discharged that her parents were allowed into a special visiting room to see her. It was so long since she had actually spoken to them that they now seemed like strangers, and Mim didn't know how to behave with them. Although the nurses and later her parents had explained time and again why she had been sent to Harold House, and why she couldn't go home, she refused to believe them. She had believed that her father was a very important person, like the prime minister, so he should have been able to rescue her. But John Squires was simply the manager of the Brighton branch of Marks and Spencer. Mim was eight when she finally went home, and by then Alice was a noisy five-year-old who monopolised the adults' attention by throwing tantrums. When Mim thinks now of her gentle, thoughtful sister, it seems impossible that she could have been such a pain as a child. Now she realises that Alice would have been as confused and anxious as she had been. Despite the fuss that was made of her back home, Mim felt that she had been replaced by Alice. She was home, but home was different, and so was she.

Some months later, still confused, Mim decided to run away from home to Australia. She was struggling at school because of all the time she'd missed, but the class was doing a project on Australia and she fell in love with pictures of koalas and kangaroos and wide sandy beaches. The beach in Brighton was all pebbles, almost impossible for her to walk on. Australia seemed like the perfect place to go. She had almost nine pounds in her money box. It seemed an enormous sum, and there was a man at the beach who took people on rides in his little boat. She would ask him where to get a boat to Australia. She packed a few clothes, her money box and an Enid Blyton book into her school bag and set off down the stairs one night when her parents were fast asleep.

The stairs were always difficult for Mim, but it was the red metal money box, designed to look like a postbox, that foiled her escape. Her savings were mainly in coins, so when she tripped and fell on the stairs it was the clanging of the coins in the tin box that brought her father rushing out of the bedroom in a panic.

A few weeks later, her parents left Alice with a neighbour and told Mim they were taking her on a special surprise trip to London. After a long drive her mother told her they were at the London docks, where long lines of people were queuing to board a huge ship.

'Look, darling,' her mother said. 'This is one of the ships that goes to Australia – that's where all these people are going.'

Mim remembers staring up at the ship, which was terrifyingly large. People were swarming everywhere, making their way up the gangplanks, walking around on the decks. Mim clung to her mother's hand, overwhelmed.

'We thought you'd like to see it,' her father said, picking her up so that she would have a better view. 'It takes a long time to get to Australia – several weeks – and it costs lots of money. You can go there when you are older; when you are eighteen, perhaps. We'll help you.'

Mim was actually in her twenties when she finally visited Australia for the first time, leaving Brighton and the spectre of the polio hospital behind. But now her head is filled with shadowy fragments of the past and she feels she is on the cusp between memory and forgetting. Was Alice right? Had she really never told her family about the misery of Harold House?

Back then she had no idea how she had got there. It seemed that one minute she'd been playing on the beach and the next she woke up in that strange and horrible place. It was several weeks before she even saw her parents through the little glass window. She was terrified, in pain, away from home and alone for the first time. The months in the iron lung were the ultimate misery. Lying on her back, barely able to move, listening to the hissing of the machines that were keeping her and the other children alive. Worst of all was the sense of abandonment. It was an emotion she couldn't name then, and she feared she was being punished for something she didn't know she'd done. She considers now that this might be why she never told her parents what it was like. As a child, she could not have articulated the depth of hurt and resentment she felt, even though she knew on some subconscious level that it was not something her parents had planned or chosen for her. She could never describe her experience to them, was never able to put it into words. Not then. Not ever.

Years later, in the days after their mother's death, Mim

and Alice had cleared out the family home in Brighton. Their father had died five years earlier, and they had agreed to sell the house and share the proceeds. Mim flew back to London Gatwick where Alice met her and they drove on to Brighton, where they spent an exhausting few days sorting, packing, filling rubbish bins, delivering clothes, bed linen and curtains to the Oxfam shop and bargaining with second-hand furniture dealers. Mim, who was by then a librarian, could only manage a short stay because she had used her annual leave earlier in the year. They had collected all the old paperwork – certificates, letters, diaries and more – into an old leather suitcase, telling themselves and each other that one day they would sit down together and go through it. But that never happened. It's years since Mim has even thought about this, and now she wonders whether Alice still has the suitcase and its contents.

Finally, Mim gets up from the bed and, with Brenda following, walks through to the kitchen and turns on the light. Sitting down at the kitchen table she puts on her glasses and writes a text to Alice.

Me again! Sorry for this afternoon. I'm so happy you're planning to come here. Please come soon and stay as long as you like. I miss you already and I can't wait to see you. Love from your grumpy sister. xxx

Chapter Fifteen

It's July and Mathias has been staying with Carla for seven weeks now. As he takes a last look around the room that has been his, he knows it's past time he went home. The house in Monbulk has been empty for too long and he has work to get on with. He's done very little here, yet the time seems to have flown by. Having discussed his plan to move with both Carla and Mim, he has been out most days familiarising himself with Perth and Fremantle, and looking at properties. He and Mim have looked at several houses together, drunk gallons of coffee and tucked into croissants or Portuguese tarts in more cafes than he can recall. It has given him a better knowledge of the area and helped him to highlight some places where he thinks he could feel at home.

Mim had seemed happy to accompany him, but he could see that she was very tired and that her strained relationship with Jodie was weighing on her. To him it sounded as though

Jodie had made the right decisions. He mentioned this as discreetly as possible and Mim had rolled her eyes at him, but as she opened her mouth to reply he had said briskly, 'Besides, it left you free to come house hunting with me.'

Eventually, from their conversations, he had learned that she was anxious about the shop, too. Mim was worried about her ability to cope with it, given her increasing mobility issues, but she couldn't really afford to take on new staff. She had admitted to him that she has some problems with her lungs as well as the more obvious problem with her leg. At the moment she works in the shop several days a week and Mathias is frankly amazed at how much she does there, though he knows it might sound patronising to say as much. Mim, he has come to realise, is fiercely concerned with independence, and this leads her to overestimate her physical competence. It's an interesting phenomenon which would make her a splendid character in a book but is something of a challenge in a friendship.

'Well, when I'm living here full time, I'd be happy to help out,' Mathias told her.

Mim had hesitated, then thanked him and said she would think more about it and might take him up on the offer. He'd been relieved that she hadn't bitten his head off.

Carla had joined them on some of their house hunting excursions, but now she is working on contract for a series of birthday cards for children and he knows that his own sense of uncertainty – some excitement mixed with anxiety – is unsettling for her.

'You can stay as long as you want, Papa,' she said when he talked of leaving. 'I love having you here.'

'Bless you, but I know it's not easy to have someone in the house obsessed with a new plan and needing to talk about it. It's time I went home and started to get things moving there.'

He finally got around to booking a flight, and then called a real estate agent in Monbulk to make an appointment for a valuation the day after he gets home.

'Well, I'm certainly going to miss you,' Mim said, when he called to invite her for dinner the night before he was due to leave. 'I've got comfortably accustomed to having you around. Now I'll have to stop hanging out in cafes and talking, and get on with some work!'

He picks up his suitcase and heads downstairs, where Carla is waiting with the car keys in her hand.

At the airport, they walk together to the check-in area and then take the elevator up to the first floor and sit looking out onto the tarmac, where luggage is being loaded onto the aircraft. They talk about the house in Monbulk which has been their home since they came to Australia.

'Are you absolutely sure that you're okay with my selling it?' Mathias asks.

'You keep asking me that,' Carla says. 'And I keep telling you that I'm fine with it. Really, I am. I'll come over for a few days before you leave, just for a last look around and some self-indulgent nostalgia, but I think you are doing absolutely the right thing.'

Mathias nods and takes her hand. Selling the family home feels like a monumental decision to him, but Carla seems to be taking it quite lightly and he's relieved about that. Whatever he has will be hers eventually, and he needs to know that any decision he makes now has her approval.

'Papa, I want you to know that I really like Mim,' Carla says suddenly. 'And I think she's very good for you.'

'That sounds like she's some sort of medicine or health food,' says Mathias, taken aback by the abrupt change of subject.

'I think she's much more than that. In all the years since Mama died, I have never seen you so comfortable with anyone other than me and Luc. It's like you have a special connection.'

'I feel . . . well, I feel very close to her. I care about her and I enjoy her company.' Mathias thinks he may be blushing. 'She can be quite challenging, too,' he adds.

'I realise that,' Carla says. 'She's not afraid to take you on about anything, and when she does, you take it seriously. Like when you told her you'd decided to move here, and she quizzed you about it.'

Mathias laughs. 'Indeed, she did, and it was good for me – she made me think more clearly about it. She sounded a bit like your mother. But please don't ever tell her I said that, she might not like it. Will you keep an eye on her for me while I'm away?'

'No!' Carla says. 'I will keep an eye on her for *me*, because I like her a lot and want to develop my own friendship with Mim while you're not around!'

*

It's almost 9 p.m. in Victoria when Mathias arrives home and, as always, he is relieved to see his lovely old house unchanged. It's a cold, wet evening – much colder than it had been in Perth – and he is shivering as he puts the lights on and walks through the house, checking that everything is in good shape. Then he takes off his coat and lights the wood stove, watching as the flames lick the logs he had set there in readiness for his return. For some time, he perches on the edge of a chair watching the flames. He has lived here more than thirty years now, and everything is familiar. The house is filled with the possessions he and Therese had brought with them from Belgium and the things they'd acquired over the years. It holds, he thinks, the story of their lives, and he loves it. But he knows that the time has come to leave.

'Are you absolutely sure?' Mim had asked him. 'You might feel differently when you get back home.'

But he doesn't. He is ready for change, for different company, and he looks forward to being closer to Carla. He no longer wants to sit here in the wooded hills when the person dearest to him is living on the other side of the country. It's time for him to be near his daughter in the place where she wants to be. It is a strange sort of handing over to the next generation, he thinks; it is his turn to fit in around her life, to support her. It's a way of seeing it that is new to him and it is something he might want to write about, he thinks: this choice to let the next generation define the future.

Chapter Sixteen

Jodie was so relieved to be going home that as the car turned into the driveway, she thought she might be sick with excitement and relief. Mim had picked her up from rehab and driven her home, and as she stopped the car and switched off the engine, Kirra opened the front door and walked over.

'Welcome home, madam,' Kirra said, trying her best to keep a straight face. 'I am your temporary housekeeper, nurse, companion and jailer.' And she hurried around to the back of the car, opened the boot and dragged out the wheelchair.

Jodie laughed and, glancing across at Mim, was relieved to see that she was laughing too. After their falling-out all those weeks ago, Mim had stayed away from the hospital and only turned up to visit when Jodie was in rehab. Her absence had been both surprising and hurtful, but when Mim did turn up, loaded with books, chocolate and fruit,

Jodie had been delighted to see her. She had been sitting in the sunroom in her wheelchair, reading, when Mim arrived, and she'd been so astonished to see her friend that she had dropped her book on the floor.

'I am so happy to see you,' she said, returning the older woman's hug, and when Mim drew back Jodie saw that she actually had tears in her eyes.

'Me too,' Mim said. 'And I am *so* sorry for my appalling behaviour. I would have come sooner, but I hoped there might be more chance that you'd forgive me if I gave you some space.'

While their rift had been painful, Jodie has to admit that it did mark a positive shift in their relationship. Mim seemed to have taken a couple of steps back, recognising that Jodie is capable of making her own decisions about what's best for her. *Perhaps we just needed that shake up,* Jodie thinks. And right now she feels good about the support system she has put in place for her recovery. She is looking forward to having Kirra in the house; the two women have worked together since Kirra first came to the practice on a work placement in the final year of her vet nursing degree. They'd got on well from the start. Kirra was bright, hard-working and keen to learn, and she had sailed through her final exams with the support of her large Indigenous family, all of whom had turned up for her graduation ceremony. When Jodie tells Kirra that she couldn't manage without her, she really means it, and she is thankful that it is Steven, not her, who will have to deal with the temporary nurse.

She clings now to the armrests on the wheelchair as Kirra pushes her up the temporary ramp to the front door. As Mim helps to manoeuvre the chair across the threshold, Jodie feels grateful that she has actually made a life for herself with its own sort of unconventional family. She might never have known or grown close to Mim or Kirra had her own family lived. And she appreciated their support all the more keenly knowing that had her own family lived they might not have accepted some of her life choices as readily as her friends did. In her final year at university, while still grief-stricken at the loss of her parents and brother, she had had a brief and rather confusing romantic relationship with a woman. When it ended, she was devastated at having lost another person whom she loved, but at least she was now comfortable with her sexuality, which might not have been the case had her parents still been alive. She thinks she would probably have been estranged from them.

It was five years before she fell in love again. Nina was a few years older than Jodie, and at first things went well. They moved in together and Jodie thought they shared a similar vision for their future. But Nina soon grew restless. She had always wanted children and, although Jodie had told her from the start that she did not, Nina frequently returned to the topic and became quite pressing. They were stuck, and although they were both thoughtful and tried to understand each other, small irritations blew up into heated arguments. There were long, resentful silences, and rumblings of discontent on both their parts. Jodie began spending more and more time at work to avoid the tension at home. Things came to a head one afternoon when Jodie had just finished operating on a labrador that had been hit by a car. Despite her efforts, the dog died, and she'd had to break the news to the devastated owners. She was washing her hands when Nina, who taught physics in a nearby high school, marched in.

'I know you're busy,' Nina said, 'but we need to sort this out right now.'

'Sort what out?' Jodie asked, drying her hands and then applying sanitiser.

'I want us to have a child and I need to know if there is ever going to be a time when you'll agree to that.'

Jodie, still distressed by the death of the labrador and under pressure to get to the next patient, responded impatiently. 'We've been over this so many times,' she said irritably. 'Right from the start, I've said I don't want children. I thought we'd got that clear.'

There was a long, painful silence while they stared at each other. Then Nina sighed. 'You are so stubborn. I thought you'd change your mind once we'd been together for some time.'

Jodie stared at her. 'Did I ever indicate that I would?'

Nina shook her head. 'I just hoped . . . I thought . . .'

'Well, you were wrong. I'm sorry, I know it's become a big thing for you. But it's a big thing for me too. It's too big.' There was a long silence. 'You said you understood that.'

'I did,' Nina said tearfully. 'But not anymore. I want a baby, and I've found a donor. He's a nice guy – you've met him, actually – and if you could just come and meet him again and talk to him . . .'

'No,' Jodie said. 'No way. That wouldn't be fair to either of you.'

There was a tap on the door and Julia, the practice receptionist, stuck her head in. 'Your next patient's here, Jodie,' she said.

'Thanks, I need a couple more minutes,' Jodie said. 'Could you put them in whichever consulting room is free and tell them I'll be there shortly?' As Julia closed the door, she turned back to Nina and took a deep breath. 'You must do what feels right for you, Nina,' she said. 'But I'm not going to change . . . and I have to see my next patient now.'

By the end of the week, Nina had moved out, and Jodie spent the next month in a state of numbness, eating large bacon sandwiches and blocks of chocolate, and watching pitiful soap operas on TV. But she knew she'd done the right thing. She had lost her whole family, and while she felt she could and would like to have someone special in her life, she knew she couldn't compromise on something as fundamental as having a baby. If she wasn't committed, it wouldn't be fair to anyone. Instead, she committed herself to developing the practice she had bought, transforming it into a modern, expanded facility, with an operating room, it three consulting rooms, an office and waiting room. Some new accommodation was added for animals who needed to be hospitalised overnight.

Now, inside her own home years later, her wheelchair parked near the window, with the wood stove burning and the smell of coffee floating out from the kitchen, Jodie feels her spirits lift. She loves this house and all it means to her: warmth, security, a place that is entirely her own. She feels tears prick her eyes and brushes them away.

She can hear Kirra and Mim talking in the kitchen, but she can't make out what they're saying. All she can hear is the rise and fall of the voices and the occasional burst of laughter. She leans back in her chair and closes her eyes, relieved that Mim has shown no sign of bearing a grudge. *I should have known it would all work out all right*, she thinks. *Perhaps this is just how families are, how it is to live with other people. Things can't always go smoothly.* In the back of her mind, she had thought it was better and safer to be alone, because if you loved people and were close to them it made you vulnerable. *Maybe I need to open up a bit*, she concedes, *let more people into my life, stop holding them at a distance in case they die and leave me alone. Maybe it is not too late to change.*

Chapter Seventeen

Carla and Mim walk through the house in silence, weaving past other people, and then exchange a glance in which each indicates to the other that it is definitely time to get out of here. Discreetly, they slip past the real estate agent and make their way out of the door and down the path to the gate.

'That was truly horrible,' Carla says once they are out on the pavement.

Mim nods. 'The absolute pits. So dark and made worse by the frankly bizarre colour scheme.'

'I think that was designed to confuse us,' Carla says. 'There were so many different colours and styles of furniture that I think they were trying to draw our attention away from other things that might be wrong with the house.'

She is thankful that Mim has volunteered to inspect houses with her. They had promised Mathias they would keep an eye on the market and view some while he was back in Monbulk. So far, they have seen nothing that would appeal to his taste in any of the areas he'd decided he liked.

It's starting to rain heavily as they get back into Carla's car.

'Come back to my place for lunch,' Carla says. 'I made some soup last night and we can grab a nice crusty loaf on the way. Then I'll run you home later.'

Mim looks at her. 'Are you sure you don't want to go to the last house on the list?'

Carla sighs. 'Only if you insist.'

'I'd rather have soup,' Mim says. 'And it's not like we're in a rush, anyway; it may still take months for Mathias to sell his house.'

Carla wonders if she should slow down the search; she is thankful for Mim's help, but she's also concerned about asking her to do too much. She knows Mim has a lot on her plate at the moment, what with the shop and helping her friend since she was released from hospital. But the fact is, the more time she spends with her, the more Carla enjoys the older woman's company – and the happier she is that Mathias has met her.

'Are you sure you're okay about this, Carla?' Mim had asked after they'd seen their first couple of houses together.

'With what?' Carla asked.

'With Mathias's decision to move here. I tried not to interfere; after all, we only just met. If you feel I've exerted undue influence on him, you should say so.'

Carla had laughed out loud. 'On the contrary, Mim – if meeting you has compelled Papa to do this, then I owe you my thanks.'

She has always been concerned about her father; while Mathias is highly intelligent and creative, a great observer of human nature, in many ways he has always seemed quite unworldly. And now that age seems to be creeping up on him, she wants him close to her, where she can keep an eye on him.

'Suppose Mathias decides it's not the right place for him after all?' Mim asks once they are back at Carla's house, preparing their lunch.

'I'm confident that's not going to happen,' Carla replies as she stirs the soup.

'He's lived there a very long time . . .'

'And now he needs to be here; near people who care about him and whom he cares about. He has me, and now he has you too – that's two more people than he has nearby at present.'

'It's such a big move, though,' Mim says, her brow creased in concern. 'Not one I'd want to take on at our age. Do you think he has any idea how big an emotional upheaval it will be? After all the years he lived there with you and your mother . . . he will be bidding farewell to a huge part of his life.'

'It's what he wants,' Carla says. 'Please don't worry, Mim. It might seem sudden but, as I'm sure you know, Papa has a lot going on under the surface, and I'm taking this desire for change as an indication that he's worked through some stuff about Mama and the past. This has been a long time coming.'

Mim nods as she piles slices of bread onto a plate.

Carla's phone rings and she looks around, trying to locate it.

'It's here,' Mim says, lifting a tea towel. 'You answer it and I'll keep stirring the soup.'

Carla hands over the spoon and picks up her phone.

'Talk of the devil,' she says, looking at the caller ID, 'this is him now. Hi there, Papa, how are you?' She watches as Mim turns down the heat on the stove and walks over to the window to look out at the rain; at first she doesn't take in what her father is saying. 'What was that, Papa?' she asks.

He repeats the news and Carla cries out in delight. 'He's sold the house, Mim!' she calls. 'Come over here and I'll put him on speaker so we can both talk to him.'

Mim sits down beside her at the table and Carla grabs her hand. 'Here's Mim,' she says. 'Now tell us all about it.'

*

Mathias puts down the phone and leans back in his chair, looking around the room in which he has done most of his work for more than thirty years. He's feeling quite emotional: they'd been so happy here, the three of them and then, after Therese died, just Carla and himself. Even alone in recent years he'd enjoyed it. It was always a haven to return to; a real home even though he lived there alone. But he's confident that he has made the right decision. It's no place for an old man on his own: it's cold in winter, hot in summer, and too far from anything and anyone else. Too far from his daughter, especially. He no longer wants to have to chop logs for the fire in winter. He would like to go out on summer evenings for a walk and see some human life around him: people sitting in cafes, bookshops open late, maybe go the cinema or theatre, walk down to the beach and look out over the sea at night. It's the right move, the right time, but part of him will always be here because this is where Therese died. He and Carla had scattered her ashes in the garden. So he's well aware that his satisfaction over the details of the sale, his enthusiasm for what is ahead, is tinged with regret at what he will leave behind.

Unexpectedly he has also realised that Luc is a factor in his decision to move. Their regular conversations on phone or Skype are precious to both of them, and Mathias feels increasingly bleak at the prospect of Luc's death.

'I don't want to be alone there without Luc to talk to,' he'd told Mim when she'd asked if he was sure about moving. 'I need to open myself up to other possibilities for friendship, not isolate myself as I have until now.'

'That sounds sensible,' Mim said. 'People here are very friendly; I can introduce you to some of my friends.'

He recounted this conversation later to Carla. 'Spending time with Mim has made me realise how nice it is to have a friend of my own age with similar interests. It seems to me that I could make other friends, make a life for myself here, without leaning on you too much.'

Now that the move has become a reality, he wants to talk to Luc, to tell him the good news. He has four weeks to pack up and move out and now he feels, quite suddenly, that he wants to do that before Luc dies. As soon as it is a reasonable hour in the Ardennes, he decides, with a glance at his watch, he will ring his old friend.

Chapter Eighteen

Alice lets herself into the house, drops a bundle of travel brochures onto the table and switches on the kettle. Then, with a cup of tea at hand, she sits at the table and spreads the brochures out in front of her, trying to decide where to start. The travel agent had asked her which airline and route she preferred. Did she want to have a stopover somewhere on the way to Perth – maybe more than one stopover – and if so, where? She hadn't considered that possibility and now she feels quite excited about it. She hasn't been overseas for a long time, but in the past she and Colin had enjoyed holidays in France and Spain, Portugal, Switzerland and Belgium. They'd also gone on a cruise around the Greek Islands, but that had been less of a success because Colin liked to be in one place; cruising was, to him, just like travelling all the time. Now the choice is hers and hers alone, but as she looks through the brochures, she realises she has become a bit like that herself. Spending time in airports and train stations and on boats does not appeal. By the time she has drunk her tea and eaten a cheese and tomato sandwich, she has come to the conclusion that what she would enjoy most would be a single stopover of a week or ten days.

Alice is increasingly excited about the trip. It actually feels like an adventure, especially as she is travelling alone and will be answerable to no one. Ever since Colin died, she has continued to live as though she is answerable to him – not that he had ever thought she should be answerable to anyone. She lives in the house that has been in his family for decades, and it's still largely furnished as it was when they first met. Alice was sharing a flat in London at the time. She had no furniture of her own, and no real sense of how one would go about putting one's own stamp on the house, as Colin had suggested she do. His first wife had redecorated when they married, but Alice had had more on her mind than decor when she married Colin. He was older, wealthy, had been divorced for five years and had a rather difficult twelve-year-old son. He was used to a wife who 'entertained', who was a prominent person in the community, sitting on lots of charity boards, president of this, that and the other. Sandra had been a debutante, had shaken hands with the Queen and danced with Prince Charles, and she never let anyone forget it. But she'd had a blatant affair with one of Colin's younger colleagues and disappeared to Spain with him.

Alice had never really understood what made Colin choose her to be his second wife. What on earth had he seen in her? she wondered, on more than one occasion over the years. They'd met on the train from London to Oxford when she was going to visit a friend for the weekend. They were alone in the carriage and Alice was reading when he spoke to her.

'I see we're both reading the same book,' he'd said. And he held up *Of Human Bondage*. 'Somerset Maugham is one of my favourite authors. I've read this book more times than I remember, and I always discover something new and fresh in it.'

Alice, timid by nature, especially around older men, blushed deeply and admitted this was her third reading.

'Third!' he said. 'That shows real commitment. Are you studying?'

She told him that she was doing a PhD in literature, and he said he was a professor of literature, and named an Oxford college. Alice was both impressed and intimidated. He asked her about her thesis, and she told him that she was studying the ways people with disabilities were represented in English fiction, explaining that she was interested because her sister had had polio as a child.

Colin had seemed genuinely interested. 'So *that's* why you're on your third reading of *Of Human Bondage*,' he remarked.

They talked all the way to Oxford, and when they arrived he invited her to lunch. And to her own surprise, Alice accepted.

They walked from the station to a small Italian restaurant which, within months, had become their special place. Despite the difference in their ages, they both knew that what was happening between them was important, and exciting.

Now, as a widow of seventy-two, Alice realises it is a long time since she has felt excited about anything. Perusing the brochures, she decides that a week or so in Bali should satisfy her unexpected craving for adventure – Ubud, to be exact. She remembers Mim describing it to her after a visit about ten years ago.

She reaches into her bag for her phone and dials her sister's number. It rings for some time, and she is just about to hang up when Mim answers.

'How would September suit you?' Alice asks without preamble.

'For what?'

'For me to arrive in Perth.'

She hears Mim gasp. 'Really? You're coming? You really mean it?'

'I really mean it!'

'Oh, Al, that's wonderful,' Mim cries. 'I'm so happy . . .'

And Alice thinks she can hear her sister's voice break a little.

'How long will you stay?'

'The travel agent said I could probably get a visa for up to six months. Could you put up with me for that long?'

Mim laughs. 'I can hardly wait,' she says.

Later that afternoon, Alice goes upstairs and enters a very small bedroom that she and Colin had used as a store-room. She shifts boxes and rummages through cupboards, and finally finds what she's looking for. It's a small leather suitcase that she and Mim had packed together, years ago, when they had sorted out the contents of their parents' house. The furniture had been valued and sold along with the smaller household items. They had made several trips to the charity shop with clothes and books, crockery and pictures. Mim had wanted just a few small personal keepsakes, and Alice the same. What they both agreed to keep was this case into which they had packed all sorts of papers and photographs and, more importantly, a pile of notebooks which had belonged to their mother, including what appeared to be a journal she'd kept during their childhood. At the time they found it, they hadn't time to give it more than a cursory look; they were too busy getting the house sorted and packed before Mim was due to fly home to Australia. So they'd agreed that Alice would keep the case until they could go through it together. Yet somehow, despite Mim's regular annual visits, they had never got around to doing it.

Now, Alice wipes the suitcase with an old duster. *I'll take it with me*, she thinks. *Six months should give us time to go through this together. It will either be a joyous discovery or a big disappointment, but at least we'll know.*

As a child Alice had never been told much about Mim's illness, had never questioned her sister's long absence, but she was instinctively aware that Mim's status in the family was different from her own. If they were invited anywhere, Alice would be taken along while Mim was left at home, and Mim was sent upstairs early if visitors were coming. She would be out of sight and out of mind. The more Alice thinks about this, the more she believes that Mim is right when she says that they had a strange childhood. Their parents loved them both, but while Alice was cuddled and spoiled by aunts, uncles and grandparents, they didn't really know what to do with Mim, nor even how to talk to her. But to Alice, that was just how life was.

When Alice started school, Mim, who was three years older, started at the same time. She had been taught some basic reading and arithmetic while in hospital, but although Mim grew to be an avid reader, she never grasped maths. Eventually, the sisters sat their eleven plus exam at the same time. Alice had tried to help Mim while they were at primary school, drawing her into groups of other girls, but Mim often shied away, which made her seem grumpy to the other children. When they started grammar school together, things were a bit easier. It was as though they were starting from the same place. They were both more confident, and there were a couple of other teenagers with visible polio-related disabilities. But Alice knew that Mim still felt her difference keenly. She thinks now that it would have been much better for all of them if they had talked about Mim's polio at home. She'd only learned much later that their parents had been warned by doctors not to talk about the polio or Mim's condition – not to Mim, and not to anyone else. She must learn to live with it, they'd been told. Drawing too much attention to the disability would be bad for both girls. Alice need only know that her sister who had been sick was now cured. The long absence in hospital was a taboo subject. The brace on Mim's leg, the pain that frequently drove her to tears and woke her at night, the impact on her lungs that left her frail and short of breath, were rarely mentioned.

And Mim and I haven't ever really talked about that since, Alice thinks now. *Perhaps it is time we finally did.*

Chapter Nineteen

Mathias stands just outside the front door watching the removal truck containing his life lumber slowly along the driveway and out onto the road. He waits for the last glimpse of it, and the rapidly fading sound of the engine, then turns back into the empty house. It is still and silent. With the departure of the removal truck, his life here has ceased to exist. Tomorrow the house will officially belong to someone else: a very friendly family escaping the city, the parents in their forties with twin boys aged twelve. Mathias liked them. He could see that they had fallen in love with the house, with its combination of beautifully preserved original features and alterations designed to maintain character and add comfort. They had loved the large sloping garden with its lawn and trees and long hazy views across the wooded hills.

'It has such a lovely feel to it,' the woman said. 'As though you were always happy here.'

And Mathias had wanted to tell her yes, they had been very happy, but sadness had become a lump in his throat and it was difficult to talk.

'We were,' he'd managed. 'We really were.'

Mathias has left them a bottle of good French champagne. It stands as a welcome on the dining room table, which they have also bought from him.

Finally, he braces himself and sets off on a last walk through the place that has been his home for so long. They had found it together, he and Therese, one Saturday afternoon just a couple of months after arriving in Australia. Thanks to the sale of the film rights for another book, they were able to buy it outright without any need for a mortgage.

This house, this country on the other side of the world, was to be his haven. It's hard now for him to remember how desperately he'd wanted to leave behind the shadows of the past. But it didn't take him long to realise that however far he travelled, the shadows followed him.

'Only you can free yourself from the past,' Luc had told him then and again, just recently. 'You let this shame – and it is not even your shame – you let it blight your life. Only you can make a decision to change this.'

Well, he might not have managed to outrun his demons, but that was not the fault of the house – and he meant what he had said to the new owners: he, Therese and Carla had been very happy here.

Mathias takes his phone out of his pocket and calls a taxi. Then he picks up his travel bag from its place on a nearby chair, takes a last look around, turns and walks out of the front door, locking it behind him, then dropping the key back in through the letter slot. As he walks down the driveway, he inhales the familiar scent of trees, damp grass and old timber.

'Here we go,' he tells himself aloud. 'New place, new home, new life.' And as his words float away into the trees, the enormity of what he is doing creeps up on him and he is seized by panic. What if Carla decides to move somewhere else? What if Mim is only being polite and can't be bothered with him? What if he finds it too hot there? What if . . . what if? But then he hears Therese's voice in his head. *It's all right, darling*, she says. *You'll cope. You like being alone. And you can always disappear into your writing when you can't face the real world. Pull yourself together and embrace this adventure.*

Mathias resolves to do just that.

Chapter Twenty

'How do I look?' Jodie asks, modelling her new jeans. After the shapeless, loose-fitting clothes appropriate to convalescence, it feels strange to be in street clothes.

'Good,' Kirra says. 'You look like yourself again.'

'Well, that's a relief. Now to see if I can sit down in them.' She lowers herself cautiously onto a chair. 'Ta da! I can do it. Although I must say tracksuit pants are much more comfortable.'

'Do you want me to help you change back?' Kirra asks.

'Oh no! I want to look cool for my visitors.'

Kirra laughs. 'Visitor, you mean – you wouldn't be preening like this if it was just Mim.'

'You are so cruel,' Jodie says. 'But yes, you're right. Do I really look okay?'

'Honestly, Jo, you look great; that silk shirt is gorgeous. Carla won't be able to take her eyes off you.'

'I think you're taking the piss.'

'Just a bit, perhaps, but seriously, you do look good.'

'Actually good, or just good for a middle-aged vet recovering from a car accident?'

'Both. Mim will be amazed.'

'Well, we know it's not Mim I'm trying to impress,' Jodie says, glancing out the window in case they are already outside.

'No, I realise that, but I thought Carla was quite impressed last time. You'd better try sitting down and getting up again, though, just to make sure you can do it without falling flat on your face.'

Jodie successfully completes the manoeuvre. 'These jeans are so tight and stiff that they will probably keep me vertical,' she observes. 'I'd forgotten how uncomfortable new jeans can be, but thanks for getting them for me.'

She lowers herself back into the chair and the dogs, having watched all this with some bemusement, amble over. They like the current situation: Jodie always home and plenty of visitors coming and going, usually with treats for them. Hoonoze jumps up onto Jo's lap and tries to lick her face while Fred, yawning widely, settles at her feet.

'Okay, I'm going back to the surgery now,' Kirra says. 'Buzz me when they get here and I'll come across and serve lunch.'

'No need,' Jo says. 'Mim'll do that.'

'No way,' Kirra says. 'You have to buzz me. I want to get a look at Carla again, make sure she's suitable for you! After all, we don't actually know anything about her – I mean, she might prefer men.'

'And you're going to find that out while you're in the kitchen with Mim?'

'Maybe!' Kirra says. 'Someone has to. So, buzz me!'

She leaves and Jodie resumes her vigil at the window, thinking about Carla, swinging between excitement at seeing her again and anxiety that she may have misread her when she'd visited with Mim the previous week. Mim had introduced them and then gone out to the kitchen to say hello to Kirra. Jo, whose first glimpse of Carla had taken her breath away, found her ability to converse naturally had vanished, but she managed to stammer out a question about Mathias, and before long they had relaxed and by the time Mim and Kirra joined them the initial awkwardness had been dispelled. When Mim and Carla left an hour later, Jodie was already wondering how she might get to see Carla again. The problem was Mim; Jodie didn't want Mim to know that she was interested in Carla, not yet. So, she had invited the pair for lunch and is hoping to summon the courage to ask Carla for her number when Mim is in the kitchen.

As a car pulls up outside her heart beats faster, and she stands up cautiously, smoothing down her shirt and jeans. She walks cautiously to the front door and opens it. Carla is standing alone on the doorstep, holding a bouquet of yellow and white roses.

'Hi, Jodie,' she says. 'It's only me today.'

Jo opens her mouth and shuts it again. 'Oh,' she says, suddenly extremely short of breath. 'Come in, Carla – it's lovely to see you. Is Mim okay?'

Carla steps inside, still holding the roses. Jodie feels as though she might faint.

'Mim sends her apologies,' Carla says. 'She texted me earlier to say that she's not feeling too well and suggested I come anyway.'

Jodie just stares at her, still stunned that Carla is here in her house, and fleetingly ashamed of feeling so happy that Mim is not.

'I hope this is okay, my coming alone,' Carla says.

'Of course,' Jodie replies. 'But you're sure Mim is okay? I mean, it's not serious, is it?'

'Honestly?' Carla is smiling. 'I think Mim is absolutely fine. She certainly sounded it. I'm pretty sure she's trying to set us up, so I got in my car and drove here as fast as I possibly could.'

Chapter Twenty-one

Mathias is sitting in a Melbourne cafe almost opposite Parliament House. He has spent five days here, sorting out his business and banking arrangements between meals with old friends and acquaintances, his publisher and his agent. Now, as a last duty before leaving for the airport, he is having coffee with Christina, a friend of Therese's who now lives in the city with her third husband. They have talked about old times, about Therese and Carla, Christina's children, mutual friends and finally Christina's current husband, who is, according to his wife, selfish and boring. For Mathias it's been a tedious conversation, and his sympathy is with the husband. He has never really liked Christina, and never understood why Therese had stayed in touch with her. But in clearing out the house he had sorted through stacks of old correspondence, paperwork and books, and had found a large envelope containing two rather worn paperback books. The books were tied with an old ribbon and a note in Therese's handwriting was tucked under it, with the reminder: *Must return to Christina asap.* He had wavered, thinking that surely if Christina needed the books, she would have asked for them by now. He was about to put them in the box for the Salvos, but then he'd opened one and seen from the inscription on the flyleaf that it had been a gift to Christina from her mother, so he'd emailed her, offering to post the books back to her before he moved. She had replied that she'd love to see him before he left and asked if he'd have time to meet for a coffee or a drink when he was in Melbourne. He was reluctant but couldn't think of a good excuse to decline. Knowing that Christina was a heavy drinker, he opted for coffee. So now here he is, sitting with a woman whom he'd never much liked, talking about old neighbours, mutual acquaintances, old times. He is on the point of saying that he really must go and collect his bags and get a cab to the airport, when Christina sets off on a new track.

'You're doing the right thing, Mathias,' she tells him. 'I'm amazed you left it so long. I thought you'd go west soon after Carla left.'

Mathias shrugs. 'I've been considering it for some time,' he says, 'but I've been reluctant to leave the house that Therese and I lived in together. It felt as though I would be abandoning her.'

'That's perfectly natural,' Christina says. 'But you must be over it now. It's time to start a new life. I did! You'll probably find yourself married again sooner than you think.'

'That's hardly likely,' Mathias responds. 'I'm in my

seventies now and I certainly have no intention of marrying again. But Carla is in Perth, and I've now made a close friend there too, Miriam. We met recently by chance, and meeting her inspired me to make the move that I've been thinking about for some time.'

'How lovely,' Christina says. 'She's a very lucky woman – you're a real catch, Mathias. So, you're moving in with her?'

Mathias shakes his head. 'Oh no, it's not a relationship,' he says. 'We're just good friends. I'm going to stay with Carla until I can find a place of my own.'

Christina laughs. 'So, what happens when you want to be more than just friends, nudge, nudge, wink, wink?'

Mathias feels his face flush. 'It's not like that,' he says. 'Friendship is what I value now, more than anything.'

'Ah yes!' Christina gives him a knowing smile. 'Well, we'll see about that. I can guarantee that the next time I hear from you you'll have moved in with her or she with you.'

Deeply embarrassed and keen to escape, Mathias looks at his watch and gets to his feet.

'Goodness me, I'm running late,' he says. 'I really must get going or I'll miss my flight.'

Christina stands up and moves in to hug him; it's a struggle not to flinch away.

'Have a wonderful new life,' she says. 'And if things don't turn out as planned with your new girlfriend, give me a call.' She gives him a provocative smile.

Mathias can't leave the cafe fast enough. It's a relief to slide into the back of the cab and flee the distasteful scene.

Had Christina always been so intrusive and crudely flirtatious? His head is muddled now, and he feels deeply uncomfortable as he goes back over the conversation and recalls the suggestions she had made about him and Mim. Does anyone else think they are entering into a romantic relationship? Does Carla? And, more importantly, does Mim? What *does* Mim think? Surely she understands that they are simply friends . . . doesn't she? But he feels his chest tighten, and suddenly his head seems to spin. Suppose she . . .

'Which airline?' asks the taxi driver.

Looking up, Mathias realises they have reached the airport. 'Qantas, please,' he says, clearing his throat.

The driver swings into the kerb and gets out to help him with his baggage.

'Have a good flight, mate.'

Mathias thanks him and stands outside the glass doors of the departures terminal, his head still spinning. His conversation with Christina offended him and has left him confused and slightly dizzy, and now he must face the horror of the airport. He would like to sit for a minute, but there is no seat out here on the pavement, so he walks to the automatic doors and steps inside.

The concourse is teeming with people hurrying in all directions. The self-service check-in kiosks are all occupied and other passengers are milling around them, waiting to pounce on the first vacant one. Over near the entrance to the departure gates, people are stacking their hand luggage onto plastic trays and dumping them on the conveyor belt. For a moment everything around him is a blur and

Mathias can't remember where he is or why. He had been looking forward to this moment, but now he feels nothing but panic. He wants to run back to his beautiful old home in the hills: safe, warm, peaceful. The place he has run to after exhausting meetings, publicity campaigns, writers' festivals and overseas trips. The place where he can sit at the computer working without noticing the hours passing. He remembers how wonderful it always felt to know he was going back there: to Therese, to his family, to privacy, to peace and, since Carla left, to a comfortable solitude with his writing and his memories. But now he is unable to see how the future will look, and he stops abruptly in the middle of the concourse. The enormity of what he is doing overwhelms him.

It's a panic attack, he tells himself. *Calm down, it'll pass.*

A woman is heading towards him; an elderly woman, short and heavily built. She has a bag on her arm, a boarding pass in her hand, and is dragging an enormous suitcase which is swaying worryingly on inadequate wheels. Mathias knows he should move out of the way, but he is frozen by the realisation that he has strayed beyond the safe confines of his life. The woman struggles on, a wheel breaks free and the suitcase takes control, lurching and swaying with its own momentum, wrenching itself out of its owner's hands and swinging her off balance, propelling her forward to crash straight into Mathias. They end up clutching at each other, teetering perilously, finally ending up in a heap on the floor.

'Oh dear, oh my goodness,' the woman says, lying painfully twisted on her side beside Mathias, who has one leg trapped beneath her. 'I'm so sorry, I completely lost my balance.'

People are gathering anxiously around them as Mathias cautiously manages to withdraw his leg. A man grabs his arm to help him up, but Mathias declines as graciously as possible, as the woman cries out that she can't think of getting up. He shifts himself onto one hip so that he can help her into a more comfortable position. The panic has gone now, and he feels sore and foolish, sitting there at the centre of the crowd.

'Are you all right?' he asks shakily.

'I will be,' she says. 'Are you?'

'Same as you. I need time to recover before I get up.'

A man in a business suit crouches down alongside Mathias. 'Let's get you up first,' he suggests.

'Not yet,' he says. He looks up at the circle of anxious faces. 'We both need a minute or two.'

'Yes,' the woman says. 'More time.'

He reaches out and grasps her hand. 'My name is Mathias,' he says. 'You don't have to move until you're ready – we're in this together.'

'Thank you,' she says, clasping his hand tightly. 'I'm Dorothy and I think I might need a wheelchair.'

Mathias turns to the man in the suit. 'Perhaps you could find an attendant and maybe a wheelchair?'

'I feel so ridiculous,' Dorothy says. 'The case was much too heavy, I should have brought two, but . . .'

'It doesn't matter,' Mathias says, 'as long as you're okay. I had a sudden panic attack and wasn't looking where I was going.'

She squeezes his hand, which is still holding her own. 'Thank you,' she says, 'thank you. We must look ridiculous, two old people rolling around in the middle of the airport. Please don't go yet.'

'I can't,' he says. 'We'll stay here until we feel a bit better.' He is surprised to note that being labelled one of 'two old people' has wounded his pride.

Eventually a pair of airport workers push through the crowd, each with a wheelchair, and he and Dorothy are helped into them. Then they are whisked away, through the baggage checks and into the far corner of the business lounge, where they are first given cups of tea, then taken to a small consulting room to be checked out by the doctor, before finally being wheeled onto their flight to Perth.

'You seem to be making a habit of picking up women in airports,' Carla says as she drives him home several hours later.

'I couldn't pick *myself* up, let alone Dorothy,' Mathias says, laughing. 'And I must say that the wheelchair was challenging – one feels totally vulnerable.'

'You *are* vulnerable, Papa,' Carla says. 'You need to remember that, especially when house hunting. No stairs, no wobbly old garden paths or slippery floors. Was it just the woman with the suitcase bumping into you that made you fall?'

Mathias sighs. 'No,' he says. 'I had one of those old panic attacks. When Dorothy ploughed into me I was already dizzy and confused. It's months – no, more like a couple of years – since I had one of those. And then it was a bit of a shock finding I couldn't get up without help.'

*

'But why were you having a panic attack?' Mim asks, the following day.

Mathias flushes with embarrassment. 'I've had them on and off since I was a teenager. This time I got over-whelmed at the prospect of making such a big change when I'm almost eighty. It suddenly hit me when . . .' He hesitates, realising he can't explain that his conversation with Christina had triggered it. 'Leaving the house and all our history there that had kept me sane after Therese died. It all seemed too much, too sudden. That must sound ridiculous. I'd been thinking of it for years and then suddenly I'd done it and the furniture had gone and I started asking myself if I'd done it for the right reasons.'

Mim nods. 'I think it's perfectly natural to feel that way.'

'You really think so?'

'Mathias, you understand human nature. You're acutely sensitive to it. If you created a character who was making this move, wouldn't you create all those emotions and reactions in him?'

Mathias frowns at her, puzzled. 'But that's fiction – it's not my own life.'

'Rubbish,' Mim says. 'Your writing is always about your-self. Since we met, I've reread some of your books. You're there on every page; not your story, but your values and beliefs, your voice. What you feel is significant. What you love, what you despise. That's the sort of writer you are.'

Mathias is silent, staring out the cafe window. He is tempted to admit that much of his anxiety had its roots in their friendship: what it is, what it might be.

'You're right of course,' he says eventually. 'Stupid of me.' He leans across the table and puts his hand on hers. 'Thank you, Mim. Thank you for talking sense to me. Now, tell me what's been going on with you.'

'Nothing much,' she replies. 'But I do have some good news. My sister Alice is coming from England next month – well, four weeks from today. She arrives on the twenty-fifth of September. It all seems to have happened quite quickly; she's stopping off in Bali for a week on her way here. I'm so looking forward to it, and she's dying to meet you.'

Mathias takes a deep breath. 'Well . . . Well, that's wonderful news, Mim. I'm so pleased for you.' What he actually feels is a return of the anxiety. The writer in him imagines the reunion of the sisters, the questions that Alice will ask Mim about him, the questions Alice might well ask *him* about why he's moved here, about . . . well . . . about anything really . . . And he's not sure he has the answers.

Chapter Twenty-two

On a Wednesday morning two weeks later, Mim is sitting in the back room of the bookshop. She has a pile of paperwork in front of her but rather than working her way through it as planned, she's watching what's happening out in the shop.

While she was in England, Doug and the other staff had moved things around a bit, and when she'd walked back into it for the first time after she got home, it no longer felt familiar. For a fleeting moment she'd felt almost as though she could happily turn on her heel and walk away from it. But once she'd walked around studying the rearranged shelves, noticing the two small tables Doug had put in the window to create special displays of books by local writers, she found her old pleasure and pride in the shop was reawakened.

Even so, she's found it difficult to get back into a routine here. Her energy seems to diminish so rapidly. Some

mornings she chooses to stay home and read or walk
Brenda down to the beach cafe for a coffee. But this lack of
discipline does not sit easily with her, so she finds herself
resenting her responsibilities here, as though the shop is
getting in the way of her living the life she wants. When
she had left for England she'd felt a sense of relief that she
would be free of it for a while. The shop was in good hands
and she could dismiss it from her thoughts, telling herself
she would do something about it when she got home. And
now here she is, facing a pile of paperwork, chewing her
pen and resenting her own shop, torn between her desire
to be elsewhere and her reluctance to let go of what she has
built. She glances over at the proposal Doug had presented
her with, outlining some improvements he thought might
be made, then looks away guiltily. She just can't seem to
summon up the interest.

'Coffee, Mim?' says a voice at the door. 'I've just made
some.'

It's Erica, who had been a customer at the shop since
the day Mim opened it. When her husband died seven
years ago, she had asked if there was any part-time work
going, and she has been working there three days a week
ever since.

'Yes, please,' Mim says, adding, 'It seems pretty busy
out there this morning.'

Erica nods. 'It sure is. It's building up nicely for the
weekend.' She smiles and heads back to the shop's tiny
kitchen.

Mim watches her go, remembering what Erica had said
when she asked for a job.

'I've no experience in bookshops,' she'd admitted, 'but, as you know, I've been coming here almost weekly for years. It's such a friendly, comforting place, I'd really like to work here, so I thought I'd ask you before I go anywhere else.'

For Mim, Erica was a godsend: friendly, likeable, smarter than she herself realised. She soon became indispensable: a solid back-up for Doug, flexible in the hours and days she worked, always happy to fill in for others and great at recruiting new customers.

'Here we are,' Erica says, returning with the coffee. 'Are you okay, Mim? We haven't seen that much of you since you got back from England.'

Mim smiles and puts down the pencil she's been chewing. 'I know,' she says. 'I haven't been here as much as I should. Honestly, I'm just being lazy. I'm having trouble motivating myself again, I suppose.'

Erica smiles. 'Yes, it's hard to get back in the swing of things.'

She heads back out to the shop floor and Mim returns to her paperwork, only to be interrupted almost immediately by a knock on the door.

'You're looking rather worn down by work,' Mathias says from the doorway.

Mim looks up, pleased. 'I am,' she says, 'but it's my own fault for having put it off for so long.'

'Would you mind an interruption? Carla was meeting a friend nearby so I thought I'd take advantage of the lift and drop in.'

'I find all this admin so tedious, I'd be grateful for some

company,' Mim confesses. 'Help yourself to coffee in the kitchen then come back and talk to me.'

He gives her a salute, turns away, and is back a few minutes later with a glass of water.

'No coffee?' she asks.

Mathias shakes his head. 'I've been well dosed up on coffee already this morning. Carla and I went for breakfast at that cafe near her house run by two of her friends. Do you know it?'

'I do. Carla took me there a few times while you were back in Melbourne. Excellent coffee and food.'

'Yes, I had an omelette with smoked salmon and spinach.'

'All right, all right, that's enough food porn,' Mim says, groaning. 'I had a piece of toast made with rather stale bread.'

Mathias laughs and sits down in the chair under the window. 'Well, I came here to see if I can be useful.'

She smiles and reaches across a pile of paperwork for Doug's proposal and passes it to him. 'Maybe you could have a look at this and give me your opinion? I think it's really good, but I seem to have lost the will to live since I read it because I don't know how to implement it.'

Mathias takes it over to the armchair in the corner by the window. 'I'm going to read this in comfort,' he says, 'and afterwards I'll walk around the shop and take a closer look. Then we can talk about it over lunch.'

Mim watches as Mathias puts on his glasses and begins to study the document. She's so pleased he made the move west; it's a relief to have him close. But she feels strangely as though she's waiting for something in her life to change, yet she doesn't know what. A second opinion on Doug's proposal will help, but she knows it won't fix what she's feeling; it's something more profound than that. She remembers feeling something similar many years ago with Derek. He was an army fitness instructor, and they'd met in a pub a few months after she'd arrived in Australia. On their third date, they ate fish and chips on the beach watching the sun go down. Mim was struggling to find a comfortable position on the sand.

'I could help you get better at that,' Derek had said. 'May I?' And he made her stand straight and still for a moment. 'Now, just do a quick scan of your body. Which limb will you move first?'

He had talked her through a slow and pain-free process of lowering herself onto the sand and getting up again. 'Try to move slowly and thoughtfully,' he'd said when she'd got it right. 'I've been watching you. You try to do things quickly, perhaps because you don't want people to see you struggle. But rushing makes it harder and it looks really uncomfortable.'

In the months that followed, he had introduced her to yoga, which helped her to slow down, move more comfortably and decisively. She grew stronger and gained confidence, and their relationship grew stronger too. A year later, they were married in Fremantle, and Mim remembers that she had felt that she was changing from within, as if in readiness for something unknown that would save her from herself, from her own negativity and what had been an often-debilitating sense of despair.

They had been married for three years when Derek died. He had gone to the memorial service for an old friend and was driving home through heavy rain along the Great Northern Highway when a teenager on a motorbike shot out in front of him. Derek's car skidded across the road and into the path of a large truck that was travelling south. He was dead before the ambulance arrived at the scene; the teenager was unhurt. When he was gone, Mim recognised that she had always feared it wouldn't last.

'Why ever not?' Alice had asked her many years later.

Mim had shrugged. 'I felt I wasn't good enough for him, I suppose. He was so genuinely good and kind, and he was strong too, mentally as well as physically.' She had hesitated then. 'I suppose I felt that I was unworthy of him. He deserved someone who was more . . .' She struggled to express herself. 'More whole – not as broken as me in mind and body. I have a broken body, and a faint heart.'

'A faint heart? There's nothing wrong with your heart,' Alice protested.

'Not physically! I mean I lack the courage and determination to take risks, to hang in there when things get tough, that sort of thing – I'm faint-hearted and it's hard for me to trust people.'

Mim remembers this now as she watches Mathias sitting reading by the window. Like Derek, he is essentially a good, kind person, but there is something else about him which she recognises in herself. It is fear, she thinks: an acute awareness of his own vulnerability that makes him cautious in the way he relates to other people.

'Are you okay?' Mathias says suddenly.

Mim sighs. 'I feel stuck,' she says. 'Stuck somewhere between the past and the present. Some days I feel I'm being devoured by regrets, while at other times I feel as though I don't care about anything.'

Mathias nods. 'I know that feeling,' he says. 'It's horrible. I often feel I am waiting, but I don't know for what.'

'That's it exactly,' Mim says. 'Anyway, what do you think of Doug's proposal?'

'From a quick flick through, I'd say it looks good.'

Mim nods. 'That's what I thought.' She's not used to accepting help – or asking for it – but she must admit it's a relief to have someone willing to act as a sounding board; someone prepared to offer her support at a time when she is feeling so unaccustomedly vulnerable.

*

Carla walks along Port Beach, watching the dogs ducking in and out of the shallow waves. Hoonoze and Fred are already soaked to the skin, and Jodie has recently adopted Pearl, a spoodle, which Carla has learned is a cross between a spaniel and a poodle.

'She's homeless,' Jodie had said, when Carla turned up at her house one afternoon recently. 'I thought you might like her.'

'I think she's gorgeous,' Carla said. 'But not as gorgeous as you. And you're standing up and walking without the boot and the stick. How does it feel?'

'Good – even better than I anticipated,' Jodie said. 'It feels like I'm getting my life back. Do you really like her?'

'I really do; she's adorable.'

'Good,' Jodie said. 'Because I got her for you.'

'For me?' Carla was shocked. 'But I've never had a dog before. I wouldn't know how to look after it – I mean her. I'm not even sure that I want to live with a dog.' She flushed, feeling awkward. 'I love your dogs, but a dog of my own? I'm just not sure . . .' She felt awful, but as she straightened up from stroking the dog's soft curly coat, she saw that Jodie was laughing.

'It's okay, I'm only kidding. Her owner died unexpectedly, so I agreed to take her in because she's so adorable. If you're not interested, I'll easily find her a good home.'

'Wow, that's a relief,' Carla said. 'I thought we were about to have our first argument – or a pretty big misunderstanding, at least.'

Thinking of this now, as she walks back along the beach to where Jodie is sitting on a rock, Carla thinks she may actually have fallen in love with Pearl – and with Jodie, too. Their relationship is still young, but Carla is already confident that she has found the love of her life. Even meeting Olivia had not felt so unquestionably right as falling in love with Jodie feels.

She had always thought that the term 'falling in love' was a little overblown, as though it could happen in an instant and your life was immediately changed. But that was what happened when she first met Jodie. And now she feels herself becoming more like the person she has always wanted to be: more confident, more loving and more open to different possibilities. They have seen each other almost every day since Carla had turned up on Jodie's doorstep with a bouquet of roses, and last night her father had commented that she seemed to have developed a thriving social life.

'Well, I finished off that painting for the council chamber,' she'd said, feeling her face grow hot. 'When you finish a big piece of work, life opens up again.'

She isn't ready yet to tell him how happy she is, in case anything goes wrong. She is aware that he is a bit fragile right now, due to Luc's deteriorating condition and the upheaval of moving. The other reason is Mim. Jodie hasn't told her yet. Like Carla, she wants to make sure that their relationship is absolutely solid before sharing the news.

While the dogs play in the shallow water, Carla approaches Jodie, who is not quite up to walking in soft sand yet.

'You look beautiful sitting there,' she says, putting her arm around Jodie's shoulder. 'How are you feeling now?'

Jodie takes her other hand and holds it. 'Wonderful. The sea air is so refreshing; I didn't realise how much I'd missed it. And you? How are you feeling? About us, I mean.'

'When I'm with you, I think I've died and gone to heaven,' Carla says. It sounds corny, but she means it.

'Me too. I'm so longing to be open about our relationship, but I still think we should hold off on telling people until we're absolutely sure that we're committed to each other and can see a future together. I . . . I've made mistakes before.'

'Me too,' Carla says. 'And that makes perfect sense to me. But I'd like to introduce you to Papa soon. He's already heard about you from Mim, of course, and he knows we're friends, though I haven't told him we're more than that.'

Liz Byrski

'I'd love to meet him,' Jodie says. 'And in the mean-time,' – she squeezes Carla's hand – 'I'm going to enjoy getting to know you better.'

Chapter Twenty-three

Alice is lying on a day bed by the hotel swimming pool. She has fallen in love with Bali: the sunshine, palm trees, service that anticipates her every need; friendly people, lots of interesting shops and salons, colourful markets, the pool, and the feel of being in an almost magically different world from Oxford. Ubud is just heavenly. She softly hums 'Bali Ha'i', imagining Rossano Brazzi from *South Pacific* heading towards her with a tall, fruit-laden cocktail. On cue, the real waiter arrives with her cocktail, bowing slightly as he puts the glass on the table beside her; sadly, he is only about twelve or fifteen at the most. Alice sighs, remembering that Rossano Brazzi died years ago. *But would you really want a man – even Rossano Brazzi – to walk into your life right now?* she asks herself. *Think of the upheaval. Think of having to share a bed again, be a wife again. Would you really want to start again in your early seventies? Would you even want a fling? Of course not!* She thinks that what she would really like is to come here with Mim, but she suspects there is little chance of that. There's the shop – and she knows that Mim found her last trip to England quite taxing physically.

Alice stretches and adjusts the back of her lounger to a vertical position so she can sip her drink. It requires some manoeuvring due to the stems of mint, toothpicks laden with glacé cherries and pineapple chunks that decorate it. Just as she puts the straw to her lips, a young woman holding a bundle of flyers approaches her.

'Good morning, madam,' she says, handing Alice a glossy brochure. 'My name is Anna, and I am letting you know about this very special offer at the hotel beauty salon.'

Alice smiles. 'No thank you, I don't really do beauty things.'

'But for all people there must be a first time,' Anna tells her. 'Please, let me explain.'

Ever courteous – not to mention a little timid – Alice submits to the explanation, listening politely as Anna lists a range of spa and beauty treatments, from manicures to massages and hairstyling. Despite herself, Alice is tempted. Perhaps she could have a massage – she's on holiday, after all. And when was the last time she changed her hairstyle?

'And for the next two days we are offering a special,' Anna concludes. 'If you book two of the treatments I have told you about, you qualify for a full makeover. One of our fashion consultants will accompany you to two boutiques associated with the hotel and assist you in finding some new outfits at twenty per cent off the standard price.'

I want it, Alice thinks. *I want it so much I could hug her.*

And right then and there she books the next available appointments.

I am going to be made over, she murmurs to herself. *I will look different; I will be different. This is the start of the rest of my life.*

But as Anna walks away, the old self-doubt creeps in. It's incredibly silly of her, she thinks, to imagine that she could change at this stage of her life. After all, she's been the same for decades. Same hair, same style of clothes and shoes, same Elizabeth Arden cosmetics that her mother used. And while she might be able to change on the outside – update her wardrobe, for instance – on the inside she would be the same: nervous, anxious, frightened of change, clinging to the past. *But I'm having fun*, she reminds herself as she drains her glass and rises from the day bed to return to her room and prepare for her appointment at the hair salon. *And who says I'm too old to change?*

Leaning back in the chair, her head resting on the basin, Alice closes her eyes and thinks of Mim, starting a conversation with a complete stranger at Doha Airport. Total strangers, neither of them looking for company, but finding it in each other. Alice has always hoped that one day Mim would find someone as wonderful as Colin, fall in love and marry him. In that respect her sister has been a serious disappointment. Apart from Derek, whom Alice had met only once, there had never been anyone else in Mim's life. She remembers a black-and-white photograph of Mim and Derek on the steps of a small church after their wedding. The photograph is memorable as Mim usually avoids

165

having her picture taken, but in this one she is smiling, holding Derek's arm, a small bouquet of flowers in her free hand. Mim was devastated by her husband's death. If there has ever been another man in her life, she has certainly never mentioned it to Alice.

'Send me a photograph,' Alice had said when Mim mentioned having met Mathias in Doha. She, like Mim, was a fan of his books. And the following day there was the photograph on her phone. She'd expected Mim to send a photo of the two of them standing side by side, smiling at the camera. Instead, it was a picture of Mathias sitting in what looked like the airport lounge; he was holding an open book and his quizzical expression made it appear that he had been caught unawares. Alice thought he was rather good-looking and had an air of sophistication. At Heathrow, she'd spotted one of his books in WH Smith and bought it to read on the plane. Staring at the author photo on the back cover, she tried to imagine Mathias and Mim together. The idea of her sister finding love after all these years seemed incredibly romantic.

Alice has always insisted that there would never be anyone else for her after Colin, but now she starts to wonder if that's really true. Has she just denied herself the love and companionship she secretly craves and that Colin would want her to have? For years Alice has dismissed the possibility. She has applied herself to maintaining the house, doing good works in the local community and maintaining a connection with her academic career by writing reviews and examining the occasional PhD. In fact, she had continued doing what she had always done, but without Colin. *Perhaps I could have a second chance at marriage or a relationship,* she thinks. *Why not? There's still time.* She hesitates. *But is that really what I want?* Thinking on it, she realises it's not a husband or a lover that she's craving; it's a different life. *And right now, I'm not sure what that would look like, who would be in it, where it would be. I need to keep an open mind, talk to Mim, consider things carefully.*

The hairdresser returns, rinses off the colour, wraps Alice's head in a towel and leads her to a chair set before a mirror. Alice leans forward, staring at her reflection. The colour looks good: a distinctive silver as opposed to its natural dull grey. Alice feels a ripple of excitement at the approach of the stylist. She feels prepared to take a risk, to try a style she might previously have dismissed as 'not her'. Shorter? Yes. Very short? No. She flicks through the catalogue the stylist proffers. *This one!*

Chapter Twenty-four

*I*n the last week of September, Mim sets off to the airport late one evening to meet Alice's flight. Mathias offered to drive her, but she has insisted on going alone; she knows she needs to set Alice straight about her friendship with Mathias before she introduces the two of them. Her sister has referred to it several times, in a teasing way, as a romance, and Mim is anxious to make sure that Alice understands that she and Mathias are just friends. *Just friends*, she thinks as she drives into the airport car park. *But what does that really mean?* She knows her feelings for Mathias are unlike those she has for anyone else, but that's only natural; it's years since she's had a man as a friend. *These things seem so much more complicated as one gets older*, she thinks, and then she wonders exactly what she means by *these things*.

She parks the car and walks towards the arrivals terminal, anticipating how it will feel to see Alice walk out through those doors for the first time. She's excited that after so many years Alice has actually decided to come. She looks forward to driving her around and showing her the place that has been her home for so many decades, taking her into the city, to the beach, to some of Fremantle's many cafes and restaurants. She is also planning a short break in the south-west after Christmas – Margaret River, perhaps, or even Albany.

Once inside the terminal, Mim edges her way towards the front of the crowd waiting behind the barrier for the doors from the customs area to open. It's awkward, as she is small and unsteady in a crowd, but she'll be fine if she can get close to the rail and hang on to that. The doors open and Mim leans forward, straining to catch a glimpse of her sister among the small group emerging. The whole crowd shifts slightly, and she is able to reach for the rail and grab it. A line of weary-looking people shuffles past, pushing trolleys and pulling suitcases. None of them is Alice.

The doors open a second time and there, at the front of the throng of emerging passengers, is Alice. But this is a very different Alice! She is striding confidently and looking unusually stylish. Her make-up is subtle and her long, messy hair has been cut in a short, chic style. And her clothes! She is wearing a black tube dress with black-and-white sneakers and a denim jacket – and she looks wonderful.

Mim makes her way along the barrier to the exit.

'Alice?' she says hesitantly as her sister approaches, as if needing confirmation of her identity. 'Alice, is that really you?'

'Of course it's me,' Alice says, hugging her. 'It's the *new* me! Do you like it?'

Mim looks her up and down. 'I love it. You do look like a new woman. What happened?'

Alice hugs her again and then grabs the handle of her trolley to stop it being jostled away in the crowd. 'I had a makeover in Bali. I've been restyled from head to toe.'

'Well, you look terrific. You can tell me all about it on the way home.'

And as Mim steers her sister out of the terminal and across the darkened car park with its scattered pools of light, she has a feeling that something big has happened to Alice, something much more significant than a makeover. Her sister seems altogether more light-hearted and youthful.

Alice is walking and talking fast, her tone excitable, and Mim struggles to keep up.

'Hang on, Al,' Mim says. 'You're going too fast for me.'

'Sorry, darling,' Alice says. When they reach the car she lifts the large suitcase into the boot and slides the smaller one onto the back seat. 'Would you like me to drive?' she asks.

'Definitely not!' Mim says. 'I'm starting to think you might be drunk!'

'Just one glass of champagne,' Alice says. 'This is just the new me: positive, forward-looking, energised.'

'Great,' Mim says, wondering if Alice has had a personality makeover as well.

On the road home to Fremantle, Alice describes her stay in Bali, with its lovely people, glorious scenery, sparkling blue water and delicious food.

'I'm determined to take you there, Mim,' she says. 'I just know you'd love it; you have to see it to believe it.'

'I've been to Bali, you know, Alice,' Mim says. 'Twice – no, three times actually.'

'Oh, that's right. Well, I can't wait to see Fremantle now – and the rest of Australia.'

'All of it?' Mim asks jokingly. 'It's a big country.'

'Why not? I'm here for a long stay,' Alice reminds her. 'You might get sick of me and pack me off somewhere. By the way, on the flight I was reading about a place I'm sure you've mentioned: New Norcia. Didn't Derek's brother live there? It sounded absolutely fascinating. Is it very far? Can we go?'

'It's an easy day trip,' Mim tells her. 'We can certainly go there.'

'Oh good, it sounds so interesting – especially the history of the nuns. I've been reading up on them lately; the different orders and so on.'

'Why nuns?'

'I don't know really. I suppose I find it intriguing how their lives are enriched as well as controlled by their faith.'

Mim laughs. 'Planning your future?'

'No, a nunnery is not for me.' Alice laughs too.

Mim negotiates a bend and then glances across at her. 'From a makeover to nuns,' she observes. 'None of it sounds much like you.'

'Well, the makeover is only a week or so old,' Alice says. 'It was a spur-of-the-moment decision. But Bali had a big impact on me. It was so entirely different, so light-hearted and colourful. It made me realise how desperately I've been locked into the past. I was shutting myself away, behaving as though Colin was still alive. Well, he's not – he's gone, he's not coming back. And as you keep telling me, he would have wanted me to have a good life after him. I more or less went into hiding, because it was the easiest thing to do. Sort of like a nun, really, though falling drastically short on faith, commitment and selflessness.'

'You *have* been living a somewhat sequestered life for the last few years,' Mim agreed. 'And you and Colin didn't go out much in the last few years, did you? I mean you never seemed to go on holidays, and you always avoided parties. Did you never want to?'

'Well, I'm not much of a party girl, never have been. We just loved being together, looking after each other. We went to movies and concerts, and while we used to holiday in Europe, Colin wasn't really much of a traveller, especially as he grew older, so we just went on daytrips in the local area or stayed home. But, you know, I feel like spreading my wings. So here I am in Australia: my first step into the future.'

'Well, that's very good news,' Mim says as she turns the car into her driveway and stops in front of the house.

They both get out and Alice faces Mim across the roof of the car.

'By the way,' she says, 'this new lease of life is largely inspired by you.'

'Me? Come on, Al, be serious,' Mim says, reaching into the car for her handbag and getting out the house keys.

'I am being serious,' she says. 'It's true. You came here all alone, built a new life on the other side of the world.

Got married to Derek and then he died, and you started all over again on your own. I'd always taken it all for granted, but I've been thinking lately how brilliant that was, how brave – taking the risk to come here alone, making this your home. You must have felt incredibly alone. And you came back almost every year, that awful journey. And when you left in May I thought, *This is my sister and I hardly know her; I have no insight into her life.* You're an inspiration, Mim.'

Mim, always embarrassed by effusive expressions of emotion, is about to say something crisply dismissive, but she resists. Instead she walks around the car and hugs her sister.

They stand there together for some moments, holding each other, and Mim is surprised by the surge of love and affection she feels.

It is Alice who steps back and breaks the silence.

'Well! Hugging you used to be like hugging a tree, but this felt different. Serious and with emotional intent.'

'Sometimes you really do talk complete rubbish, Al,' Mim says. But she is laughing as she turns away to unlock the back door and usher her sister inside.

Chapter Twenty-five

Mathias's car, which travelled from Melbourne by train, had arrived in Perth with a nasty dent on the bonnet. No one at the station either in Perth or Melbourne seemed able to explain it, though it was clear something heavy had been dropped on it during the journey or when it was loaded or unloaded. The argument over who was responsible for the damage has gone back, forth and sideways for weeks now, but finally the insurance company had agreed to take responsibility and now he is driving out of the Volvo dealer's yard with a gleaming new bonnet. It feels like driving a new car, but with the comforting reassurance of its familiarity, its connection to his earlier life.

His phone rings while he's stopped at a traffic light and, glancing at it, Mathias sees it's a call from Luc. 'Hold on,' Mathias tells him, 'I'm in the car. I'll just pull over and call you back . . .'

He parks by the verge and returns the call. 'Okay now,' he says. 'How are you, my friend?'

'I journey on,' Luc says, 'but with some difficulty. Each day is now quite hard work.'

'Are you getting lots of rest?' Mathias asks.

'I am in a constant state of rest,' Luc replies. 'Sometimes I think I must have died already and am being held in a waiting cell until the Lord makes up his mind what to do with me. And you, Mathias? What about you?'

'The move was unsettling at first, as I told you,' Mathias replies. 'But that feeling seems to have passed now. I'm still looking at houses, and this morning I've picked up my car at last and it looks like new. It's so good to have it back again.'

'So, soon things will be calmer and you can focus on ridding yourself of the burden you carry. Have you told Carla yet?'

'I haven't told anyone,' Mathias admits. 'I am a coward. Each time I come close to it, I start backing off again.' He hears Luc's sigh of frustration. 'Yes, yes, I hear you, Luc,' he says. 'But it's easier to think about it than to do it – to suddenly say to someone, *Look, I have been keeping something from you*, and then to tell a story I have kept hidden for more than sixty years.'

'Do you realise that people can see that you are burdened?' Luc asks. 'Not only people who know you well, but those you meet for the first time. It is as though you are carrying a tray of precious crystal glasses and you are afraid of dropping them.'

'That's just how it feels, although the possible cost seems far worse than the loss of a few glasses.'

'What about the book I gave you?' Luc asks. 'Have you read it?'

Mathias admits that he hasn't.

'You must confront this, Mathias, open it up. I know it was traumatic for you, but it is so long ago now that no one cares, except perhaps a few annoying historians. These days people would be fascinated by your story; they would see it as nothing more than a quaint little piece of history. Tell your daughter: she has a right to know. And tell your friend Mim; talk to her about it.'

'All right,' Mathias says, 'all right. I'll think about it.'

'And how many times have you said exactly that and done nothing?'

They talk a little longer, until Luc says he is growing tired and must rest.

Mathias drives on, replaying the conversation in his mind, wishing he could see his past through Luc's eyes. His friend makes it all sound so simple and sensible. Some part of him knows that Luc is right, and that moving here to Western Australia could be more than just a change of location; it could be the catalyst for a change within himself. If he were the hero of his own book – well, not a hero, but the main character – he'd probably deal with it that way. He'd mark this move as a turning point at which the main character opens up about the devastating secret he has kept since his teens. He suspects that most people would think his endless secrecy and silence was ridiculous, and his fear even more so. Perhaps he should talk to Carla, as Luc had urged. But would she really want to know? Maybe it's not a good time to spring it on her. Recently, Mim had told him that she suspected Carla and Jodie were now a couple, and he'd been alarmed. It was too soon for Carla, he insisted. She needed time to recover from the Tracey disaster, needed distance.

'Oh, do stop it!' Mim had said. 'It sounds to me as though Carla was over Tracey the day it ended, if not before. Not completely, of course, but essentially. She made the decision, and she knew afterwards she'd done the right thing, even though it was painful.'

'Well . . . yes, that's true, I suppose,' Mathias conceded. 'But these things take time.'

'It takes time if you part from someone whom you loved and were happy with for years,' Mim said. 'Probably you don't ever fully recover from that. But Carla's situation is very different from your loss of Therese.'

He shook his head. 'But Carla hasn't mentioned it to me at all.'

'She's probably waiting for the right moment, giving you time to settle in, and giving herself time to work out what she hopes for from this new relationship. Anyway, I'm not certain about it; I just get the feeling that something is happening there, and they have to work that out. So don't go barging in giving her advice.'

Sometimes Mim sounds very much like Therese; it's one of the things that draws him to her. She is very realistic, speaks her mind and doesn't mind disagreeing with him.

But Mathias isn't convinced that she's right about what is best for Carla. *I'm going to ask her about Jodie,* he decides. *I'll do it as soon as I get home. I'll tell her I have a right to know.*

But as soon as he hears the words in his head, he knows he's wrong. He hears Mim reminding him that it is *not* his right to know. Carla has her own life, and it is not his place to interfere. He is so distracted by his musing that he misses the change of a traffic light and sails through the red light to a screech of tyres and a horn blast from a driver who was about to turn in front of him. *You sort yourself out and let Carla sort out her own life,* he tells himself. And he makes up his mind to be more diligent about his property search so that Carla can have her house to herself again as soon as possible. *I must respect her decision – she will tell me when she's ready. And maybe then I will tell her my own old secret.*

Aware that he has managed to shelve the problem yet again, he swings into the driveway and sees that Carla's car is missing, though in its usual space is a gleaming, dark green Land Rover. Mathias hesitates, wondering whose car it is, and decides that it must belong to Nick or Paolo. He parks, gets out and sticks his head inside the partly open front door.

'Hello,' he calls. 'I'm back. Do we have visitors?'

'Hello,' someone calls from the kitchen, and as he steps inside the door a stranger appears wearing Carla's apron.

'Oh, wow,' she says, wiping her hands on the apron. 'You must be Mathias. We weren't expecting you home just yet. I'm Jodie, a friend of Carla – and of Mim too; she introduced us.'

Mathias stares at her; she is so unlike the woman he'd imagined. He knew Jodie was a vet, and even though Mim had told him her friend was younger, he'd presumed she must be in her late fifties, sixties even. Instead, this woman with mesmerising green eyes seems to be about the same age as his daughter.

'Ah! Yes, well, this is a surprise . . .' He hesitates. 'A good one, of course – a very good one.'

'Carla just popped out for some wine. It's so nice to meet you, Mathias.'

They shake hands and are standing there awkwardly when there is the sound of a car in the drive. 'Ah! Talk of the devil!' Mathias says with some relief. 'Here she is. I'll go and give her a hand with the wine.'

'It's only a couple of bottles,' Jodie says, 'I'm sure she can manage it. Could you come and stir this sauce for me while I get on with the vegetables?'

Thankful to have been given a task to mask his discomfort, Mathias follows Jodie to the kitchen and takes her place at the stove. 'It smells delicious,' he says as he stirs. 'What is it?'

'It's from one of my mother's old recipes,' Jodie says. 'She always made it to go with fish. It's –'

'Hi, Papa.' Carla appears in the doorway holding two bottles of white wine. 'I see you've been put to work already.' And she crosses the floor to kiss him. 'I tried to call to let you know Jo was coming for dinner, but you must have been on the phone. Have you two introduced yourselves?'

'We have,' Jodie says, 'but Mathias has only just arrived. Perhaps you could pour him a drink? He's not allowed to stop stirring yet.'

Mathias laughs, relaxing a little. Jodie is not only younger than he expected, and prettier, she seems very open and friendly.

'Is Mim coming to dinner too?' he asks.

'Yes, Mim and possibly Alice,' Jodie says.

'Mim but *no* Alice,' says a voice.

They turn to see Mim walking into the kitchen. 'Alice has jet-lag and is going to bed early, but she thanks you for the invitation and is looking forward to meeting you all. So, you'll just have to put up with me – but I brought dessert.' She hands Carla a round baking tin. 'Custard tart, it's still warm. Now, what can I do?'

'Thank you, Mim, you know I love your custard tarts,' Carla says. She draws a cork from one of the wine bottles. 'But Jo and I can manage dinner. You and Papa should take the wine and go sit outside. We'll call you when it's ready.'

'So, what do you think?' Mim asks as she and Mathias sit down at the table in the garden.

'She seems very nice,' Mathias says, 'but I had only just met her when Carla turned up and then you. I was expecting someone older.'

'Because she's my friend?'

'I suppose yes, because of that. Do you think they are planning to make some sort of announcement?'

Mim shakes her head. 'I think this is just a chance for you to meet Jodie. It would be helpful if you could relax a bit, take some deep breaths, smile and stop worrying. Have a drink and don't say anything at all about it.'

Mathias sips his wine. 'I can't think of anything else.'

Mim rolls her eyes. 'Just imagine this is a book you're writing,' she says. 'Think about how the daughter would want her father to behave in this situation.'

He looks at her for a long moment. 'She would want him to mind his own business,' he says. 'And how did you know I work things out like that in my head?'

She leans towards him. 'Because I read books, Mathias – lots of them. Enough to know a bit about people, and writers, and anxiety.'

Mathias continues staring at her, then picks up his glass. 'And you are a witch,' he says.

'Indeed, I am – so do as I say or I'll put a spell on you!'

Chapter Twenty-six

Mim is planning to take Alice into Perth to see the city and do some shopping. She rarely goes into the city herself, which is why she's left it so long – it's mid-November already. Alice is clearly keen to have a look around the city and has been studying a map on her iPad.

'Roughly where will we be going?' she asks at breakfast.

Mim puts on her glasses. 'We'll go on the train, because the parking will be horrendous. So, from the station – here – we'll walk across to Hay Street Mall, where the big shops are. And there are some nice little arcades leading through to Murray Street. When we've had enough, we can get an Uber up to Kings Park. The views are spectacular, and we can have lunch there. I suggest we get up and go early. If we get a train about nine, we'll be there about nine thirty.'

*

The following morning, they catch an early train into the city. It's a bright day but there's a gentle breeze, for which Mim is grateful; she is not keen on shopping or going into town, especially in the heat, but better now than next month, when it will be hotter, and the schools will be breaking up for the Christmas holidays.

Alice is looking very elegant in a pale blue linen dress. Mim has been impressed by the difference that the Bali makeover has wrought. Her sister looks younger, slimmer and very relaxed – the latter, she says, is because quite suddenly she has stopped worrying about her size, which has been the bane of her life.

'I feel better as well as looking better,' she tells Mim as the train whisks them along the line from Fremantle to Perth. 'I wish I'd done it years ago. I feel as though I have a future now.'

'It's really good to see you so happy,' Mim says. 'But didn't you feel you had a future before? You didn't think you were likely to die soon, did you?'

'Oh no. It's just that I felt there was nothing left for me except more of the same, and that I didn't have any other options. Like I said, you're the one who changed my way of thinking.'

'But how?' Mim asked. 'I don't understand what you mean. I've been doing the same thing for years too, so I don't see how I can have inspired you.'

'No, not that. Remember how you said that I was still living the life I had with Colin, and that was not something he would have wanted? Well, I took that on board; now I'm trying to live a new life without him.'

'Well, I'm glad I could help,' Mim says. 'But it's really yourself you should be thanking. It's all very well me telling you what you should do, but none of us can change unless we want to.'

A small boy who has broken free from his mother charges down the centre of the carriage, stumbles and falls at Mim's feet. She leans down to help him up, and his mother, clutching a baby, comes to collect him.

'I'm so sorry,' she says, holding on to him with her other arm. 'He just loves the train so much; he gets overexcited.'

'I'd have been a hopeless mother,' Mim says, watching as the woman juggles the baby and the little boy.

'Me too,' Alice says. 'I don't have the patience.'

'Do you ever wish you and Colin had had children?'

'Occasionally,' Alice says. 'But I never wanted them at the time. Michael was such an obnoxious kid that it put me off the idea. By the time he went to live with his mother, I was so glad to see the back of him I never gave it any thought, and Colin had certainly had enough by then.'

'Do you hear much from Michael these days?'

'Hardly ever, although he did come down from Edinburgh last month. He brought his new wife, the third one. He walked around the house like it was his own home, peering at things, and then said to the wife, Jennifer, "All of this will be ours eventually." He's like a rat, you know, a big greedy rat, just like when he was a kid. So, I said, "Actually, Michael, some of these things belong to me. In fact, with the exception of your father's artworks, which you will inherit, the entire contents of the house was left to me."

And Jennifer – who really seems rather nice – told him not to be so rude and arrogant, and that she wouldn't consider taking anything out of "Alice's home" – until such time as it was no longer "Alice's home". And later, while he was on his mobile, she said quietly, "Alice, I think you should make a list of the things that are yours or that you want to keep and leave it with your solicitor, so that everything is absolutely clear. I'm learning that Michael is quite ruthless about getting what he wants, whether it's possessions or just his own way. He's very self-centred and I hadn't realised that until recently. Don't leave anything to chance, or goodwill, because he hasn't much of the latter." I was staggered! I suspect either she'll change him or, more likely, she'll leave him.'

'Is there anything you'd want to take from the house?' Mim asks.

'Very little, but I'd like to keep Michael guessing. Just in case I decide to move.'

'But you won't move,' Mim says. 'You've said many times that you want to stay there.'

'Mmm. Well, I might be changing my mind. I've been thinking about a change. That's why I'm here. You've been suggesting it for years, so I thought I'd come and check it out.'

'Here?' Mim gapes at her. 'You mean you're thinking of coming here to live?'

'Possibly. Would that bother you?'

'*Bother* me? I'd love it, you know I would. Were you thinking about it before planning this trip or is it part of the Bali makeover?'

'I've been thinking about it for quite a long time, really. I suppose I just felt strange about leaving the house, as though everything might fall into a hole if I wasn't there. But if I did move here, I wouldn't interfere with your life; I'd get a place of my own.'

'But there's plenty of room in my place. You could have the room you're staying in now. We wouldn't be tripping over each other.'

Alice shakes her head. 'I really appreciate that, Mim, but I need a place of my own, and it's not as though I can't afford it. Besides, there's Mathias to think of.'

'Mathias? What's he got to do with it?'

Alice shrugs. 'Who knows what might happen with the two of you?'

'Mathias is my friend,' Mim insists, 'and please don't infer anything else when he's around. I would die of embarrassment.'

Alice raises her eyebrows. 'Okay, okay! But you two are very close, and anyone can see that you get on like a house on fire.'

'We do,' Mim agrees. 'But as I've told you any number of times, we're just good friends. I'm very fond of him, but I must admit I don't always understand him. He's quite private, you know. I often sense a deep sadness in him, as if something is weighing on him. It might just be that his oldest friend in Belgium is dying, but I think it's something more than that. Anyway, we have a lovely friendship, which is all I want. Now tell me,' she says, to change the subject, 'if you did move here, where do you think you might live?'

As the train slides into the station and they step out onto the platform, they discuss the possibilities. Mim is truly delighted about the prospect of her sister living nearby.

'I haven't made any firm decisions yet, Mim,' Alice reminds her. When they reach the street, she stops suddenly outside a cafe and glances at her watch. 'Let's have a quick coffee,' she says, ushering Mim towards the door. 'Look! They even have almond croissants, your favourites.' And she steers Mim inside and into a chair while she goes to the counter to order.

Mim does as she's told, even though she senses that Alice is up to something. *Go with the flow*, she tells herself.

But Alice doesn't say anything as they drink their coffee and eat their croissants. It's only as she is picking up her bag to leave that she says, 'Actually, I have a surprise for you. If I've read the map correctly it's quite near, so let's go or we'll be late.'

Mim is startled. 'What are you talking about? Late for what?'

'Just trust me,' Alice says. They step out on to the pavement and Alice takes Mim's arm and looks around, trying to orientate herself. 'This way,' she says. 'I can see the place I was looking for. Come on!'

Mim suddenly finds herself being pushed through the heavy glass doors of an upmarket hair and beauty salon. 'No!' she cries. 'No, Alice!'

'Yes!' Alice insists. 'Give it a go, Mim.' And she approaches the black marble reception desk, holding tight to her sister's arm so she can't escape.

'I called yesterday to make a reservation for my sister, Ms Squires,' Alice says.

The woman at the desk studies her computer screen. 'Oh yes,' she says. 'Style, cut and colour, and a facial.'

'No!' Mim says again, starting to panic.

'Come on, Mim,' Alice says firmly, 'don't make a fuss. I think you're stuck, just as I was.'

'But I'm older,' Mim protests, 'and I –'

'I know,' Alice cuts in. 'You are three years older, and you have post-polio syndrome. I understand – I do. But why not take a risk? All it will cost you is a few hours. And who knows? You might even enjoy it!'

Mim's whole body was stiff, knotted with tension, resistance and hostility. If she hadn't been so thrilled to hear that Alice was considering moving to Australia, she would have marched out of the salon. But something had opened up in Mim as she considered the prospect of having her sister close by. That Alice was even considering the possibility was totally unexpected, and remarkably uplifting. It gave her a feeling of warmth and security. She didn't even start worrying about the time it would take, the bureaucratic hurdles and mountains of paperwork that would be put in their way. Even before the various treatments were applied to her face, neck and hair she just felt lighter, younger and stronger.

'I love it,' she tells her sister as they leave the salon. 'It makes me look so much younger. Not that I actually mind my age; seventy-five is not the end of the world. I wish I'd done something like this years ago.'

'I told you,' Alice says. 'That's just how I felt in Bali. And we're not done yet. Now we're off to David Jones. You definitely need a wardrobe makeover, too. Don't worry – we'll start slowly, just get a few nice things today. Then you'll be gorgeous for Christmas.'

Mim rolls her eyes. 'Gorgeous? That'll be the day. And I haven't done my Christmas shopping yet. I could do that this afternoon if we skip the clothes.'

But Alice is insistent. Mim has never seen her like this; she is positively bossy! Bossy is Mim's own thing: she is used to telling people what to do and how to do it. But not this time.

'Did you boss Colin around like this?' she asks as they walk up the street.

'Quite a lot. Especially towards the end,' Alice says. 'In the early days, he was really active, you must remember that – how much he loved going on hikes, and he played tennis and golf for years. But in the last ten years or so it was hard to get him moving. He became very passive. His arthritis was a problem, and we had long painful conversations about how important it was to keep moving. But Colin had all sorts of arguments and invented all sorts of reasons not to exercise and started to get grumpy with me, so I gave up. I think he was just ready to go in the end.'

Once in the store Mim follows Alice obediently to the ladieswear department and once again puts herself in her sister's hands. She is steered into changing rooms to try on trousers and tops, dresses and skirts that she would never have considered in other circumstances. She is shocked by the number of times Alice urges her to try something that she thinks most unsuitable only for it to look surprisingly good. Eventually she has to call a halt, because she is simply exhausted. Soon they are sitting on the train surrounded by carrier bags.

'How long is it since you went clothes shopping?' Alice asks.

Mim shrugs. 'No idea – years, probably. And even then it was usually just a quick dash into Kmart and out again as fast as I could.'

'You weren't always like that,' Alice says. 'I remember going shopping with you when we were younger.'

'Oh, yes, but that was such a long time ago,' Mim says.

'I think we've both been stuck in a rut,' Alice muses. 'Mum brought us up to think that clothes must be practical, ladylike and last a long time. And we were taught to avoid drawing attention to ourselves. She always did her own hair, and it was always the same. And everything she wore came from Marks and Spencer. Neat, clean and modest.'

'That's right – it was so important to be modest. She always said we were not to get above ourselves or try to be noticed. Do you remember that?'

Alice nods. 'I do. I suppose it was the post-war attitude. She always looked rather dull and middle-aged, now that I think about it, when she could have looked much younger. Poor Mum; I wonder if she minded.'

'If she'd minded, I don't think she would have made such a thing of it,' Mim says. 'She loved us and wanted us to be safe and responsible – solid, she used to say. You're right, it was that late fifties thing when little girls were

191

supposed to become little ladies. The fifties, and even the early sixties, were so boring.'

They sit in silence as the train stops and new passengers get in.

'Do you think she was happy?' Alice asks.

Mim considers this. 'I suppose in her own way she was. She didn't have high expectations or expensive tastes; and she hadn't had the sort of education that we got.'

'Do you remember those horrible cardigans she knitted for us? The Christmas ones?'

'Oh my god, weren't they the pits?' Mim says, laughing. 'I hid mine several times, tried to tell her that I'd lost it at school, but she always found it in the end.'

'I still miss her, you know,' Alice says.

'Me too,' says Mim, turning to her sister. 'I really regret that I didn't spend more time with her towards the end. I spent so long resenting her and Dad for putting me in hospital and then hiding me away at home that I never really allowed myself to understand and forgive them. It was always in the back of my mind that they could abandon me again.'

'They really did love you, Mim,' Alice says. 'The way they talked about you, the things they said about you when they didn't know I was listening. I know it didn't feel that way to you, but you were their precious first child.'

Mim nods but stays silent. A small part of her believes that Alice could be right, but the remembered experience still denies it. She pauses, looks out of the window and changes the subject.

'Well, Al, despite the mortification of being handled by so many people, this has been a really lovely day. Thank you for dragging me out and shaking me up.'

Alice nods. 'We must do some more sisterly things; I'll have to think of some more ways to torture you!'

Some hours later, alone in her bedroom, Mim stands looking at herself in the mirror. The loose wide-leg pants fit perfectly and make her look taller. The pale grey silk shirt that she'd resisted at first looks and feels wonderful, especially with her new haircut, which seems to have worked magic. *I look totally different, but I still look like myself,* she thinks. She tries on two other pairs of trousers, another silk shirt and a couple of cotton tops. Then she decides to risk the dresses. It's years since she wore a dress and she had tried to demur, but Alice had been insistent. She steps into a sleeveless dress in lemon linen and is surprised by how good it looks – even better than it had looked in the shop.

Mim stands there looking at herself for a long time, and slowly she feels her mood change; she is on the brink of tears. Her excitement at her new look and new clothes has morphed into sadness. She has a painful sense of the lost opportunities, a glimpse of what could have been a different sort of life. Has she really always seen herself as defined by the damage of polio? Her right leg, usually in a brace, her rather stiff and awkward arms, and the obvious way that she tips slightly to one side when she walks. Did she adopt this attitude of not caring how she looks in order to protect herself from the disappointments of the fitting-room mirror and the reactions of others? Was it her way of guarding against that? Because now it seems to her to be more like giving in: setting herself apart from others so she couldn't be compared with the girls with the pretty hair and dresses, their stilettos and miniskirts. She had tried to turn herself into a different sort of person; refusing any interest in fashion, refusing to indulge in beauty treatments and modern hairstyles. Yet what she sees in the mirror now is a pleasant-looking, attractively dressed older woman with a very cool haircut and discreet makeup. *How might I have looked?* she wonders now. *Why did I never even take the smallest risk of trying to find some sort of style? Why did I let myself become a dowdy old woman who has never really had the confidence to play to her best side?*

She sits down abruptly on the bed, puzzled and angry with herself for drifting too easily into decades of a sort of self-abandonment. *Why did I give up so quickly?* But she knows the answer; she has always known it. The polio, its lasting physical and psychological effects, had made her feel unattractive, different, somehow less than other girls and women and, worst of all, unlovable. At school she had been painfully slow to make friends and never became part of a group, although Alice and her friends tried to include her. It was the boys who turned school into misery for her. 'Watch out for the crippo,' they'd yell. 'Where's yer horse, Hopalong?' On the worst days, when she needed her crutches, they called her Hunchback, or Toad. None of it made sense, but who cared about that? Sometimes boys would kick away a crutch then run off, screeching with laughter, as she struggled to get up.

'Take no notice, dear,' her mother had told her. 'It's just ignorance, don't dignify it by responding.' Easily said, but not easily done.

She admires her reflection one last time then slips off the dress and hangs it in the wardrobe. Alice had said that Mim inspired her to change her attitude to life; it might turn out that her sister has returned the favour.

Chapter Twenty-seven

*C*arla is growing anxious about Christmas. Mim has invited her, Mathias and Jodie for Christmas Day. Carla has grown very fond of Mim, and she's sure she'll like Alice too, but it is all going to be so different from what she is used to – out in the sun on Mim's wide verandah with its view of the sea. It will be a far cry from the cool, quiet Christmases at the old house in Monbulk, under the deep shade of the trees and surrounded by blissful silence. But it's not just the break with tradition that disturbs her; it's the thought of a long day spent with other people. She has become less sociable the older she's got, and like Mathias she is most at ease with one or two people, so the prospect of five of them being together the whole day and into the evening takes her out of her comfort zone.

'It'll be fine,' Jodie had assured her a couple of days ago, when she'd realised that Carla was less than enthused about the idea. 'In fact, it will be really lovely. Mim loves doing Christmas; she's a great cook and very organised, and I bet Alice is too. It won't be at all formal. And we can escape to the beach with the dogs if it all gets a bit much.'

'It still seems a bit intimidating,' Carla said doubtfully. 'I like Mim a lot, but I haven't a clue about Alice. And Papa says he thinks Mim's neighbours are coming as well. That's quite a lot of people.'

'Clare and Andrew are coming late in the afternoon for a drink before dinner, that's all. They'll be there an hour at the most. And do you have any idea how intimidating you and Mathias can be, especially when you're together? You're quite a formidable pair. You are both so . . .' she hesitates, 'so self-contained, so assured and in control of yourselves. And here's me: I talk too much, get carried away with silly ideas, talk to animals as though they're humans. I'm messy, undisciplined in everything except my work. My emotions are up and down from day to day.'

Carla thinks back over the conversation – explaining her feelings to Jodie had forced her to put them into words. Since they'd met, she'd felt something within her that had been dormant since the loss of her mother coming back to her; there had been a slow unwinding of tension, and for the first time in a long while she is feeling a sense of inner peace. But it's precarious still, made more so by her awareness of Mathias's unspoken pain, or fear – or whatever it is; she can't quite put her finger on it. But his mood affects her own. She just wishes she knew what was troubling him.

She wanders out into the garden and sits in her favourite basket chair. It is as though Jodie opened a door to a different sort of life, something she had desperately needed, almost without knowing it. This is something she's never felt before: a sense of certainty and commitment and an utter lack of doubt. And the more certain of her future with Jodie she feels, the more she wants those close to them both to know. She wants to claim this part of her life openly, to show her pleasure and pride in it, especially to her father.

*

Jodie, sitting at a table outside the restaurant, sees Carla walking along the pavement, scanning the crowded tables, trying to find her. She gets to her feet and waves, and Carla waves back and heads swiftly towards her. They hug and then settle at the table as Carla sighs with relief.

'That was a big sigh,' Jodie says. 'Bad day?'

'Well . . . not really. I've just been thinking about Christmas . . .'

'Are you still feeling overwhelmed by the idea of celebrating Christmas with so many people?' Jodie asks.

'It's partly that. But it helps to know that we'll be there together. I know we've talked about taking things slowly and being sure, but I think I'd feel better if people knew about us. I think we should tell them.'

'Okay,' Jodie says, relieved that Carla seems as certain about their relationship as she feels. 'Let's order some food and a drink and we can talk about it. But I have to confess – and I know I should have told you sooner – Kirra knows about us.'

'Oh, I realise that!' Carla says, laughing.

'I think she knew how I felt about you even before I did! That day you turned up alone without Mim, I'd asked Kirra to go out and buy new jeans for me. She even helped me to get ready; she was totally into it all.'

They are still laughing about this when the waiter arrives to take their order. He returns swiftly with a bottle of wine.

'So,' Jodie says, as she pours them each a glass, 'what's really bothering you?'

Carla sighs. 'It's difficult to explain, because I'm not sure I understand it myself. I've been wondering why it is that I'm so uncomfortable in big groups of people, and I think it's something I get from Papa. He's always been a bit of a loner, and I know Mama used to worry that his reserve, and his fierce sense of privacy, might affect me. I heard her tell him more than once that he needed to open up more, for my sake. I'm starting to think that there was something more to it than just a character trait. It's almost like Mama was meaning he should be open about something specific, though I have no idea what that could be. But I came to a rather extraordinary realisation when I was thinking about Christmas. I realised that it's not just myself I've been worrying about; I've been worrying about Papa. And then it occurred to me that I am more anxious when he is with me than when I'm alone.'

Jodie nods. 'I've noticed that. I mean, it's obvious that you're very close and love each other very much, but sometimes . . . Oh no, scrub that, it's not my business; after all, I hardly know Mathias.'

'Tell me please, Jo. Tell me what you were going to say.'

Jodie takes a deep breath. 'Okay, well, sometimes, when you're together, I feel like you're both waiting for something terrible to happen.'

Carla stares at her for several long moments without speaking. Then she nods. 'Yes,' she says. 'Yes, that's exactly how it feels – but it's really only when we're with other people. How clever of you to pick up on it.'

'I feel as though I could be drawn into his anxiety, or his sadness, or whatever it is that seems to travel with him,' Jodie elaborates. 'I sense that same anxiety in you from time to time, but it's much stronger when you're together.'

Again, Carla is silent, this time staring into her glass.

'Have I upset you?' Jodie asks cautiously.

'No! No, not at all,' Carla says, reaching out for her hand across the table. 'I'm just gobsmacked that you could . . . well, that you were able to . . . to articulate it so well.'

Jodie gives her a small smile. 'Well, I've been watching you closely. It seems to me, though, that the anxiety or the fear belongs to Mathias, and it's something you take on. I mean, it's not *your* fear, is it? It's your response to *his* fear or anxiety. Because you're so close to him, you take it on as your own, as if to protect him somehow.'

'You're sounding like a therapist,' Carla says.

'Sorry – I worried that I might be overstepping; that's why I haven't said anything before.'

'No, you're not overstepping,' Carla says. 'I think . . . no, I'm *sure* that you're right.'

'Good, because I'm sure I'm right too! And it is a real thing, you know, taking on someone else's burden. We see it all the time in animals: dogs who live with people who are nervous or frightened or have a serious illness, for instance. And horses can detect all sorts of things in their owners.'

Carla leans back in her chair and finishes her wine. 'So, what do I do about it? I have no idea what it's about. When Papa said he wanted to move here I was really happy, because I thought it would be better for him in his old age if we could live closer to each other. But now things are changing. I feel that weight moving in on me. It's as though I am sharing a huge burden and I don't even know the cause of it – but I do know that I don't want to carry it anymore.'

'Then I think you have to tell Mathias that. He lives here now; that darkness is only going to grow more significant for you. I'm sorry to be so blunt, but I worry that if you don't deal with it, this will affect our relationship in the long term.'

Jodie is worried that she's gone too far. She holds her breath until she starts to feel dizzy. Carla is staring at her empty glass; she stares without moving or speaking until Jodie can hold on no longer.

'Talk to me, please.'

Carla takes a deep breath and looks up.

'Oh, Jo, I'm sorry – I'm just so amazed by your insight. I can see exactly what you mean and I'm sure you're right. I have no idea what this thing is, but the more I think about it it's so clear that Papa is haunted by something. And that's why it's hard for him when there are other people around. I don't mean crowds; he has his public persona as a writer and he seems comfortable playing that part. It's more with people he knows, people with whom he has some level of intimacy. It's as if at a certain point the shutters come down. He's always pulling back, as though there is something about himself that he doesn't want them to know. And yet I've noticed that he is more relaxed when Mim is around.'

'Do you think Mim knows what it is that's troubling him?'

Carla tilts her head, thinking. 'No, I don't think she does. But I do think something about her – her briskness, perhaps, her forthrightness and independence – makes him feel safer, just as Mama did.'

Jodie nods. 'I think she has that effect on quite a few people. Me, for one.'

The waiter is approaching with their food.

'I will talk to him,' Carla says. 'I promise. I need to think some more about how and when I'll bring it up, but I'll do it soon.'

*

The following week Carla and Jodie are sitting outside Nick's cafe, studying the breakfast menu.

'Is it healthy or decadent this morning?' Nick asks.

'Decadent,' Carla says. 'I'll have the pancakes with maple syrup.'

'Well, I don't want you to be alone in your decadence,' Jodie says. 'I'll have the same please, Nick.'

Nick nods and drops a brochure on the table. 'Right you are. Now, this is the Perth Festival brochure. Paolo and

I wondered if you'd be interested in coming with us to a couple of things. We've already marked a few events we're interested in.' And he heads back inside the cafe to put their order through.

Carla looks at Jodie and raises her eyebrows. 'Would you be okay going to something with them? I usually do.'

'I'd love to,' Jodie says. 'I think I've fallen in love with Nick and Paolo already.'

'So, it's not just me anymore?'

Jodie laughs. 'You are on a pinnacle.'

'Phew! That's a relief.' Carla opens the brochure and starts to leaf through it. 'What about this?' she asks, stopping at a page and pushing the brochure across the table to Jodie.

By the time Nick comes back with their coffee they have marked several items on the program.

'You know,' Carla says to Jodie, 'I think we're going to have to tell them about us before Christmas.'

'Tell who?' Nick asks.

Carla rolls her eyes. 'My dad, of course, and Jodie's friend Mim!'

'Tell them? But they know already.'

Jodie shakes her head. 'No, we haven't told them yet,' she says. 'We were planning to make an announcement on Christmas Day.'

Nick laughs out loud. 'But they *do* know. At least, Mathias does. He came in here for breakfast a few days ago and asked Paolo and me what we thought of your new girlfriend, Carla. Of course we told him how wonderful Jo is.'

Carla shakes her head. 'Sneaky old devil. But how did he find out?'

'Perhaps he just suspected, and you and Paolo confirmed it for him, Nick. Or maybe Mim said something,' Jodie speculates. 'We both know she set us up in the first place.'

Paolo shook his head. 'So, if Mim knows, and Mathias knows, what are you guys waiting for? It seems the only people who are concerned about telling people are you two. Get your act together and make it official already.'

'Maybe,' Carla says. 'Or we could let them wonder for a bit longer!'

Chapter Twenty-eight

Mathias is trying to buy Christmas presents in Fremantle, but he can't seem to focus on what he should buy for whom. He's never had to worry about shopping for anyone other than Therese and Carla and he finds he has no idea where to start with anyone else. This must be why Therese always made a list, he thinks ruefully. Finally, after about twenty uninspired minutes, he decides he'd better follow her example. He slips into a cafe, orders a long black at the counter, then sits down at a pavement table. The trouble is that he's not a Christmas sort of person. His years of quiet Christmases at home with Carla in the old house suited him perfectly, but he realises it's unfair to think they could keep on like that. Carla has a new life now – which reminds him that he must also find a gift for Jodie. He is relieved to find that he likes Jodie very much; she is the perfect match for Carla. If only they would just say so! He and Mim have talked about this; they are both finding it frustrating that Carla and Jodie are obviously in a serious relationship but are pretending they are just good friends. And speaking of Mim, what about her and her sister Alice, whom he's only met briefly? What should he buy them?

The waitress brings his coffee, and as he sips it he stares out at the street, which is busy with people of all shapes and sizes, colours and languages. He likes this about Fremantle: the diversity of the community and its visitors, the combination of old and new, traditional and modern. He's been feeling more and more at home here; moving was definitely the right decision. But it's hard for him to relax when Christmas seems to have taken over his life. He will feel no peace until he has found appropriate gifts. Carla is fairly easy to buy for; she loves unusual jewellery and he knows of a shop she likes. He's sure he'll find something there.

He opens his backpack and takes out a pen and notepad. What about Jodie? Trying to choose something that's right for her feels like a test he has to sit. He is thinking about this when he remembers a painting he saw in the window of an art gallery: a watercolour of dogs playing on the beach by a local artist. It had caught his eye and he'd stopped to look at it. Yes, he thinks, that could be right for Jodie. Good . . . Now, Alice and Mim. He barely knows Alice, but Mim has mentioned that she is a big reader, so perhaps a book – maybe something Australian, as she mentioned she had read very few Australian novels. He is feeling more confident, although he still hasn't thought of anything for Mim; he wants it to be something significant, something that defines their friendship in some way, but he's aware that he's setting himself an impossible task. Still, having even an incomplete list is reassuring, and he feels more relaxed now, able to sip the rest of his coffee and watch the world go by without stress.

He has just put his pen and notepad away and is preparing to leave when his phone rings. He drags it out of his pocket and peers at it, but the sun is hitting the screen and he can't make out the caller ID.

'Hello?' he says.

'Mathias?' a woman's voice asks. 'Is that you, Mathias?'

And he recognises Patrice's voice and feels a shiver of foreboding.

'Yes, Patrice – it's me. Is everything all right?'

'Dearest Mathias, I am so sorry to tell you . . .' She pauses, and he hears her repress a sob. 'Our beloved Luc has gone. He passed away during the night.'

Mathias grabs the edge of the table and sits down again, resting his head on his free hand. Patrice is sobbing, telling him that Luc passed peacefully in his sleep. She knew that he would want her to tell Mathias how much he had loved him, that their friendship had been the most important of his life.

'You were like brothers,' she says. 'He loved you like a brother.'

Mathias tries to say the right things, the selfless things, tries to focus on what Patrice must be feeling. They talk slowly and sadly, and Patrice tells him that their children are arriving soon, everyone is devastated, although they all knew that he was close to the end. Mathias asks if there is anything he can do, and she says she thinks not. She urges him not to try to come for the funeral.

'Come later, when the worst of our grief has passed and we can enjoy our memories.'

Mathias says he will think about it and that he will call again tomorrow. He puts down the phone, buries his face in his hands and weeps.

After a few minutes he takes several deep breaths and, feeling the warmth of a hand on his shoulder, he looks up.

'Are you okay? Can I help you at all?' A young man, vaguely familiar, is standing beside him. He moves a little to sit down, reaches for Mathias's hand and holds it. It is a strong hold, warm and comforting. Mathias grasps it tightly.

'Thank you, but no, I am not okay,' he says. 'I had such very sad news. My oldest friend has died. We spoke often, but we did not have a chance to say goodbye.'

'I'm so sorry,' the young man says. 'That's a great loss.'

Mathias nods, unable to stop the tears from streaming down his face.

'I think you need a drink. Brandy, perhaps?'

Mathias nods. 'Please, a small brandy and some water.'

The young waitress who had brought his coffee is nearby, and the man signals to her.

'This gentleman has had a very bad shock,' he explains as he orders the brandy.

'We knew each other since we were fifteen years old,' Mathias says. 'We were at high school together in Belgium and then went to the same university. Despite living on different sides of the world, we have always stayed close.

We talked often, met frequently – for more than sixty years.' He shakes his head. 'And now he has gone. I've dreaded this moment. I wanted to be the first to go, not to be left alone – he was so much wiser and stronger than me.' He hesitates. 'I'm sorry, you don't want to hear all this; it's so very kind of you to sit here with me.'

'It's nothing,' the young man says. 'Such sad news at any time is hard to bear, but it's even worse when you are alone . . .'

The waitress appears with a glass of brandy and sets it on the table. 'The manager sends you his condolences and says the brandy is on the house.'

Mathias thanks her and she heads off to take another order.

The young man gestures to Mathias's glass and says, 'You should drink to your friend.'

Mathias nods. 'Indeed. To Luc . . .' He hesitates, wanting to say more, trying to find the words to express what Luc meant to him. 'The most beloved friend, the wisest mentor.' He raises his glass. 'I loved him as a brother.'

He chokes back a sob as he feels the warmth of the brandy moving down his throat. The stranger is still there, gentle, calm, his presence strangely reassuring. He can't be more than twenty-five, Mathias thinks. Tall, with grey-blue eyes, wearing beige jeans and a leather belt with a large buckle in tooled steel. Mathias feels sure they must have met before, but he is too ragged with grief to ask.

'I've heard it said that great loss can make one stronger,' the man says. 'That we adjust ourselves – our behaviours, opinions and attitudes – to keep us in harmony with those we love. It begins with our parents, and sometimes when someone to whom we are very close dies, we find ourselves changing.'

Mathias considers this. 'Yes,' he says. 'That makes sense. But I wouldn't want to change much from the person I have been because much of it is thanks to Luc. I always admired him so much as a man and a scholar that I ran many decisions past him, sought his opinion on my work, consulted him on aspects of my life. Now I will have to make my own decisions without his counsel. I feel, in this moment, that I won't know who I am now that he has gone.' He is surprised to find himself talking so freely to this stranger, allowing himself to appear so vulnerable.

They sit for a while in a comfortable silence for which Mathias is grateful; it gives him time to muster some strength and he feels under no pressure to make conversation. Eventually the man breaks the silence.

'It's a wonderful gift, a friendship like that,' he says. 'A tribute to both of you that your love for each other lasted all this time. Such friendships are rare.'

Mathias nods. 'He was the only person who knew a secret, a terrible secret that I have kept from everyone else, except my late wife.' And as he says it, he knows this should provide relief – there is no one left who knows – yet he can feel nothing but grief.

They sit in silence for a few minutes. 'How do you feel now?' the man asks. 'Can you get home all right?'

'Yes, thank you, I'll be fine. I parked my car nearby. You've been very kind.'

They both get to their feet, Mathias standing with one hand on a chair back to steady himself.

'Goodbye, Mathias.' The young man extends his hand. 'Take care – my condolences on your loss.'

'I'm sorry . . . I don't know your name . . .' Mathias says, shaking the proffered hand.

But the man has gone. Gone impossibly quickly, before Mathias can question him further; he seems to have disappeared into thin air. Mathias looks in all directions, but he can't see the man anywhere.

Bewildered, he sits down again at the table.

The waitress comes by to collect his cup and his glass. 'How are you feeling now?' she asks. 'Would you like another brandy, or some coffee perhaps?'

Mathias shakes his head. 'No, thank you, nothing more, but I wonder – the young man who was sitting here with me, do you know who he is? Is he a regular customer?'

She frowns at him. 'I'm sorry, I don't know who you mean.'

'The young man who ordered the brandy for me.' He points to the chair. 'He was sitting there.'

The waitress is bewildered. 'But you were the only person at this table,' she says. 'You had a cup of coffee, and then you got some bad news – a bad shock, I think you said; you'd been talking on your phone. Then you ordered a brandy and some water. There was no one else here.'

'But you spoke with him.'

'No, sir, only with you.' The waitress looks at him closely. 'Are you sure you're all right?'

Mathias nods. 'Yes. Yes, I am . . . I think . . . I'm so sorry, I'm rather muddled.'

'It could be the shock,' she says.

'Yes, yes, the shock, of course. That must be right.' He doesn't believe it; he knows the man was there. He thanks the waitress, picks up his backpack and walks slowly away.

As he walks in the direction of his parked car, he looks back several times, but nothing has changed. *He was there*, he tells himself, *I saw him, felt him take my hand. I knew him; he was like a part of me.* He stops walking, leans against the wall of the nearest building, tucks his thumb behind his belt buckle and remembers as he does this that the young man had done the same thing: tucked his thumb in his belt, fingering the buckle. He looks down at his own belt, and the large steel buckle. Goosebumps rise and a shiver of recognition runs up his spine. He presses himself back against the wall, dizzy again, his heart thumping in his chest, waiting until he is calmer. Then, with new and purposeful energy, he walks swiftly to his car.

He drives straight back to Carla's house, dumps his backpack on the floor and goes directly to the lounge room, where he picks up a framed black-and-white photograph. There it is, the photograph of himself with Luc, taken by Therese on his twenty-fifth birthday. In the picture, he is wearing a belt with a buckle of tooled steel – a birthday present from Luc. He is wearing the same belt today. The leather is smoother, softer now. It's so soft he has often considered abandoning the belt and fitting the buckle to a new one, but he never has.

'You need a new belt, my friend,' Luc had said when they last met. 'Be careful or your trousers will fall down.'

Mathias studies his own face in the photograph and sees, just as he expected, that it is the face of the young stranger whom he had encountered earlier.

He sinks down onto the sofa, still staring at the photograph. It was so real: the warm hand on his shoulder, the words spoken in a voice he recognised. And he is overwhelmed by sadness, by frustration and confusion. *No one will ever believe this*, he tells himself. *They would think I was losing my mind – and perhaps I am.*

*

A few days later, on a beautiful, warm December evening, Carla lays the table out on the terrace. She has prepared grilled salmon with a salad and opened a bottle of rosé. She calls to Mathias, but there is no response, so she walks back into the house and calls again. Still nothing. Finally, she walks upstairs to tap lightly on his bedroom door.

'Dinner's ready, Papa.'

There is a mumble from within and then Mathias opens the door, clutching a book. 'Sorry,' he says. 'I was reading.' And he closes the book and drops it onto the bed.

Carla sees he looks tired and sad, as he has since Luc's death, and this makes him seem older even than when he had arrived back from Europe. They go down the stairs together and out onto the terrace and now, in the dimming light, she sees his age not only in his face but in his body, in the way he moves. It shocks her and for a moment she has to look away. Can he really have changed so much in just over a week?

She remembers visiting her maternal grandmother with Therese, many years ago. It was the first time they had been back to Belgium for a visit since they moved to Australia and Carla found herself face to face with someone who was at first unrecognisable. Carla was shocked, embarrassed. Yet her home still looked familiar, and when she had bent to kiss and hug her grandmother, the scents of perfume and face powder were exactly the same as she had remembered. But what had moved her most, and made her struggle to hold back tears, was the sense that her grandmother's personality seemed to have melted away. She seemed to lack the will and desire to participate in the life going on around her.

'When you see someone every day,' Therese had told her daughter later, 'you don't see the slow, subtle changes that happen over years and months – especially to older people. It's only after an absence of a few years that you really see what time has done to a person.'

Carla reminds herself that she has seen her father on a fairly regular basis, so perhaps she has simply not noticed the small changes that have shaped him into an old man. It was as though grief had quite suddenly drained all vibrancy from his face and body and, in doing so, had diminished him. She wonders if she will ever again see him as he had been a few days ago, before Luc's death.

Mathias picks up his glass and raises it to her. '*Santé*,' he says and sips his wine.

'*Santé*,' Carla says in return. 'How are you doing now, Papa?'

'I'm still here, although perhaps a little less present than usual,' he says, smiling.

She nods. 'I noticed that your hands are shaking a bit.'

He holds up his right hand and looks at it, spreading his fingers, obviously concentrating on keeping it still. 'Sometimes yes, but not all the time.' He smiles. 'Fortunately, I can still use the keyboard. I am getting old, Carla – losing Luc has reminded me of that in a very brutal way. Today I talked with Patrice. She told me they will have a very small funeral and she insisted once again that I should not try to go there. I doubt I would have been able to get a flight so close to Christmas anyway. She asked me instead to visit in the northern spring, when the weather is warmer, and we can go for walks in the hills. She asked after you, and I told her about Jodie. She was so happy to know that you have found such a wonderful person. She sends you her love.'

'It would be good to see her again,' Carla says. She is taken aback by his mention of Jodie.

'Maybe you and Jodie would come? I would invite Mim, too. You youngsters could have a wonderful holiday in the Ardennes and we old crocks would keep out of your way.'

Carla smiles and pats his hand. 'That would be lovely,' she says.

'You mustn't worry about me, Carla,' he reassures her. 'I'm working through this, but it takes time. And now I realise I have broken the silence. I am supposed to pretend that Jodie is just a friend. I'm sure she is much more to you than that, but Mim says we must wait for you to tell us.'

'And Jodie tells me that we must wait to tell you,' she says. 'But, of course, you're right. It's been a few months now and we both feel . . .' She hesitates, wondering how to describe it. 'We love each other, Papa, and we want to be together. This time I really feel that I have found the person I'm supposed to be with. I've never felt that before.'

'Then it's a gift,' Mathias says. 'And she feels the same?'

'She does!'

Her father twists his glass in his hand, tilting it back and forth as the flickering light of the table candles changes the delicate rosy shade of the wine.

'You'll want to live together now,' he says.

Carla draws a deep breath. 'Well, yes, we've discussed it. I'm going to move in with Jodie. It would be easy, and not too expensive, to create a studio for me on her property. There's an old, unused building close to the house that would be ideal. You must come with me to see it, tell me what you think.'

'You are the artist,' he says. 'You know better than I what you need.' He smiles wryly. 'Even so, as a man I am compelled to interfere and offer unwanted advice. And this house?'

'Well, eventually I'll sell it, but there's no hurry. You take your time finding your own place; stay here as long as you want. And of course, if you want to stay here for good, that's fine too.'

Mathias puts his glass down and watches as Carla refills it. 'Thank you, I will appreciate having time to find a new home. As for staying on permanently . . . well, I would like to be closer to Fremantle. Mim has some new plans for her shop, and I want to be involved in that. And I would like to be near the sea; I've often thought how wonderful it would be to get up early in the morning and walk to the beach.'

Mathias leans across the table to where Carla's phone is sitting on top of the newspaper. He pushes the phone closer to her. 'Could you ring Jodie and ask her to tell Mim about the two of you as soon as possible? I'll be in trouble if I know before she does.' He gets up from his seat and starts to walk away from the table.

Carla, seeing there are tears in his eyes, feels a wave of panic. 'Papa, where are you going? Have I upset you?' She gets to her feet to follow him.

Turning, he says, 'Upset me? Of course not, why ever would you think that? I am going upstairs to get my own phone so that I can ring Mim after Jodie has spoken to her. Besides, we haven't finished our dinner yet.'

But Carla follows him. 'You have tears in your eyes,' she says, putting her arms around him.

'Tears of happiness for you, darling. Which is much better than the tears of sadness and loss I have shed over the last few days.' And he returns her embrace briefly, then continues on into the house to fetch his phone.

Chapter Twenty-nine

Mim is not really looking forward to Christmas, but she is trying to look keen and interested as Alice seems quite excited. She is rummaging through a box of Christmas decorations so that they can decorate the tree – which, as Alice has pointed out, they should have done at least two weeks ago.

'Crikey, Mim,' she says, 'these are ancient. Some of them look like the old decorations from home.'

'That's because some of them are,' Mim says. She is exhausted, and the last thing she wants to do is decorate a tree. She had been into Life Support today and it had been full of holidaymakers and Christmas shoppers.

'Did you take these when Mum died?' Alice asks.

'Take what?'

'These decorations.'

'What? You think I *stole* them?' Mim says, suddenly

angry. 'Do you honestly think that I would steal decorations from our mother?'

'Mim!' Alice says. 'That's not what I said and it's not what I think.'

Mim sniffs and turn away. 'Well, that's how it sounded. I've had them for decades. Mum made me take a few each time I went home to visit. By then they were spending Christmases with you and Colin, so they weren't decorating at home. I think Mum wanted me to have something from home here in Australia, so I could have an English Christmas.'

'And did you?'

Mim shakes her head. 'Never. I took some of them to the shop one year and Doug put them up. They looked lovely, but they were getting a bit tatty so this year he bought some new ones.'

'Mim,' Alice says cautiously, 'it never crossed my mind that you would have stolen the decorations.'

Mim looks at her, ashamed. She had known the moment she blurted it out that Alice wasn't accusing her. 'I know. I'm sorry, Al, I don't know why I reacted like that.'

'Speaking of the shop,' Alice says, 'I've always assumed that you were there more or less full-time, but you don't seem to be going in all that often. I think today was the first time this week.'

Mim feels her face grow hot with embarrassment. 'Yes,' she says, and she pulls a string of coloured baubles from the box and hands them to Alice for the tree.

'So that's it?' Alice says. 'Just yes?'

Mim sighs and sits down on the arm of the sofa. 'You're

right; I've been more or less avoiding it. I haven't really felt like going back there since I came home from England.'

Alice looks up at her with surprise. 'But that's ages. What's changed?'

Mim shrugs. 'I don't know really. I went in quite a lot when I first got home. I checked that everything was in order with the accounts and the stock, and I spent some time chatting with the customers. But it felt very strange; I found it quite hard and exhausting. Then Jodie came out of hospital, so I was back and forth between her place and mine quite a bit. Then I was looking at houses with Carla, and with Mathias since he's come back to Perth. So, yes, you're right – I've hardly been there.'

'Can you afford *not* to be there?' Alice asks.

'For a while I can, but not for long. I just can't seem to summon the enthusiasm or energy for it, though. Something in me has changed, Al. I came back from England feeling . . . well, I can't really describe it . . . I just feel different. I don't want to give so much of myself to the shop, yet I don't want to give it up either.'

'Is it possible that it's too much for you now?'

'I think that's partly it, yes, but not entirely. I do still love the shop, but it also feels like a burden on a day-to-day basis . . .' Mim's voice trails away. 'I haven't told anyone this, but I'm considering finding someone to take on the lease and buy the stock and the fittings,' she says eventually. It's devastating to hear herself say it aloud.

'What? You mean get out of it altogether?'

Mim nods. 'Perhaps. It's a bit of a local institution and the turnover is pretty good, so I don't think I'd have any trouble selling it. But at the same time, I still love it and don't want to part with it. I just want to make time and space in my life for myself, for something else.'

'What sort of something else?'

Mim sighs and walks over to the window to look out to sea. 'Honestly, Al, I have no idea.'

There is a long silence, then Alice gets to her feet. 'Well, I think you need to work out what it is you want before you start making any big decisions.'

'I know. But there are also other considerations. I'm getting old and my memory is getting rather dodgy. I can't remember titles and authors the way I used to. A few years ago, I could answer customers' questions immediately, find the books they were looking for – all that knowledge was stored in my head. But now things leak out very quickly. Sometimes I feel I'm getting in Doug's way.'

Alice sits down beside her. 'Have you talked to anyone else about this? Jodie, perhaps, or Doug himself?'

Mim shakes her head. 'Not yet. I thought I might talk to Mathias about it. Doug has presented me with a proposal for some improvements and I gave it to Mathias to read. He was impressed, and said he'd be happy to be involved if I needed the help. We were going to meet with Doug, but I kept putting it off, and then Mathias's friend died and he's been very distressed, so the discussion hasn't happened yet.'

She flops down off the sofa arm onto the seat and leans her head back against the cushions, relieved at having told her sister, but also dreading the possibility that Alice might start to offer suggestions and solutions and encourage her to be more positive, when what she really wants is for someone to take the responsibility away from her. Before her sister can speak, she says, 'I think that I just need to live with this confusion until I get some clarity. So, please don't be hurt or offended, but I'd rather you didn't try to advise me. I have to find my own way through this.'

Alice says nothing for some time and Mim, while at first relieved, starts to wonder why. The silence seems laden with unspoken questions.

'Actually, Mim, I think you're right,' Alice says eventually. 'This is something you need to work through yourself without interference. I went through something similar when Colin died. I didn't want people trying to cheer me up, to suggest things I could do, offer hospitality I couldn't return, make me cakes or take me to the movies . . . well, you get the picture. I wanted to sit with what had happened, to wait in that space for as long as it took for me to work out what I wanted. And the shop is something very close to your heart; the prospect of giving it up must weigh on you heavily – almost like grief. But whatever you decide to do, it has to be right for *you*, not just for the shop.'

Mim gives her sister a small smile. 'I know I said I didn't need your advice, but thank you – you're very wise.' She lifts her head from the cushion and says, 'And that's not the only clarity you've offered me. The makeover you treated me to really opened my eyes. When we got back home that day, I tried my new clothes on again in front of the mirror and, Al, when I saw how I looked I couldn't stop crying. I realised that I had given up on myself years ago, because every time I looked at my reflection I saw the ugly names I was called as a child. A cripple, a hunchback, a toad. It's not something you forget. Even before post-polio syndrome rolled into my life, I still saw myself in those terms. I've tried to be strong and I know I am. I have been. Derek helped me enormously; he thought I was brave and beautiful, and he helped me to see myself through his eyes. But when he died, I just went back into the protective shell I'd built around myself before I met him. Holding people at arm's length, always dressing in a way that didn't draw attention to myself as a woman. But now . . .'

'But now?' Alice prompts her.

'Now, after seeing myself in those new clothes, I felt . . . well, I felt – what a waste. What a waste to let those childish slurs define me. To have lived so many years believing that I'm somehow less than the people around me, that I have to work harder to seem normal or acceptable. I've put so much energy into pretending I don't care how I look and what people think of me when, to be honest, I have cared too much.' She stops, swallowing hard, and wipes her hands over her teary face. 'I don't want to be that person anymore.'

*

Later that evening, they sit on the verandah eating cheese on toast. Alice looks around her and sighs with pleasure at the peaceful surroundings.

'I love it here,' she says. 'I should have come years ago.'

Mim smiles. 'Well, the important thing is that you're here now.'

'I've been doing a lot more thinking about the idea of

moving here, and I have to say, I do think getting away from my old life in Oxford is the best thing I've done for myself since Colin died.'

Mim puts down her toast. 'Really?'

Alice nods. 'Yes. I've decided that this is the right place for me to be.'

'Oh, Al, how wonderful. I was so happy when you told me you were considering it, but I didn't want to push you.'

'And I'm very taken with Fremantle. It would be good to have a look around the area and see what kind of properties are available.'

'I've seen quite a few places with Mathias,' Mim says. 'There are some interesting new places being built further down past the dog beach. We should have a look there.' Her phone rings and she glances at it. 'It's Jodie,' she says before answering.

Alice smiles and picks up their plates. 'I'll make some tea,' she says and walks back to the kitchen.

She puts the plates in the dishwasher and fills the kettle. As she waits for it to boil, she looks out through the trees to the sea, still glimmering in the fading light. She feels a pang at the thought of leaving Oxford; it feels, in a way, like leaving Colin behind. *But I love it here and I love being with Mim,* she tells him. *I still miss you so much, but I guess that's not going to change wherever I am.*

She gets the mugs out of the cupboard and spoons tea-leaves into the teapot.

I wish you could see Mim now. She's so at home here, and she has lovely friends and neighbours – and you'd just love her shop.

I can imagine you going in there day after day until she gave you a job to do to get you out from under her feet.

She goes to the fridge and takes out the milk, thinking now of Colin and how fond he had been of Mim, and she remembers, suddenly, a conversation she'd had with him some years ago. She had been grumbling about Mim still being so caught up with the effect of polio on her body and her life.

'I don't think you're being fair,' Colin had said. 'It's a brutal disease, and back then the doctors were still working out how to deal with it. I'm a good bit older than you and I remember it clearly. It did take over people's lives and define their futures in many cases. I think it's perfectly reasonable for Mim to be as she is. She still experiences a lot of pain – especially now that she's been afflicted with post-polio syndrome – and it still limits what she can do. It's really part of who she is. I think you should stop trying to shake her out of it, stop telling her to let go of it. Maybe try stepping inside, seeing it through her eyes.'

Alice recalls the scene so clearly now. Colin had been standing in the lounge at the time, a copy of *The Guardian* in one hand, a glass of red wine in the other.

'You'll need to keep an eye on her as she gets older, Alice,' he'd added. 'My guess is that it'll be hard for Mim to accept some of the natural effects of ageing, because she is so driven by her determination to overcome the legacy of polio. She'll end up fighting old age too. She'll probably end up running herself into the ground unless you can help her to live with it.'

Alice sighs remembering this now. She'd not given it

much thought at the time, but she can see now that Colin was right, that things had eventuated just as he predicted. For years Mim had fought the effects of her disease. Now that she was ageing, the battle had become that much harder.

Alice pours milk then tea into two mugs, and carries them back to the verandah, where Mim is still on the phone, but just about to hang up.

Mim smiles up at her. 'Okay, see you tomorrow,' she says, ending the call. 'That was Mathias,' she tells Alice. 'He called after I hung up from talking to Jodie.'

Alice puts the tea down beside her sister and sees the huge smile on her face. 'He makes you happy, doesn't he?' Alice says.

'What? Oh yes, I suppose he does, but the main thing is that Jodie rang to tell me about her relationship with Carla, which of course we all knew about but were being careful not to mention until they were ready to tell us. But Mathias accidentally let it slip to Carla, so now it's out in the open. I'm so happy for them and so is Mathias.'

'That's wonderful,' Alice says. She turns to go back to her own chair but Mim catches her arm.

'Thank you, Al,' she says.

'What for?'

'For coming here, for being with me right now when I need it. I've missed you so much, for more years than I can remember. And now you're here and it makes my world so much better.'

Chapter Thirty

Mathias wanders around the house, walking into and out of every room, checking the views from the windows, the ways the sunlight falls, wondering how it would feel to live here alone. Carla has done that for several years now and it is certainly a delightful place. But is it as delightful without Carla in it? Last night she had stayed over at Jodie's place, something he realises she has probably been longing to do over the last few months. To him this will always be Carla's place, so it doesn't suit him to be here alone. The location is lovely, but he prefers Fremantle. Being able to walk to the beach would be good, and to walk into the town too, and stop for a coffee on the way. When he and Carla had talked, he'd told her that he wanted to be near Mim's shop. But, really, he means that he wants to be closer to Mim: to be able to walk to her place, spend time with her, help her at home and in the shop. But it's not just about a place to live, but how to live, and who he will be in this new place. Luc's death has robbed him of the person who knew him the longest and the best. He was a safe haven; with him Mathias could be himself and know who that self truly was. What is he now, without that precious point of reference? Something about Mim makes him feel that he needs to be near her. And although he has told her very little, it is as though she knows and understands who he is.

It's a relief for him to think about this. The first few days after he had heard the news from Patrice, he had been locked in grief. He needed to spend time alone reflecting on the past, reliving their parallel lives: the times they had fallen in love, married, had their children. They'd made each other's lives richer, and as they passed middle age their reflections on life, on politics, literature and philosophy, had become especially acute. Throughout their lives they had aimed to meet at least once a year. Mathias and Therese had occasionally holidayed in the Ardennes, and a couple of times Luc and Patrice had ventured to Australia. Mathias, who travelled quite often to Europe as a guest at writers' festivals or conferences, would always make time to visit them.

He stands now at the window of Carla's lounge room contemplating the future.

The loss of his oldest, closest friend, the one person who knew his deepest secret and kept it all his life, has made him vulnerable. Without Luc's support, he fears exposure and rejection more than he has ever done. He is haunted by dread.

'You must learn to trust others,' Luc had told him, time

and again. 'You have everything out of proportion. When you trust someone with this, you will find that what you see as your terrible secret is not so terrible at all. We all have secrets, Mathias, we all fear that one day something from the past will catch up with us; that we are at risk of something private showing up in public and changing everyone's opinion of us. For you this has become a demon that rules your life. But suppose one day someone does tap you on the shoulder?'

Mathias had shivered at that prospect but said nothing.

'See?' Luc continued. 'You have no realistic response to this. You anticipate that tap on the shoulder which releases the truth as though it is the match that sets the house on fire. Instant disaster. So, you are always waiting for the worst to happen. But it doesn't have to be that way. Instead of a fire that burns down the house, that spark of truth could simply be folded into history, setting you free.'

Mathias wants to be able to enter fully into his life here in Western Australia but having lived for decades in the shadowy peace of his home, he feels now that he has stepped into the harsh and unforgiving light of a very different place. He feels raw and unsafe, just as he had felt after he and his mother moved from Bruges to the Ardennes and he was faced with a classroom full of strangers, challenging, hostile, boisterous.

'You must show them something of who you are,' a boy murmured to him. 'Show them you are proud and confident.'

'But I am neither of those things,' he'd whispered. 'I don't know how to be here.'

'But you can pretend,' the boy said. 'Pretend you are strong and confident. Step into the space with confidence. Say little but sound as though you know much more than they can ever know. As though they are irritating flies, and you can brush them away in a moment.'

That was the first time Mathias met Luc, and the best lesson he was ever taught in grasping the future and taking control. Becoming a writer had been a part of it. Sometimes he is able to remind himself that it helps him to distance himself from others. People are fascinated by how writers work, how a story grows, and why he chooses a certain topic or creates a particular type of character. The answer is, of course, that he can hide behind his characters. Almost everyone thinks that the writer must be hidden among the characters: the villain, the hero, the stalwart friend, the loving parent or partner, the subtle bully. But they can never really find him.

Now, he thinks, *I have to learn who I want to be here, how I will step across the chasm into a new life, a different life, and make it my own.*

*

'Are you sure you'll be able to work in here?' Jodie asks anxiously, looking around the spare room. 'There's the view across to Fremantle and, um . . .' She hesitates, trying to think of an additional advantage. 'I mean, I know it's very different from your studio.'

'Jodie,' Carla says, 'we've been through all this. I love the room and it won't take long to get the old stable renovated so I can work there. It will be lovely, rustic, quiet. And who knows? I might just take a bit of a break from working in the meantime. I've done well this year, despite the fact that I've been distracted by thinking about you all the time! So, do stop worrying. I love you. We're going to live together; I'm moving in after Christmas.' She walks across the room and puts her arms around Jodie's waist.

Jodie sighs and leans into her. 'I so want it to be right for you.'

'And I want it to be right for you too. It makes sense to be here. You've built such a great place here. It's perfect. I love having the dogs around. I like looking out of the kitchen window and seeing the old horses in the pasture and knowing that you are madly working away in the surgery. Steven is great and Kirra is an absolute gem.'

Jodie nods, appeased. 'It's exciting to be starting our lives together. Wasn't Mathias lovely about it?'

'He was, and I think he's glad to have some time to himself so he can work out what he wants. And he's accustomed to living alone.'

Jodie wants to ask a question that she has been turning over in her mind for some time.

'Do you think there's something between Mathias and Mim? Something more than friendship, I mean.'

Carla rolls her eyes. 'They're not sleeping together, if that's what you're asking. At least, I don't think they are.'

Jodie flushes. 'But if they were, would you mind?'

Carla shakes her head. 'Why should I? It's up to them. I just want Papa to be happy.'

'So, if they were, it wouldn't bother you?'

'Not at all.'

Liz Byrski

Jodie smiles. 'Well, I think they're probably too old for that anyway, aren't they?'

'Too old to share a bed, or too old to have sex?'

'Both. Either. The latter mostly.'

Carla raises her eyebrows. 'Who knows what might happen? I don't know Mim well enough to say, but I don't think Papa would be looking for that now. It's her company, her friendship, that he values. And Mim makes him laugh – that's something he loves. Not many people get him the way Mim does. But why are we talking about this? I really don't want to have to start visualising that!'

Jodie flops down in a chair and pulls Hoonoze towards her. 'I was just wondering. I mean, obviously you're concerned about your father, and although Mim's not my mother, she has become a sort of mother figure for me in the last few years. That wasn't something I ever looked for – and in fact I resisted it, at first – but now it feels rather nice. I want her to be safe and happy.'

'I want them both to be safe and happy,' Carla says. 'If they could be that together, I think it would be lovely.'

Jodie gets up and walks over to the window, looking out to the field where two elderly horses are grazing.

'Mim has always said to me that she would never, ever have another intimate relationship.'

'I can't really comment on that, but my father is not the sort of man who gets close to women as a rule. And you've told me that Mim doesn't really have male friends. I think something just clicked between them when they first met. They actually seem like old friends.' She shrugs. 'Well, who knows what will happen? All I know is that

236

I'm so grateful to have met you, and I can't wait to move in here!'

The following day is Christmas Eve, and Jodie is in her office writing up notes from her last consultation before they close the practice for Christmas, with emergency calls being diverted to the twenty-four-hour veterinary practice at a nearby university. Steven left a couple of hours ago and only Jodie and Kirra remain – along with Hoonoze, who is under the desk with his head on Jodie's left foot, fast asleep.

Jodie finishes the notes, puts away the files and tidies her desk, thinking as she does about the progress of the practice this year, and her own recovery. It reminds her that the slim stack of paperwork about her accident and treatment can now have its own place in the filing cabinet. She breathes in deeply, thinking back to that bleak night when she had set out to deliver a foal and ended up in hospital. It hangs in her memory like a fuzzy nightmare that she has still not been able to banish. The darkness, the rain beating onto her windscreen, and then the steep bend that she'd so badly misjudged. She sits down in her chair again and extends both legs outwards, bending her knees and then circling her ankles. She's so fortunate to have recovered so well, she thinks. And how amazing that from such a strange, painful and worrying time had come her new life with Carla. So much has changed . . .

A knock on the door interrupts her thoughts.

'Come on in,' she calls.

'I was thinking I might head off home now,' Kirra says, popping her head around the door. 'All the paperwork is finished, and the cleaners have gone. So, if it's okay with you . . .'

'It's fine with me,' Jodie says, 'but before you go, do you have time for a Christmas drink with me?'

'Of course,' says Kirra.

Jodie slips out of the office to the small kitchen, returning with a bottle of champagne and two glasses.

Kirra has opened the door that leads out to the narrow balcony overlooking the paddock at the back of the house where the two elderly horses graze.

'We'll have to find homes for those two after Christmas,' Jodie says.

'I think I've found someone who might take them,' Kirra tells her. 'He's up in the hills. I can't remember exactly where but I think it's near Mundaring. He's already got two horses that he rescued from somewhere, and he's prepared to consider taking a couple more. He's going to think about it and call me back between Christmas and New Year.'

'Really? That's great news, Kirra. How did you find him?'

'Gumtree,' Kirra says, sipping her champagne. 'I checked with the local vet up there and she said she knows him well. She assured me he'd give them a good home.'

'Kirra, you really are worth your weight in gold!' Jodie exclaimed. 'No, no, don't laugh, it's true. You've been amazing this year; I don't know what I'd have done without you. And your final exam results were brilliant. Not only that, you kept me sane after the accident, *and* you managed Steven. I know he can be a bit abrupt sometimes, but he's a good vet and he thinks a lot of you. He told me you're the best nurse he's worked with. So, I wondered whether you're planning to leave now that you've qualified?'

Kirra is clearly shocked. 'Leave? No, definitely not. Why would I want to do that? Do you want me to go?'

'Of course not,' Jodie says. 'I just thought that you might be feeling it's time to move on to bigger and better things.'

'No way, I love it here. I love working with you.'

Jodie laughs. 'Well, I'm relieved to hear that, because if you're keen to stay on I was wondering if you might be interested in sharing some of the practice management with me. We could get another student nurse in, and maybe another qualified nurse could come in part time to take the pressure off you.'

'Really? That would be fantastic!'

'Good. Let's sit down and work out the practicalities after Christmas. Steven's going to continue on a couple of days a week, because I want to reduce my hours. Carla will be moving in after Christmas and we've had some quite good quotes for the renovation of the old stables into a studio for her. So to have you here in a more senior role while that's going on would be great for me. I know I can rely on you.'

Later, when Kirra has left, Jodie strolls around the building, considering how to reorganise the space so that Kirra can have a room of her own that would double as both an office and allow her to undertake minor treatments.

After living alone for so long, Jodie knows it will take some adjusting to share her home and life, and she knows that cutting down on her working hours will help with that.

'I'd like to have more of a life outside of work,' Carla had said. 'When you live alone it's easy to let work take over. We can rescue each other from that.' She has booked tickets for events at the Perth Festival and suggested a couple of movies they can go to between Christmas and New Year. Jodie likes the idea that she will finish work a little earlier and have the occasional weekend off. No more running herself ragged at the surgery; no more late nights eating cold baked beans out of the tin.

'Carla has made you grow up almost overnight,' Mim had commented a few days ago.

Now, she steps outside and walks over to the horses, with Hoonoze and Fred racing ahead of her. Dick and Dora, the old horses, ignore the boisterous dogs as they stand there in the fading sunlight blinking, tossing their heads to shake off the flies, occasionally stamping a hoof and swishing their tails. Jodie walks over to pat them.

'I suppose we *could* just keep you both,' she whispers, resting her head on Dora's neck. 'You don't cost much, and I've grown very fond of you.' She thinks of the man up in the hills that Kirra had told her about, providing a home for old and unwanted horses. 'We could do that too, I suppose – keep you two and take a couple of others as well.' The more she thinks about it, the more she likes the idea. *Who doesn't want to feel safe and comfortable in their old age?* she asks herself. *I'm so fortunate, the least I can do is give some horses a good home in which to spend their final days.* And she locks up and walks down the path to the house.

Chapter Thirty-one

Mim wakes early on Christmas morning, but Alice has insisted that she is to stay in bed and wait for tea and toast to be brought to her. She sits up slowly, looking out of the window, between the branches of the trees that frame a clear view of the ocean, with Rottnest and Garden Island, in the distance. It was the view that had convinced her to buy this house more than twenty years ago. And she did well, she thinks. The block of land is large enough that it would comfortably accommodate two houses, and she has a beautiful garden, attractively overgrown with native plants, and some old trees that provide welcome shade to the verandah. The land slopes downwards, and in the far corner of the garden a cluster of bushes and trees conceal a small stone cottage which the previous owner – the architect who built the house – used for a studio. The house he designed has been her sanctuary, a source of peace and satisfaction. It is, she believes, a place where she can live safely alone in her old age. She has poured money into it over the years, renovating some parts, extending others. And it has been worth every penny.

She slides out of bed, walks over to the window and looks out again between the trees to the sea. Christmas Day, she thinks, and on the other side of the country people are watching as their homes are burned to ashes by the fearsome bushfires which seem unstoppable. They have been forced to seek refuge with friends and relatives, to sleep on folding beds in church halls and schools, or in sleeping bags in their cars or even, in some cases, on the beach. Mim, thankful to live on the other side of the continent, thinks of the families and the firefighters who will not have time and energy for Christmas this year but will live and work in fear until the infernos can be brought under control – and then they will have to confront the terrible loss and damage.

Mim can hear Alice in the kitchen and she is reminded that Christmas this year will be very different from what she is used to. Usually, she and Jodie spend the day alone, but this year there will be five of them. Alice and Carla are in charge of the food, while Mathias has been tasked with organising drinks and managing the barbecue. He has also made a huge Christmas pudding. Jodie is in charge of all the dogs, as well as loading and unloading the dishwasher, making tea and coffee whenever needed, and fixing the lights on the tree, which are playing up.

Things have changed considerably, she thinks, remembering those quiet days spent with Jodie, and wondering now if she had held her friend back when she might rather have been doing something with younger friends. This Christmas will be a challenge for all of them: Mathias and Carla have always spent the day in a similarly quiet way in the Dandenongs. But this will be an Alice-driven Christmas: more traditional, more organised, more work, more Christmassy. When Colin was alive, Alice often had guests for Christmas. Mim had spent a few Christmases with them and was impressed by her sister's skill in creating the meal, cooking and serving it with ease and confidence. She had loved being a hostess, making people comfortable and treating them with genuine warmth. Mim is thankful that she has been banned from doing anything except perhaps setting the table. As sisters they are totally different in so many ways.

Since Alice arrived here, Mim has been learning more about her sister. She had never really been aware of the extent of Alice's generosity of spirit, her competence in the house and garden, her ability to step into someone else's painful space and offer support. She wonders now why she has never really taken all this in before, never thought deeply about it, nor considered what this might have cost her sister in terms of physical and emotional energy. *I've taken her so much for granted,* she tells herself now. *Despite seeing her almost every year, I never really took the time to get to know her properly.* She has relished the time they have spent together over the last three months, growing ever closer.

'Merry Christmas!' Alice says now, appearing in the doorway with a tray on which there is a pile of toast, and two mugs of coffee.

'Oh, Merry Christmas, Al,' Mim replies. 'Are you having your breakfast in here with me?'

'Only if I'm invited,' Alice says.

'You are more than welcome,' Mim says. She returns to the bed, shifting over to one side to make room. Alice hands her the tray and climbs cautiously onto the bed beside her.

'Thank you for looking after me,' Mim says when Alice is settled. 'I love having you here – not only because you're looking after me, but because you're you, and I think I haven't fully appreciated you in the past.'

'I know what you mean,' Alice says. 'I feel that too – I haven't appreciated you. Haven't really thought about who you are, what your life is like.'

They are silent for a moment. Alice picks up her coffee and sips it.

'I really do want to come and live here, Mim, but I'm dreading the process: going back to the UK, doing the paperwork, waiting for a decision. This must sound awful, as I've been so lucky having a beautiful home to live in over there, but I could happily just walk away and never go back to Oxford again.'

'I could go back with you, help you, wait with you, if you want,' Mim says. 'If you think it would make a difference.'

'It certainly would, but first we have to sort you out, get things organised at the shop. Mathias has promised to help. He's very concerned about you.'

'You told him? Oh, Al, how could you!'

'Don't be ridiculous; he's your friend. He told me that you and Carla are the reasons he moved here.'

'Did he really say that?' Mim asks.

'He did, and he meant it. You need to stop behaving as though you don't need love and support, Mim. You've been doing it all your life and now is the time to stop. Allow people to love you – lots of us already do!'

There is a long silence while Mim stares at a piece of toast.

'Do you think I don't let people love me?' she asks at last.

'I know you don't. You never have. This time we've spent together is the first time in our adult lives that I've felt free to show you and tell you that I love you. You've always maintained an emotional distance. Perhaps it's because you're in your own place, or just because we're getting older, but it feels like you've finally let me in. Maybe you haven't even realised it.'

Mim doesn't know what to say. She turns and looks out to sea, and they sit in the silence.

Eventually, Alice swings her legs off the bed. 'Hand me the tray, will you? I need to go and get on with the preparations.'

'No!' Mim says, grabbing her arm. 'Don't go yet. Please stay for a minute.'

Alice gets back onto the bed.

'You're right,' Mim says. 'You're absolutely right. I don't know why I do that. I suppose I push people away before they push me away.'

'When they might actually be trying to draw closer?' Alice suggests.

'Yes,' Mim says, looking at her in surprise. 'I never planned it or thought about it until recently. It's just been part of who I am – and that's not just the effect of the polio; it was losing Derek too, I think. I didn't want to risk losing someone else.'

'And you have to soldier on, as Dad would have said. Soldier on until you get to the other side. But life doesn't have to be like that, Mim. You don't need to do that and it's certainly not what we want for you or from you: me, Mathias, Jodie and Carla. We all love you; we want to do what we can for you. There are things you can no longer manage, and you should no longer try to cope alone. You're seventy-five years old! Accept it, and stop behaving as though nothing's changed.' She hesitates. 'Sorry, if I've said too much. I know I said I wouldn't interfere.'

Mim is silent, thinking of the times she has refused to consider her age with anything but determination. Long ago she had made up her mind to be totally independent, to do whatever needed to be done until she dropped dead. She would never let herself be dependent on anyone else.

'I know you are determined to hang on to your independence, and what Colin called your singularity. He thought you always feared rejection and so you were determined to appear totally competent, able to take on anything, and never put yourself in a situation where you might show weakness or incompetence and then be abandoned.'

Mim looks at her. 'Colin said that?'

Alice nods. 'Several times.'

Mim is silent, struck by Colin's insight. 'I sort of wish he'd said that to me,' she says. 'I might have been smart enough to listen to him.'

'I doubt it,' Alice says through a mouthful of toast.

'You would have flown off the handle at him for trying to analyse you or interfere with the way you lived. Especially as he was a man.'

'But Colin was an exceptional man . . .'

'Yes, but be fair, Mim, it was about twenty-five years ago that he first made this observation to me. Back then, you wouldn't have been so open to hearing it, even from an exceptional man.'

'Well, I wish he was here now,' Mim says, taking hold of Alice's hand. 'For your sake and for mine.'

When Alice has gone to the kitchen, taking the breakfast tray with her, Mim swings her legs out of the bed and goes back to the window. For years she struggled to appear strong and competent; an example of how someone with a disability can overcome the hurdles if they really want to. But deep down she's felt that polio had left her flawed and unlovable, and she had longed to be loved.

'You must never let people know how difficult things are for you, Mim,' her father had told her once. 'Don't let them see it; don't expect or accept special treatment. You are better than that.'

He had loved her and believed that this was the key to an independent life for her. But she has known for some time that it was as crippling as the polio itself. She had needed to be herself: a frightened, lonely and confused child, not a plucky little survivor, always in fear of the consequences of missing the next step.

What does it mean – that recognition for which she has fought all her life? What is it worth? What has it cost her to maintain her apparent confidence, her pretence of strength, durability? Her father had given her a role to play, and she can see that she played it far too well; solitary struggle had become her way of being. So, what now? she wonders. And all she can think is that if she is to change, she needs energy. Right now, she feels drained by a combination of her physical difficulties and the onset of old age. *Wait!* she tells herself. *That's all I can do. Wait and rest, get some energy back, and then perhaps I can make my life more manageable. I have to stop pretending that I can do everything myself all the time.* Closing her eyes, she takes several deep breaths. *I need to learn to let go.*

She rises, walks into the bathroom, steps into the shower and turns on the taps. She stands there, eyes closed, saying it again and again – *I need to learn to let go* – as the warm water cascades down her body.

Chapter Thirty-two

Mathias has made a Christmas pudding. It is his mother's recipe and she had made it every year. She'd said it was a traditional English Christmas pudding, that the recipe had been given to her by a friend, and he had never questioned this, nor asked who the friend was. It was enough that she made the pudding, which was always wonderfully rich and moist, thick with fruit and soaked with brandy. He has followed her recipe to the letter. Now, as he takes the pudding, wrapped in a white cloth, and puts it into a basket, he thinks of his mother.

Theirs had been a difficult relationship, defined, in his teenage years, by his father's abandonment. When his father had disappeared from their lives, his mother's main concern seemed to be what others might think, and how she and her family's standing in the community might be affected. But while she had seemed obsessed with the opinions of outsiders, he felt she had never taken into account what it meant to him. He drags his thoughts away from those times, the memories still so confused and painful for him, and starts to pack the food and wine into his car, along with a box of wrapped presents and six bottles of champagne. Then he walks back into the house to make sure he hasn't forgotten anything. The house is still and strangely bleak now that Carla often stays overnight with Jodie. He feels her absence acutely, and he stores this emotion away for future use. He thinks he might like to write about this sense of loss that has haunted him since Luc's death and Carla's departure to begin a new life with Jodie. Two endings without a new beginning. The idea takes him by surprise; it's the first time in months that he has even thought about writing again.

He parks his car alongside Mim's and Carla's at the back of Mim's house, and when he turns off the engine and gets out, he can hear the dogs barking in the garden, and the sound of women's laughter floating out from the kitchen. Fred, the beagle, hears him first and comes out, barking ferociously until he recognises Mathias, at which point he stops barking and bounds over to greet the new arrival, with Hoonoze close behind. Brenda eyes him suspiciously from the doorway.

'Mathias, you're here!' cries Jodie. 'Merry Christmas!' And she pushes past Brenda and walks straight to him, hugging him tightly. 'We were waiting to see if you wanted to go to the beach with us and the dogs for a walk and a swim?'

He hesitates; it's the last thing he wants to do this morning, but he doesn't want to start the day by hurting anyone's feelings. 'Are you all going?' he asks.

'All except Mim. She says she needs to stay home this morning.'

'Then I shall stay here with Mim,' he says with relief. 'I will either keep her company or annoy her, or both. Could you help me bring in the things from the car, please, Jodie?'

And together, they carry the food, drink and presents into the house and Mathias feels his resistance to the day slipping away with the realisation that he is, after all, part of something bigger than himself and his grief.

'Where *is* Mim?' he asks, looking around.

'Right here,' she says, walking into the kitchen. 'I've been sitting on the verandah while everyone else does the work. Happy Christmas, Mathias.' And she reaches up to kiss him on the cheek, then slides her arm through his and leads him out to a seat in the sun.

'They'll be gone soon,' she tells him, as they listen to Alice, Carla and Jodie organising themselves and the dogs. And minutes later there is a collective shout of farewell and off they go in their sunhats, carrying towels, the dogs barking with excitement.

'Ah! that's better,' Mim says of the sudden stillness. 'They get on so well, those three, it's exhausting.'

'Everything seems to happen so quickly,' Mathias agrees. 'I often have to hide the fact that I'm struggling to keep up.'

'Me too,' Mim says, taking his hand. 'And you're also coping with grief. This must have been a very hard time.'

Mathias nods. 'And I felt so bad, because in the upheaval of selling the house and moving here, I hadn't called Luc as often as I had in the past. Patrice says he would have been too sick to talk much anyway, and he was very hazy in the last few weeks, but I feel I abandoned him. He's been a crucial part of my life, and now he's gone, and we didn't really say goodbye.'

Mim starts to say something but he stops her.

'Mim, please don't reassure me, I know he will have understood and forgiven me. I'd like to tell you more about him, and our friendship, but it's still too raw for me at the moment. But I do want to tell you something before the others come back.' Mathias hesitates, but if anyone will understand, he reasons, it's Mim. 'It's something that happened to me just after I got the phone call from Patrice,' he says. And he tells her about his experience with the young man in the cafe, which is still so clear in his mind, still so disturbing.

'And then we shook hands and he was gone,' Mathias finishes. 'But no one else saw him. The waitress who spoke to him said she hadn't seen him, that she spoke only to me. That *I* had asked for the brandy . . . but *I heard him, Mim.* I felt his hand on my shoulder, he shook my hand. And then, when I got home, I looked at a photo of myself and Luc when we were young, and I realised: the man I had met . . .' He looks at her, suddenly cautious, anxious that she might think him ridiculous.

'Was it your younger self that you saw?' she says.

'Exactly!' he says in amazement. 'How did you know?'

'Well, I didn't *know* it,' Mim says, 'but I've heard of

such things happening before. I believe it happens more often at night, in dreams, but it can happen the way you've described, too.'

'I've wished so much that it had been Luc I saw.'

'Yes, but it's powerful that you saw yourself and you supported and comforted yourself. That seems right to me, because you're such a strong individual, and you're a loner at heart. I don't think you ever rely on other people, do you? And if people give you advice about yourself, you'll trust your own opinion rather than theirs. So it seems only natural that, in a crisis, you turned inwards.'

There is a long silence, during which Mathias, thinking hard about what Mim has said, stares out towards the sea. Eventually he turns back to Mim. 'Perhaps we see what we need to see,' he says. 'Maybe we create it for ourselves.'

A gull lands on the verandah rail, turning its head sharply from right to left, its beady eyes sizing them up.

'Buzz off, Trump!' Mim says, waving her arm, and the bird squawks back at her and shifts further along the verandah rail.

'Trump?' Mathias asks.

'Yes, because he won't shut up. He's here day after day, squawking at me, and he's so arrogant and hostile, he never stops. It seemed an appropriate name. He even wakes me up in the mornings.'

Mathias laughs out loud. 'Oh, I've missed you these last couple of weeks, Mim. Although we've spoken on the phone, it's not the same as meeting face to face. But I've been a mess, and I know you're exhausted. I hope you are getting some rest now; Alice has been worried about you.

You know, I can be quite a useful person. I can cook and shop and drive you anywhere, and I would love to help with the shop. Doug's proposal makes a lot of sense. It would require some financial investment, but that's something I would like to help with too. I have plenty of time to help out in any way you want.'

'But you have your writing,' she says.

Mathias shakes his head. 'I haven't written anything since I finished editing my last book. I thought perhaps the muse – if there ever was one – had deserted me, but I did have the germ of an idea just this morning. Maybe the urge to write is not really lost, but is resting. And at the moment I find I am less interested in writing about life and more interested in living it.'

*

The dog beach is busy with walkers and swimmers both human and canine. To Alice, who has never owned a dog or even thought about the existence of dog beaches, it all looks a bit wild. It's decades since she has ventured into the sea. Carla and Jodie let Fred and Hoonoze off their leads and, barking with excitement, the dogs race down to the water while Brenda is cautiously progressing in a slow and stately manner to the water's edge, where she stops to observe her surroundings. Alice admires her obvious determination not to get caught up in all the silliness of the younger dogs.

'I'll stick with Brenda,' she says, paddling in the shallows.

'Oh no, Alice,' Jodie says, 'do come in, it's really lovely.'

She walks back through the water towards her and takes her hand. 'Come a bit further – I won't push you in, I promise.'

'I feel so silly,' Alice says. 'I don't know how long it is since I've been on a beach. Several decades at least. I didn't even try it out in Bali; I just stuck to the pool.'

'Then it's definitely time to give it a go again,' Jodie says. 'Carla will stay with the dogs, so they don't get in our way.' And she draws Alice's arm through hers, leads her into knee-high water and stops. 'Okay?' she asks.

'Beautiful,' Alice says cautiously. 'The temperature is lovely.'

As they walk towards the deeper water, Alice feels herself adjusting to the roll of the waves. Trusting herself to walk alone, she slides her arm out of Jodie's and presses onwards. How old was she when she last swam in the sea? Forty, perhaps? It seems like a lifetime ago that she relished the freedom of the sea, how it tempted her to test herself in all sorts of ways.

'It's wonderful,' she calls to Jodie. 'I'd forgotten how wonderful it is.'

'Great,' Jodie calls. 'But take it slowly – this is the Indian Ocean, not the English Channel!'

Moving her arms in the old familiar motion, Alice lifts her feet from the sand and is thrilled to discover how well she can still swim and keep afloat. 'I'm fine now,' she calls, swivelling around to wave to Jodie and Carla, who are cheering her on. A wave catches her, dragging her back towards the shallows. She stumbles a little as she gets to her feet, but she quickly recovers and heads once more for deeper water, revelling in the sheer energy and power of swimming. She feels her age and weight releasing her and she is young again, swimming with friends in the Mediterranean, while Colin watches anxiously from the beach. She grasps the memory of how it felt to be young, fit and strong; to plunge into the depths and rise to the surface, just in time to catch a new breath and dive again. Down she goes again, and up, and down again, trying to touch the seabed with the tips of her fingers, before rising to tread water in the waves. Eventually she makes her way back to the beach, exhausted and exhilarated.

'It was wonderful out there, so exciting,' she gasps. 'But you're right – the current is quite strong.'

'You're a really strong swimmer,' Carla says, putting an arm around her shoulders. 'I'm so impressed.'

They lie on their towels at the back of the beach, and Brenda flops down alongside Jodie while the other two dogs romp along the sand closer to the water. Alice, stretched out flat, her eyes closed behind her sunglasses, is still heady with the excitement of her swim. She half opens her eyes to look up at the sky. *So, what did you think of that, my darling?* she asks. *I wish you could be here now, lying on this beach, reprimanding me for being reckless. I miss you so much, but it was magnificent out there.*

*

Christmas Day rolls out gently once the swimmers and the dogs are home. They eat a light lunch on the verandah, and then Jodie and Carla take the two young dogs with them to meet Nick and Paolo in nearby Cottesloe. Alice checks that everything is ready for this evening's dinner and then retires to her room. Mathias lies reading in the hammock at the end of the verandah. Mim, meanwhile, stays on the recliner with Brenda beside her.

The day has a sort of magic for her: the conversation with Alice, and later with Mathias, the pleasure of being surrounded and cared for by her favourite people.

'This is such bliss,' she murmurs to Brenda who is fast asleep on an old towel. 'I could even become a fan of Christmas.'

Since Mim first left home in her early twenties, she has always tried to sidestep Christmas. She hates the commercialisation, the superficial talk around it, the ridiculous expectations and, while not part of any organised religion, she feels that the beliefs at its heart are cynically trivialised on the altar of consumerism.

Today seems vastly different: she is banned from doing anything other than relaxing and enjoying herself, which she thinks is self-indulgent, though she has to admit it's really all she feels capable of. Now her mind drifts back to her first Australian Christmas, about six months after she had arrived to settle here for good.

She'd been to Australia a year earlier, travelling with a friend. It was an adventure, the one she'd always wanted. Mim had fallen in love with the country and with Fremantle in particular. She felt she could have a new life here and after returning to England decided to migrate. She was twenty-six by then and had worked for several years as a librarian. On the ship she made a new friend in Sandra, a teacher from London's East End. They found a small flat, moved in together, and within the first month they had both found work.

By the time Christmas came Mim and Sandra had both made friends. They spent the day at the beach with half-a-dozen other young people, got horribly sunburned and spent Boxing Day lying in a dark room getting in and out of a cold bath.

As she lies here now on the verandah, under the shade of the eucalyptus, she feels a warmth inside her body, in her painful limbs and, strangely, in her mind. She thinks of Derek, whom she had loved and lost, and wondered where they would be now had he survived . . .

She sits up straight and looks around; she must have drifted off. Brenda is still asleep beside her on the towel, but Mathias's hammock is empty, his book left open, face down on the nearby table. She can hear faint sounds from the kitchen, the kettle rising to the boil, the clink of cups and saucers, the door of the fridge being open and closed. And then Mathias appears beside her with a cup of tea and a slice of Christmas cake.

'You walk so quietly,' she says, as he tucks a cushion behind her back. And she attempts an awkward joke about feeling like the Queen.

'You are obviously unaccustomed to being cared for,' Mathias says. 'May I sit here with you?'

She watches as he settles himself, feeling her earlier sense of warmth and wellbeing increase. She thinks of Alice, to whom she feels closer than she has ever felt before, and of Jodie and Carla; she has treasured Jodie's affection and companionship for years, and she is growing fonder of Carla every day. And then there is Mathias. She's known him only a few months, but she feels she has known him for decades. *Does love feel different in old age?* she wonders. *Is this love or just a close friendship? What does Mathias think it is?* She knows only that for most of her life she has protected herself from love, fearing it would render her vulnerable, but now something has shifted.

I need to change, she tells herself now. *I need to learn to live peacefully, free of the darkness of my own fears and limitations. I must begin again.*

Chapter Thirty-three

It's just turned half-past four when Alice wakes from what was supposed to be a half-hour doze on her bed before getting back to the kitchen; Mim's neighbours Clare and Andrew would be calling in for a drink any minute, and she hadn't finished putting together the tray of canapés. She has emerged from a dream of swimming in stunningly clear water, with shoals of tiny, multi-coloured fish darting around her as she swam back to the shore where Colin was standing. It was a glorious feeling of freedom and she'd woken knowing it was essential that she lie absolutely still to retain the peace and lightness of the moment. Even once she was fully awake, she kept her eyes closed, unwilling to surrender the remnants of the dream, that had its roots in their honeymoon on the Mediterranean island of Corsica.

She listens for a while to the gentle sea breeze rustling the leaves of the trees and the low tones of voices at the other end of the house before she sits up, forcing herself into the present. Since arriving here, she has thought more lovingly and more often of Colin and she thinks that it might be because she is not at home, not living in the house they had shared for so long. It's a contradiction, really; in Oxford, she had convinced herself that she should live a life as close as possible to the one they had lived together. To make any significant change had seemed not only too hard, but also disrespectful of her marriage. She had said as much to Mim, who had listened patiently.

'But Alice, Colin loved you,' Mim had said. 'He certainly wouldn't have wanted you to feel tied to a particular way of life for his sake.'

Now she knows that Mim was right, and she wishes she had taken the leap and come here sooner. Had she done so, she could be living here in Fremantle already, in her own house, walking on the beach every day, helping Mim in the shop, building a life of her own instead of living a life that could never be complete without Colin.

There is a tap on the door.

'Come in,' she replies, running her hands through her hair to tidy it. 'Oh my goodness, look at the time – I slept for almost two hours.'

'You must have needed it,' Carla says. 'I've brought you a cup of tea.' And she puts the tea and a slice of Christmas cake on the bedside table.

'Thank you, Carla. Why don't you sit down?' Alice pats the bed beside her. 'I think that glorious swim knocked me over. I needed the exercise, but I haven't been in the sea for years.'

'It's really energising, isn't it?' Carla says. 'Have you been to Rottnest yet?'

Alice shakes her head. 'Mim says we should wait until after the Christmas holidays. I'm really looking forward to it. Apart from a trip with Mim into Perth to get her hair done and buy her some new clothes, we've mainly spent our time here in Fremantle. We've been to the Arts Centre and walked Brenda along the groyne most days. It's been lovely and peaceful. And Mim has really needed to rest.'

As she sips her tea, she sees that Carla is looking slightly uncomfortable. Alice leans forward. 'Is anything wrong?' she asks.

'No. No, of course not. It's just that . . .' She sighs. 'Oh dear, I'm no good at this. Alice, can I ask you something in confidence? It's about Papa and Mim.'

'Well, you can ask, but I doubt I'll be able to tell you anything you don't already know.'

'Jodie and I have been wondering what's going on with the pair of them.'

Alice shrugs. 'I've been wondering that myself. Well, they're obviously good friends, but I have no idea beyond that. Why? Are you concerned about Mathias?'

'No, not really,' Carla says. 'It's Jodie more than me. She's concerned about Mim – especially this last week, since she told you how exhausted she is.'

'That was a good thing I think,' Alice says. 'She needed to admit it to herself. It's made her realise that she needs some support and that it's actually okay to accept help. She's always been fiercely independent, but I guess we all have to learn that ageing is a challenge which demands that we accommodate it.'

Carla nods. 'I've noticed something similar in Papa. She and Papa get on well, don't they? I haven't seen him so at ease with anyone since my mother died.'

'He's a lovely man, and I know Mim is very fond of him. She really enjoys his company.'

'And he enjoys hers.' Carla hesitates. 'So, you don't think there's anything else – like, well . . .' She hesitates, flushing, obviously embarrassed.

'If you're asking if they're sleeping together, I doubt it,' Alice says. 'But either way, it's none of our business.'

*

Jodie has cleared up the dogs' dishes and washed them in the laundry sink. As she goes back to the kitchen, she sees Mathias, Alice and Carla clearing up the dining room and spots Mim beckoning her from the verandah.

'Come and join me,' Mim calls. 'We haven't had a chance to talk for ages.'

Jodie fetches them each a drink then goes out to join her.

'It's been a lovely day,' she says, suddenly aware of how much she has missed her regular time with Mim. 'Very different from our usual Christmas. I'm sorry I haven't been around much recently, Mim. Everything's been a bit overwhelming – first of all getting back on my feet, liter-ally, and then meeting Carla. For which, by the way, you are entirely responsible. That day when you were meant to be coming to lunch with her and she turned up alone, you weren't really unwell, were you?'

'Guilty as charged.' Mim smiles. 'But I couldn't spend another lunchtime watching the two of you making eyes at each other, so I thought I'd speed things up a bit.'

'Was it really as obvious as that?'

'It was positively steamy. As I'd hoped it would be!'

Jodie leans back in her chair. 'I'm so happy, Mim. I never thought I'd fall in love again. I didn't even want to! Anyway, enough about me; how are you and Mathias getting on? He seems to have become such a good friend to you.'

'He has. I thoroughly enjoy his company. He's still struggling with the loss of Luc, but I think it helps him to talk about it. You know, I've never really met a man that I actually wanted to spend time with, not since Derek. I've relied on women friends and I'd forgotten about the different conversations, and how it feels to have a male friend.'

'Good,' Jodie says, nodding. 'I'm so pleased.' She realises she is nodding excessively. 'And you . . . ?'

'And me . . . what?' Mim asks.

'Er, I was just wondering if, well, if you and he . . .' She blushes and, glancing over at her friend, sees that Mim is trying not to laugh. 'I mean, the two of you: are you . . . well, are you a couple?'

*

'You wouldn't believe how embarrassing it was,' Jodie tells Carla on the way home that night. 'She knew just what I was asking but she refused to buy into it, so I ended up feeling ridiculous.'

'We *are* ridiculous, both of us,' Carla says. 'I did much the same thing with Alice. If they tell each other about it, they'll be laughing their heads off by now. Promise me you'll never ask me to do something like that again.'

'I promise,' Jodie says. 'But I'd still like to know. You don't think Mim will say anything to Mathias, do you?'

'Oh no,' Carla says. 'I'd never even considered that! He'd have a fit. I can't believe I let you talk me into it. You owe me for this, and I promise you I'll think of some truly horrible revenge.'

Chapter Thirty-four

Christmas has come and gone. It's New Year's Eve and Mathias is feeling restless and unsettled. He has seen dozens of houses, but nothing yet that appeals to him, and the temporary nature of his situation is beginning to disturb him. And unless he feels calm, he won't be able to write. Some days he tells himself he is vain and foolish to think that it would matter if he never wrote another book. On other days he is acutely distressed because he knows that he would be bereft without the promise of the glowing reviews, the congratulations, the pleasure of seeing his new book at the top of the bestseller lists. He would miss the letters and emails from readers, the reassurance that people were talking about his work, that it was being placed on syllabuses in schools and universities in Australia and overseas. Mathias would never admit any of this aloud, because he feels it is embarrassingly prideful, and it reveals a side of him that he would hate for anyone to see. But he is aware that it is about more than ego; knowing his books are loved and well regarded around the world makes him feel safe: less vulnerable, worthy of some respect.

Eventually he decides that some exercise will soothe his troubled mind – temporarily, at least – and he drives to the local swimming pool. Half an hour later, he is ploughing up and down his lane as though his life depends on it. After twenty laps, he heads for the shower, his equanimity restored for the time being. He is on his way back to his car when his phone beeps with a text message. Mim and Alice have decided to have lunch at a cafe by Bathers Beach with some old friends of Mim. Would he like to meet them there? He swiftly replies in the affirmative, glad to have a sense of purpose.

Fremantle is heaving with tourists, and he starts to worry that he won't be able to find a park, but luck is on his side: just as he nears the cafe a car pulls out in front of him and he is able to slip into the space.

He spies Mim and Alice at a pavement table with a couple who look to be around the same age.

Mim half stands to introduce him. 'Mathias, these are my friends Chris and Soula. They used to be regular customers at the shop until they retired and moved down the coast to Busselton.'

'It's good to meet you, Mathias,' Chris says, getting to his feet to shake hands. 'Mim tells us you've recently moved here from Melbourne.'

'Yes, I'm staying in my daughter's house, looking for a place of my own,' Mathias says, walking around the table to shake hands with Soula.

'Are you looking for somewhere in Fremantle?' Soula asks.

Mim steps in to describe the search for a house, and while the women move on to the topic of the ideal size for a garden, Chris turns to Mathias. 'So, Mim tells me you are originally from Europe. France, was it?'

'Belgium,' Mathias says. 'I grew up in Bruges.'

'Ah, Bruges . . . such a beautiful town. The collection of Flemish art is superb – and, of course, it's home to Capo. Do you know *The Adventures of Capo*?'

'Ah . . . yes,' Mathias says, shooting Mim a questioning look.

But before she can intervene, Soula joins the discussion.

'Our kids adored Capo,' she says, 'and now our grand-children love him too. We offer them other stories but it's always Capo they want. You must know the books, Mathias; the author is from Bruges too, I think. What was his name, Chris? Oh, I know – he's a Mathias too. Mathias . . .' She stops suddenly. 'Oh my god, it's you, isn't it? I thought you looked familiar; I've seen your photo in the back of the books. You're Mathias Vander!'

There is an awkward silence as everyone waits for Mathias to respond. He can feel Mim's eyes on him and doesn't want to let her down.

But Chris puts a hand on his arm. 'I'm so sorry if we've embarrassed you,' he says. 'It's just that we are big fans of your work. Not just the kids' books, but your adult novels too. How wonderful to meet you!'

Mathias, who is usually deeply embarrassed at being treated like a celebrity, is surprised to find that he is rather enjoying the couple's obvious appreciation of his work. Before long another bottle of wine is ordered, and any discomfort Mathias was feeling soon evaporates. It's almost four o'clock before they leave the cafe.

'Come home with us now, Mathias,' Alice urges. 'It's a waste of time for you to go home and then drive back down here this evening to go to Jodie's place.'

Mathias, whose first instinct is to seek solitude, hesitates.

'Oh, come on, Mathias,' Mim says. 'Don't be a stick-in-the-mud.'

Mathias stares at her in amazement, then he starts to laugh. 'Change my plans at the last minute, Mim? Be spontaneous? Remember who you're talking to!'

'Is that a yes?'

'It is.'

*

It's seven o'clock when the three of them set off in Mathias's car, laden with champagne, cakes and chocolate. Mim, who hasn't celebrated New Year in Australia for decades and is usually tucked up in bed by nine thirty, is surprised to find she's looking forward to the evening. The tradition of New Year's Eve has always seemed rather silly to Mim. How often had she made a resolution that lasted more than a fortnight? Never, probably. And come the next year, she would have forgotten what that broken resolution was.

In the front seat, Alice is telling Mathias something about their parents.

'How about tomorrow, Mim?' Alice asks, twisting around to speak to her.

'What about tomorrow?'

'I was telling Mathias about that pile of papers and photographs I brought with me from when we cleaned out the old house after Mum died. New Year's Day seems a good time to start going through it, don't you think?'

'It certainly does,' Mim says. 'Let's do it.'

The front door is open when they arrive at Jodie's house, and as Mathias pulls into the driveway Brenda, who is in the back with Mim, sits up and starts to take an interest. As they come to a halt, Mim opens the car door for her and she leaps out. Fred and Hoonoze bound over, barking excitedly.

'Wow,' Alice says. 'Brenda's certainly got the party spirit.'

The racket of the dogs brings Jodie hurrying to the door to greet them. They are the last to arrive, and she leads them through the house to the back garden where Carla, Nick and Paolo are already sipping champagne with Jodie's doctor friend, Rosemary Parks, and her cardiologist husband Bill. There are introductions all round and the glasses are topped up. Rosemary greets Mim, kissing her on both cheeks and commenting on how well she looks.

Later, as she stands on the terrace with her drink, Mim spots the shadowy shapes of the horses in the paddock and sets off cautiously down the path to see them. It's a beautiful evening; the light is warm and rosy, and the horses come to the gate to meet her, swishing their tails as she talks to them. She puts her glass on top of a nearby post and leans against the fence, the stillness and silence broken only by the rough breath of Dick and Dora and the occasional stamping of a hoof. She strokes their heads and their velvety ears, wondering how old they are, and from what horrible fate Jodie had rescued them.

'I'm glad you're here,' she tells them softly. 'This is a good place to be. Jodie and Kirra love you, and Carla is starting to love you too. It's what we need as we get older, isn't it? Someone to love us. It might be a bit dull here, but you can't go on pretending that age hasn't changed you or changed what you need. I should take a lesson from you two. You live in the moment, in your lovely field, dozing in the sun, taking gentle walks and eating. I think I have a lot to learn from you.'

'Very sensible,' says a voice behind her and Mathias appears to stand beside her at the fence. 'Animals are so much better than us humans at understanding the basics.'

'You made me jump,' Mim says, retrieving her glass from the fence post. 'You must think I'm losing my marbles, having a conversation with two horses. But I always talk to animals. I talk to Brenda constantly.'

'I know,' he says, putting his arm around her shoulders. 'I've heard you discussing the weather with her. But right now, I've been sent to tell you it's time to eat.'

*

It's almost ten o'clock, and Mathias is running out of steam. They had told Jodie and Carla that they wouldn't be staying until midnight, and it's clear that Mim is now as tired as he is, although Alice still looks as though she could last all night.

'Shall we make a move now?' he whispers to Mim.

'Definitely,' she says, and she catches Alice's eye. 'We're thinking it's time to go.'

Alice nods and starts to say her goodbyes to Rosemary and Bill.

'Are you guys going?' Nick asks. 'Not staying to see in the New Year?'

'We're leaving that to your generation,' Mathias says.

'Okay, but just hang on a moment, Mathias,' he says. 'I've got something for you.' And he goes back into the house and returns with a book which he hands to Mathias. 'I saw this in a book sale recently. I thought it might bring back some memories for you. Happy New Year.'

'How kind of you, Nick, thank you,' Mathias says, reaching for his glasses. He looks down at the cover and catches his breath.

'You'll recognise that, of course,' Nick says, pointing to the photo on the front cover. 'Although I doubt anyone else will.'

'I do,' Mim says. 'It's that thing from the Brussels Exhibition, back in the fifties. Look, Al, you must remember it. What was it called, Mathias?'

'The Atomium,' Mathias says with difficulty, unable to lift his eyes from the book jacket.

'Oh yes!' Alice says. 'I remember now. But I can't remember what it represented. Mathias, do you know?'

Mathias hesitates, overwhelmed by heat; he feels the sweat crawling down his neck, and swallows, feeling that his throat is closing over.

'Yes . . . er . . . yes, I do,' he says, struggling to get the words out. 'It's a scale model of an iron crystal cell, magnified more than one hundred and sixty billion times.' His heart is beating fiercely, pounding so hard in his chest that he is sure everyone must be able to hear it.

'Were you there, Papa?' Carla asks, peering over his shoulder. 'Did you go to the exhibition?'

'I did.' Mathias nods. 'Thank you, Nick,' he says, anxious now to get away. 'I'm sure I'll enjoy this very much.' He wonders if the tightness he feels in his throat is affecting his speech.

'We went on the train, didn't we, Mim?' Alice says. 'With Mum and that friend of hers – I can't remember her name.'

'Me neither,' Mim says. 'Isn't that a coincidence, Mathias? We might have been there at the same time. We might even have walked past each other without ever knowing it!'

His head is pounding now, and he desperately needs to leave, but there is no quick escape from the hugs and kisses, the good wishes and promises to meet again.

'Are you okay, Mathias?' he hears Mim ask as if from very far away. 'You've gone very pale. Here, let me help you.'

He clasps the book to his chest as Nick guides him to a chair and Carla calls for Bill and Rosemary.

Chapter Thirty-five

It's after three in the morning when Mathias wakes up, confused at first, and then remembers that he is in Mim's spare room. A shaft of moonlight gleams between the curtains and he thinks he can hear the sound of the sea. Rolling over onto his back, he stares up at the ceiling, remembering with a sinking heart the sudden horrifying moment when he almost collapsed at Jodie's house. Had it not been for Nick helping him into the chair, he would have fallen to the floor, shaking, as he had done at the airport in Melbourne.

Mathias heaves himself into an upright position and tucks the pillows behind him. There is a glass of water on the bedside table and he drinks it quickly, then rests his head back against the wall. He remembers Rosemary producing a stethoscope from somewhere, and then recalls that she went to her car to get her medical bag before ushering everyone back to the lounge room or the verandah to give him some space, leaving him alone with Bill.

Mathias closes his eyes again, remembering Bill checking his pulse, listening to his heart, shining a light into his eyes, taking his temperature, asking about medications, alcohol consumption, recreational drugs . . . and more.

'Has this happened before?' he'd asked finally.

Mathias nodded. 'Many times. Most recently when I was at the airport for my flight here.'

'A panic attack?' Bill asked.

'Yes. But it's not usually as bad as this. At the airport I was suddenly overwhelmed by the enormity of moving across the country.'

'And tonight?' Bill asked, sitting down beside him. 'Do you know what triggered it?'

Mathias felt trapped. He searched his mind for some excuse to divert Bill, but there was none. He took a deep breath. 'The book,' Mathias says. 'It was the book that Nick gave me.' And he leaned forward and picked it up from the floor where it had fallen.

Bill said nothing, obviously waiting for more information, but Mathias stayed silent.

'So, it was the book,' Bill prompted gently. 'The cover photograph is the Atomium at the Brussels Exhibition. Was that it?'

Mathias closed his eyes, feeling his anxiety levels rising again. 'I can't talk about it,' he whispered. 'Nobody knows, not even my daughter.'

'I see. Have you ever discussed it with anyone?'

'Only one person: my oldest friend. He died just before Christmas.'

'But you've never seen a doctor, or a counsellor? A psychologist, perhaps?'

Mathias shakes his head.

'Hmm,' said Bill. 'Well, you're pretty fit for a man of your age, Mathias, but your blood pressure was through the roof just now, and at your age the risk of falling and perhaps losing consciousness is increased. You do need to deal with this. Talk to someone about it. Your daughter, for instance. Or you could ask your doctor to refer you to a psychologist. If you're not comfortable with either of those options, you are welcome to talk to me, but it would be as a friend, not a patient, as mental health is not really in my line of work.' He took a business card from his inside pocket and handed it to Mathias. 'You told me earlier that you were looking forward to starting a new life here. Coming to grips with the cause of your anxiety should be your first step, or you may not be around to enjoy it.'

For several minutes Mathias watches the shimmering blade of moonlight, then he swings his legs off the bed and gets up. He's still wearing his shirt and trousers, and he walks barefoot out of the bedroom then opens the glass doors to the verandah and sits down in Mim's recliner. Mim and Alice had brought him back here, insisting he stay the night so they could keep an eye on him. He had willingly handed over his keys to Mim, and as Carla clung to his arm, he could see that she was profoundly shaken.

'We'll look after him, Carla, I promise,' Mim told her. 'And one of us will let you know immediately if he collapses again. Otherwise, we'll call you in the morning.'

Mathias sighs. There will be questions now, and the only way to prevent Carla from worrying about his physical or mental health is to tell her the truth. Luc had warned him about this.

'Imagine you die without having told Carla,' he'd said. 'You are a well-known person, and some journalist somewhere, writing an obituary, could easily discover this bit of family history and publish it. Do you want her to find out that way?'

No. He knows that he has to be the one to tell her. But he is still haunted by the anger and misery on his mother's face; can still hear her imploring him, *Never speak of it, Mathias. No one can ever know.* But of course, the whole world knew, though over time people lost interest.

He leans back in the recliner, closes his eyes and allows his memory to take him back to 1958 when, at fifteen, he had begged his father to take him to Expo, the Brussels Exhibition. Everyone was excited about Expo. Belgium, a comparatively small country, had won the right to host this significant post-war international exhibition over other, larger capital cities, including London and Paris. It was an outstanding achievement for such a small country to take the lead in this particular push to reunite post-war Europe. Viktor Peeters was full of himself, having been a leading member of the organising committee and its spokesperson.

Mathias, a quiet and studious boy, was both awed and intimidated by his father. Viktor was a tall, distant and domineering man who had very high standards. Although never physically violent, he had a vicious tongue and frequently crushed his son with violent and abusive language. Fortunately, Mathias did not have to spend much time in his company. Viktor worked in Brussels, while the family's home was in Bruges, almost ninety kilometres away. Mathias's father kept an apartment in the capital, living there during the week and returning to Bruges at weekends. Viktor eventually agreed that Mathias could join him in Brussels for the Expo. He arranged for Mathias to be a volunteer guide, helping visitors find their way around, answering questions, distributing leaflets. Mathias was beside himself with excitement, and he spent hours poring over the instructions for the guides, the locations of the various countries' pavilions, their shapes and sizes, and their flags. He looked every day at the uniform waiting in his wardrobe. Another student from his school in Bruges was also to be a guide and together they practised their welcome greetings in Flemish, French, English, Dutch and German. Already an anxious boy, Mathias's greatest fear was that he might mix the languages in his head and greet a guest inappropriately.

He had prepared himself well, but nothing could have prepared him for the incredible sight of the gleaming stainless-steel Atomium, more than one hundred metres in height, each of its nine stainless-steel spheres, connected by huge steel tubes, more than eighteen metres in diameter. Mathias remembers shivering in the chilly April sunlight, struck by the size and brilliance of the structure and, beyond it, the multiple walkways and pavilions arranged across the vast site.

A couple of days later, those pathways and pavilions were packed with visitors from around the world, the bars and restaurants bursting with people. Mathias was posted near one of the entrances. He was thankful that he had worked so diligently to understand the layout of the exhibition, and the best routes to certain particularly significant sights.

He saw little of his father in the next three weeks, but he made friends with other guides and some of the construction workers who were on standby. When he made his way home in the evenings on the bus with the other guides, Viktor was often absent, or heading out for dinner with overseas guests. Mathias enjoyed the sense of independence and of doing something for his country; it felt like history was being made, and he was part of it.

One morning, two days before Mathias was due to go back home and to school, he woke to find that his father, who had left the previous evening to meet some colleagues for dinner, hadn't returned. His bed had not been slept in, and Mathias assumed he must have stayed somewhere else. He got dressed, ate some cereal and went downstairs to catch the bus. On the way out of the building he asked the concierge whether Viktor had left a message for him, but he hadn't. And when Mathias returned from the Expo that evening, there was still no sign of him.

He'd barely slept that night, lying stiff and alert in his bed, waiting for the sound of Viktor's key in the door. Early in the morning, he used the phone to call downstairs to the concierge, but there was still no news, so he called his mother. She told him not to worry. 'Your father will have been out drinking and stayed somewhere else overnight.' Years later she told him she had long believed her husband had a mistress in Brussels.

Mathias was not reassured, but he got dressed in his uniform, ate breakfast, and was about to leave the apartment when there was a knock at the door. It was thrust open before he could answer it, and the manager of the apartments entered, together with another man in a brown suit and two uniformed police officers.

Mathias, already made anxious by Viktor's long absence, was now terrified. The men were courteous, but they informed him they must search the apartment and told him to wait with the manager. It was only when the men searched his father's bedroom that Mathias learned his father's clothes and personal effects were missing. Had they been there the previous day? He didn't know; he had only glanced into his father's room to see if he was home.

Now Mathias feels a familiar sinking in his stomach as he sits upright in the recliner, then stands, walks to the verandah rail and looks down into the shadows of Mim's garden. He remembers his rising fear as the men finished their search of the apartment and began to pepper him with questions for which he had no answers. Finally, they left him alone with the man in the brown suit, who introduced himself as Axel.

'We will be taking you home to Bruges, Mathias,' he said kindly. 'I'm sorry if this has been upsetting for you, but it is essential that we find your father. Are you sure there's nothing you can think of that might help us?'

Mathias shook his head, trying to hold back tears.

Axel sighed. 'We've known for some time that your father has been spying for Russia, and we believe that he has used the cover of the exhibition to defect. You understand what that means, don't you?'

Mathias, more than sixty years and fourteen thousand kilometres distant, feels tears running down his cheeks now just as they had then.

'It is likely that Viktor is already in Russia by now,' Axel told him. He went on to explain that his colleagues in Bruges were speaking with his mother, though she was not under any suspicion. 'If you would like to speak to her, you may telephone her now.'

At the memory of that phone call, Mathias feels physically ill.

'You are an idiot!' she screamed at her son. 'You should have stopped him, useless boy. You could have stopped him. Your father would not have left if you asked him not to.'

Mathias stands rigid in the darkness, holding his breath until he feels giddy, recalling the bitterness of her words, his shame and confusion at what his father had done, and the terrible sense of guilt and isolation from which it took months to emerge and which still haunts him today in his darker moments.

*

Mim is woken by Trump, squawking irritably as he struts along the verandah rail outside her bedroom.

'Shut up!' she calls.

But Trump, true to form, refuses to be silenced and screeches back at her.

Then, through the fine mesh of the white curtains, she sees the silhouette of a figure rise and shoo the bird away.

'Mathias?' she calls. 'Is that you?'

When there is no answer, she gets up, pulls on her dressing-gown and opens the French doors.

'Mathias, shouldn't you be resting?' she says, stepping out onto the verandah.

'I woke early and couldn't get back to sleep,' he says.

Mim thinks he looks terrible – even worse than when she and Alice had brought him home with them after his panic attack the night before. His face is pale, and when he goes to pick up a glass of water from a side table his hand is shaking so much he can barely grasp it.

'You stay right here,' Mim orders. 'I'm going to make you some coffee and toast. You hardly ate anything at dinner, and you need something in your stomach.'

Matthias shakes his head. 'No food, thank you, but coffee would be greatly appreciated.'

'You are going to eat something,' Mim insists, 'even if Alice has to hold you down while I shovel it down your throat.'

Mathias smiles wanly. 'In that case, I had better attempt to eat the toast myself.'

'That's the spirit,' Mim says.

*

Mathias leans back in the recliner again and listens to the comforting sounds coming from the kitchen: Mim filling the kettle, the clatter of china, the click of the toaster. Then, hearing a faint scratching on the boards of the verandah, he glances around to see Brenda walking towards him, her tail wagging as though she's glad to see him. She walks right up to Mathias and rests her head on his thigh. He speaks gently to her, strokes her head, and she drops down beside him, closing her eyes against the sun.

He closes his own eyes now, resting his head on the back of his chair, wishing he could sit here forever, listening to the faint sounds of the sea, the birds in the trees and the burble of the kettle coming to the boil. Even Trump, chattering irritably further along the verandah, contributes to his sense of calm. But he knows that this peace is short-lived. Today is the day he's been dreading for decades: he must finally tell the truth about his past.

He hears Mim's footsteps approaching, and then she is beside him with a tray bearing mugs, a plunger of coffee and a jug of milk. She sets these on the table, then says, 'Don't move,' and returns to the kitchen with the empty tray, reappearing moments later with toast, a pat of butter, a selection of jams, some marmalade, plates, cutlery and serviettes. 'You promised you would eat something,' she reminds him.

And to his surprise, Mathias realises that he is hungry.

For a while they both pretend there is no elephant in the room. They talk about Carla and Jodie, how happy they seem together, what a lovely evening it had been until – whoops! – they steer away from that to discuss Jodie's plan to take on another two elderly horses.

Eventually, Mim folds her napkin and pours them each another cup of coffee.

'Okay,' she says. 'Let's get down to business. Tell me about these panic attacks of yours, Mathias – and what was it about the book Nick gave you that triggered one last night?'

There is a long silence. Mathias looks out at the sea, trying to muster the strength to relive those awful days once more.

'I was so excited to be going to Expo,' he begins. 'My father was a prominent member of the organising committee and he was able to arrange a position for me as a volunteer . . .'

Mim's eyes are fixed on him unwaveringly as he recounts the days leading up to his father's disappearance and the knock on the door that fateful morning. When he describes the phone call with his mother, he sees them fill with tears.

'Oh, how awful for you,' she says. 'So, what happened then?'

Mathias takes a deep breath and continues his story.

'As Axel had promised, he drove me home to Bruges. Outside our house there was a crowd of reporters and photographers. They descended on the car, shouting questions, cameras flashing. Axel gave me a newspaper to shield my face and steered me through the crowd and in through the front door.

'Inside, my mother was frantic. She was still blaming me. *How could you let him go? Why didn't you stop him? You should have made him come home.* It was my fault, she insisted, my failure – and that was when I collapsed with my first panic attack.

'The next morning, we were front-page news. There were photos of Axel ushering me into the house. Photos of my father at various ages surrounded by important people who were now all talking about their disappointment, distress and anger on learning that this trusted employee of the government had betrayed his country. We were publicly disgraced. Our neighbours shunned us; foul graffiti was scrawled on the walls of our home. I was bullied at school, beaten up by other boys – even beaten by a teacher when I tried to defend myself.

'Eventually, my mother packed up our belongings and we went to stay with my maternal grandparents, who lived in the Ardennes. We changed our name from Peeters to my mother's maiden name, and I started at a new school as Mathias Vander. That was where I met Luc, on the first day, and from the beginning we felt like brothers. The irony is that it was my father's treachery and my mother's blame that brought us together.'

*

'What did Mim actually say?' Jodie asks as Carla drives towards Fremantle. 'Is Mathias okay?'

Mim had called Carla fifteen minutes earlier, as she was making coffee in the kitchen. Jodie, sleeping off the excesses of the night before, wasn't even aware Carla had got up until she was shaking Jodie awake.

'Mim just rang,' she'd said. 'She's been talking to Papa, and he wants to talk to me. I'm going to get dressed and go straight over. Do you want to come with me?'

It was the last thing Jodie wanted to do. She had drunk

more than she was accustomed to the night before. Her head was aching, she felt nauseous and she could do with at least another fourteen hours of sleep. But the anxiety on Carla's face told her that she couldn't let her go to Mim's alone.

As she turns onto the Canning Highway, Carla says, 'Apparently Papa told Mim about something traumatic that happened when he was a teenager. It's what caused his first panic attack.'

'Well, it's good that he's talking about it, isn't it?' Jodie says.

'I think so, but I feel very jittery about what it might be. I mean, suppose he committed some terrible crime and he's been in hiding ever since?'

'Mathias? A criminal?' Jodie says. 'No way. He's the most honest, trustworthy person I've ever met. He has too much integrity. You're more likely to be a closet criminal than your father.'

'Gee, thanks for that! Your assessment of my character is incredibly flattering – not!'

Jodie laughs. 'Oh, come on, you know what I mean. If Mathias was given ten cents more change than was due to him, he'd go back to the shop as soon as he realised it. You can't possibly think he's guilty of some atrocity.'

Carla shrugs. 'I can't imagine what it could be; I'm just trying to prepare myself by thinking of worst-case scenarios.'

'I'm sure it's nothing like that,' Jodie reassures her. 'Whatever happened in the past, you know the man Mathias is now – a good man, an honourable man. So take some deep breaths and calm down.'

Eventually they turn into Mim's driveway. Carla parks the car and turns off the engine, just as Alice comes out through the back door with her sunhat and beach bag.

'Happy New Year,' she says, kissing them both. 'And thanks for a lovely evening. I'm going to the beach for a swim with Clare. I'll see you both later.' And she heads off along the path to Clare and Andrew's house.

'Good morning,' Mim says, emerging from the kitchen as they enter the house. 'Mathias is on the verandah, Carla. Why don't you go and talk with him while Jodie and I make some coffee?'

Chapter Thirty-six

Alice and Clare are sitting side by side on the beach. They have done this several times since Mim had introduced them over dinner one evening. Sometimes Andrew joins them, but Alice likes it best when, as today, it is just herself and Clare. This morning she is happy to be away from the house while Mathias talks to his daughter and Jodie. She thinks it will make things easier for everyone. Spending time with Clare has made her realise that she misses the women friends who have drifted away in the last few years. Deaths, sickness and moves to other parts of the country on retirement have meant she now has only a couple of friends in Oxford with whom she can talk about books, go to movies and share meals. Both Clare and Andrew have recently retired from universities, where they taught in disciplines similar to her own. They have many interests in common, so their conversation flows naturally – and alone with Clare, Alice finds that it is also easy to talk about personal matters.

This morning she is feeling restless. She has fallen in love with Fremantle and is determined to move here, but the practicalities are daunting.

'I can't quite make up my mind how to do it,' she says to Alice. 'I can either stay until my visa is about to expire, then head home and lodge an application. Or I could return to the UK sooner and get my application under way while I sort things out in Oxford. Mim thinks I should wait, but I'm inclined to go sooner.'

'I agree,' Clare says. 'You should start the ball rolling as soon as you can. I can see how keen you are to move. I suspect Mim doesn't want you to go yet because she's enjoying having you here. How is she now?'

'A lot better, I think,' Alice says. 'She finally gave in and agreed to rest more, and that seems to have helped.'

'Well, when you do go back to the UK, we'll keep an eye on her. I've often urged her to get one of those things you wear around your neck so you can call for help if you have a fall or are unwell. She always says it's a good idea, but I don't think she's ever done anything about it.'

'That doesn't surprise me,' Alice says. 'You know how independent she is. But I'll talk to her about it again and see if we can organise something before I leave. And I'd like to help her sort out what she means to do with the shop, too; I think she's been quite stressed about it.'

'I really admire your energy, Alice,' Clare says. 'You never seem to stop. I think we're about the same age, but you leave me standing.'

Alice hesitates, watching a small child toddle down to the water's edge to fill a bucket.

'It's really only since I've been here,' she says. 'When Colin died, I felt as though all my energy and enjoyment of life had been sucked out of me. But my stopover in Bali and then coming here to Fremantle has been just the kind of shake-up I needed.' She stands. 'And speaking of shake-ups, it's time I went back to Mim's to see how everyone's going.'

*

Back at home that afternoon, Jodie goes out to check on the horses while Carla flops down into a hammock in the garden. She'd listened intently as her father described a teenage boy who had been so excited about his trip to Expo with his father, only to be left frightened and alone, his world turned upside down. She could see how he might have internalised the guilt and blame his mother projected onto him.

'But why?' she'd asked him. 'Why would she blame you?'

'Darling, I wish I knew. I think it was just her terror. Perhaps she was thinking that had she been there herself she would have stopped him. It's ridiculous, of course, because no one could have stopped my father from doing anything he decided to do. But she was hysterical. She was a rather difficult woman, not easy to get along with, and she was traumatised by the shame of being married to a spy and traitor. She believed we were somehow implicated in my father's actions, and now I realise that at some fundamental level I have always believed that she might have been right. It was only as I recounted the story to Mim that I realised how deeply ingrained was the guilt and shame of a frightened boy – and how little relevance it has to my life today. My father's actions were his own, and the guilt and shame were all his; they should never have been my cross to bear.'

'I always knew you carried some sort of emotional burden, Papa, but I never imagined something like this,' Carla said. 'When did you tell Mama and Luc?'

'I told Luc when we'd become close friends at my new school in the Ardennes, and I told Therese as soon as I knew I wanted to marry her. She reassured me that it didn't change how she felt about me, and so did Luc. Yet the anxiety that has plagued me all my life has its roots there, in 1958. It rears up whenever I am anxious about other things. That panic attack at the airport recently, for example, when I contemplated the enormity of the move to Western Australia. It was almost as though my secret had been safe in the Monbulk house, but I was leaving the place that had been my sanctuary and that made me feel vulnerable.'

Now, as she stretches out in the hammock, eyes closed against the sun, Carla is torn between relief at finally understanding the cause of her father's anxiety and anger at her grandmother's treatment of her son.

'Carla, are you okay?'

As Jodie puts a hand on her shoulder, Carla wakes with a start.

'Goodness,' she says, struggling to sit up. 'How long have I been asleep?'

'Less than an hour,' Jodie says. 'Are you feeling okay? You look awfully pale.'

'I'm fine, just tired – and a bit churned up emotionally, I suppose. I was reflecting on Papa's story and I must have drifted off. It was such a revelation, and it makes sense of his behaviour over the years.'

Jodie nods. 'I was wondering whether he'll write about it now. It's an interesting story, and maybe writing about it will help to give him some distance from it. Perhaps that sounds silly – I know nothing about the writing process. It's just a thought I had while I was feeding the horses.'

Carla looks at her. 'That's an interesting idea. I might ask him about it.'

*

Mathias carries the small suitcase Alice has brought out of Mim's spare room and hands it to her.

'A new year and a journey back into the past,' Mim says. 'Now it's our turn to rake over our family history.'

She places the suitcase on an old tablecloth she has spread over the dining room table. Alice undoes the clasps and opens it, and the two women gaze at the contents. There are bundles of papers stuffed into large manilla envelopes, some old diaries, a plastic folder bulging with old school reports, even a file with some of the sisters' childhood paintings. And, of course, there are lots of photographs. They look at each other, eyebrows raised.

'This looks like fun,' Mim says doubtfully.

'Or possibly not,' Alice says with a sigh. 'Are you joining us, Mathias?'

Mathias smiles. 'I think this is a family matter,' he says. 'I'll take my book out onto the verandah.' Mim has insisted he stay another night after his ordeal, and to her surprise he agreed readily.

'Did I tell you that Mathias's mother blamed him for not stopping his father from defecting?' Mim asks when he is safely out of earshot. 'I suppose she was so terrified of what might happen to them that she wasn't thinking straight. But Mathias has carried the burden of that accusation all his life. He's such an intelligent, logical person, yet he wasn't able to face the memory of that time, unpick it and set himself free. I'm sure his mother was terribly distressed and frightened; she probably never gave a thought to what her attitude might do to Mathias.'

'So, she never retracted what she said about it being his fault?' Alice asks.

Mim shakes her head. 'Apparently they never discussed the whole affair after they moved away. It was a taboo subject. How dreadful for both of them. Thank goodness I never had any children; I'm sure I'd have made a hash of it.'

'That's ridiculous, you'd have made a wonderful mother,' Alice says. 'Anyway, let's get on with uncovering our own family secrets – if there are any.'

'I don't think there's any really orderly way of going about it, do you?' Mim asks, gazing at the jumble.

Alice shakes her head. 'No, not really. I wish we'd done it years ago, but we both kept putting it off. I suppose we could just have a bonfire and burn the lot.'

'No,' Mim says. 'We must do this, even if it does all end up in the bin. Who knows what we'll find?'

Mim fetches a plastic laundry basket into which they can dump anything that is clearly rubbish, then sits down beside her sister and gets to work. Old invoices and receipts go in the basket, as do old business letters, chequebooks and bills.

After a while, Alice sits back and groans. 'Can we stop now?' she asks.

'No,' Mim says. 'We've only just started.'

And on they go.

After a while, Mathias comes in from the verandah and offers to make some tea for them. When he brings the tea to the table, he asks if they mind if he joins them after all.

'Are you sure you can handle more family history?' Mim says with a smile.

'Well, yours looks like more fun than mine,' he replies, picking up a black-and-white snapshot of the two sisters in checked cotton dresses with puffed sleeves, sitting on the steps of their old home.

'Look at this,' he says.

'That can go in the bin,' Mim says, and Alice agrees.

'No!' Mathias cries in dismay. 'It's so sweet. May I keep it?'

Mim and Alice exchange a look, and Mim shrugs.

'Of course, you can, if you really want it. But show it to anyone else and we will never forgive you.'

'Not even Carla and Jodie?'

'Especially not them,' Alice says.

The afternoon wears on and twice Mathias has to empty the plastic basket into the rubbish bin outside. They've all had enough by now, but Mim insists they carry on until they're done. Mathias is allocated the task of putting each sorted pile into a manila envelope and labelling it. Alice decides it's time for a drink and goes to the kitchen to fix them each a gin and tonic.

Meanwhile, Mim picks up one of the old diaries that they've put aside for further examination. She flicks through pages filled with her mother's small, cramped handwriting, then puts it down again.

'How are you feeling now?' she asks Mathias.

'A lot better, thank you. But rather like a plant that has lived in a certain spot for years and has now been dug up and replanted elsewhere!'

Mim smiles. 'Well, I hope you'll soon adjust to the new soil,' she says. 'It's going to be much healthier for you. But I can imagine how strange it must feel to put down that weight you've been carrying and try to walk away from it.'

He nods. 'I should feel on top of the world, but actually it's quite disconcerting. Who am I without that albatross hanging around my neck? Only time will tell, I suppose. You were right to urge me to talk to Carla this morning, Mim. It made all the difference.' He leans over to take her hand. 'Thank you for listening and for caring. I can't begin to tell you what it means to me.'

Alice returns carrying a tray with their drinks and some nibbles.

'Let's take this onto the verandah and finish the rest of the sorting tomorrow,' she suggests.

'Good idea,' Mim says, finally giving in.

Outside, Mathias picks up the book he has left on the table so Alice can put the tray down. 'I've been looking at the book Nick gave me,' Mathias says, holding it up to show them.

'Oh, look,' Alice says, pointing at one of the photos. 'It's the British pub they constructed for the exhibition. Mum took us there for lunch, Mim, do you remember?'

Mim laughs. 'That's right. She was so relieved to find a place with English food. She wasn't at all adventurous when it came to what she would eat.'

'I think that was a typical English attitude at the time,' Mathias says.

'Mum always said that you couldn't trust what terrible things the French might serve up – let alone the Germans!' Alice recalls.

Mathias directs their attention to the map, points out the various places where the guides were stationed. 'We were told to be friendly and helpful, and we were taught how to greet visitors in their own language. Most of us could only speak French or Dutch, of course. The aftermath was so dreadful, I'd quite forgotten how much fun it all was, feeling so important in our uniforms, having our photos taken with the tourists. Flirting with the girls – even kissing some of them.' He looks up from the map and smiles at Mim. 'Maybe I even kissed you,' he says.

'Oh, I do hope so,' she says, laughing.

Chapter Thirty-seven

On the first Monday after New Year, Mim goes back to work at Life Support for the first time in a few weeks. As always, she gets a little shiver up her spine as she enters the shop, knowing that it is hers. The shelves are orderly, and on the circular table near the window there is a display of books by local writers. Soft music is playing in the background, and there are fresh flowers in an old china jug on the counter. Mim has always wanted a few comfortable chairs where people can sit for a moment, and Doug has put small wooden stools beside them with a selection of books of various genres: romance, sport, gardening. Mim thinks the shop is even more inviting and welcoming than when she was managing it herself. She has always rejected suggestions that they have music, because she felt it would be too distracting, but now she has to admit that it is rather soothing.

The shop is quite busy, she is pleased to see. There are

several people who look like holidaymakers, and a few regulars whom she recognises and stops to exchange greetings with. Doug, who is behind the counter chatting to a customer, lights up when he sees her. Mim browses a shelf while he finishes with the customer, and then they head into the back room together, leaving the other staff to handle the sales.

'I can't tell you how much we've missed you, Mim,' Doug says. 'All of us, but me especially.'

'Likewise,' she says. 'But I can see you've been doing a terrific job. It's a joy to walk in off the street into what feels like a world of books.'

Doug makes coffee and they sit at the table and talk about the shop, the great pre-Christmas sales and, finally, the future.

'I know I should have talked to you a long time ago about your proposal, and I am very sorry to have left you hanging,' Mim tells him. 'Mathias and I have both looked it over and all your suggestions for improvement and expansion are excellent. Mathias is quite keen to invest in the shop financially so that we can make those changes, and I'm inclined to accept his offer. The only problem is, well, me. The fact is, I'm seventy-five now, and I'm no longer as physically fit as I was – especially with, well, you know . . .' She gestures to her leg. 'I was feeling pretty hopeless about it a few weeks ago, thinking I might just have to let the shop go, but I've had a good break over Christmas and I'm feeling much better. So, if you're happy to handle things on the floor, I'll get on with some of the paperwork.'

Doug returns to the shop floor and Mim switches on the computer. When she is prompted to enter her password, she hesitates. What was it again? After a couple of failed attempts, she finally hits on it. 'At last!' It is not just the physical effort of running the shop that she has been finding exhausting, she admits to herself; the mental effort is also significant. She struggles sometimes to stay on top of the administration, to remember what has to be done when. She decides that it will help her to feel more in control if she were to set up a spreadsheet listing the daily, weekly and monthly tasks. She opens Excel and brings up a blank spreadsheet, but as she stares at the blinking cursor she realises she can't remember what to do next. It's as though the business part of her brain has gone to sleep and won't wake up. *Come on, come on,* she urges herself. *You know how to do this; you've done it for years and you can do it again.* But she can't.

Defeated, she picks up her handbag. Telling Doug that she has suddenly remembered an urgent appointment, she hurries from the shop. As she drives home – a distance which until recently she used to be happy to walk – Mim feels heavy with sadness. The shop had looked lovely and everything seemed to be running smoothly, and she knows it has much more to do with Doug than herself. *He's got such a sound grip on the business, he could easily take over,* she tells herself. *But of course, it's been that way for a long time, only I refused to let myself think about it.*

Back home, she finds a note from Alice saying that she's gone shopping with Clare in Fremantle. Mim makes herself some tea and takes it out onto the verandah. For a while she just sits there, staring at the sea. Then she pulls herself together, gets up from her chair, searches in her bag for her mobile and dials Mathias's number.

'I can hear birds,' Mim says when he answers. 'Are you out somewhere?'

'I'm sitting on the terrace reading,' he says.

'I wondered if you were free this evening to come over for a meal?' Mim asks.

'I'm free and I would love to. I've become very attached to your company.'

Mim, touched by the warmth in his voice, feels close to tears. 'And I yours,' she says somewhat awkwardly. 'Come as soon as it suits you. I've come to a sort of reckoning about the shop and I'd like to talk to you and Alice about it. So, it's to be a round table meeting as well as dinner.'

'Excellent,' he says. 'And why don't we order in? Uber Eats is very good or –'

'Uber Eats!' Mim exclaims. 'Who am I talking to? That's a bit, well, cool and modern, isn't it?'

'I am a very cool person,' Mathias says, laughing, 'though clearly I have very old-fashioned friends. When did you last have takeaway? No, don't bother to answer, it's probably years ago.'

*

Sitting on the verandah later that evening, there's a knock at the door and Mathias gets up to open it for the Uber driver.

'Your first Uber meal,' he says, carrying the food from a local Indian restaurant out to the verandah table and sorting out their separate orders. 'Welcome to 2020!'

'I can't remember when I last had takeaway,' Mim says. 'I had pizza once, I think – but it was a long time ago.'

'It just never occurs to me to order meals to be delivered,' Alice says. 'But I have to admit this looks good.' She closes her eyes and inhales. 'And it smells divine!'

Mathias watches them both with amusement. 'I can't believe that you single women don't do it regularly,' he says. 'It makes life so much easier.'

Mim and Alice exchange a knowing look across the table. 'Our mother would not have approved,' Alice explains. 'She thought it was a woman's duty to feed herself and her family – although she would occasionally break the rule for fish and chips.'

'This is delicious,' Mim says, tasting her butter chicken then patting her mouth with her serviette. 'If she were here, I suspect she would have changed her views by now, especially if she tasted this.'

There is a short silence while they tuck into the food, and then Alice says, 'I know we need to talk about the shop, Mim, but there's something I need to tell you first: I've booked a flight back to England for the end of the month.'

'Oh no, Al!' Mim says, putting down her glass. 'That's so soon!'

'I decided I couldn't afford to leave it too long, because none of us really knows what's going to happen with my application or with the COVID business. I looked online and it says that it can take up to a year for residency to be approved, so I think I should get started as soon as possible. I think I'll have to go for an interview too. There are simply so many unknowns, but I keep coming back to believing that this is the best way to do it. Go back and get started on it. Sort things out in the Oxford house while I wait. The sooner I do it the sooner I'll have an answer. Please don't be upset with me, Mim.'

'Oh, Al, of course I'm not upset; I'm just being selfish because I want you to stay. I'm going to miss you so much. I've loved having you here; I feel we've got to know each other so much better in these last couple of months.'

Alice grabs her sister's hand across the table. 'Thank you,' she says. 'I feel exactly the same. These last few months have been so special, and the best thing is that we're going to have lots more times like these ahead of us.'

Mathias is silent watching the two women, unwilling to involve himself in a matter that is essentially none of his business. As they talk, he gets up and takes the dishes to the kitchen, putting them in the dishwasher.

On his way here earlier, he had stopped at a bakery in South Fremantle and bought a strawberry tart. Now he puts it on a plate and takes a carton of ice cream from the fridge.

'What are you doing out there, Mathias?' Mim calls.

'I'm bringing you dessert,' he says.

'You are a saint,' Mim says, when he carries the tart out. 'Thank you. And now I guess we'd better talk about the shop.'

She tells them about her visit to Life Support, and her conversation with Doug. 'He's been doing a great job,' she says. 'The shop is looking better than it has for some time, and it feels so nice when you walk in from the street.' And she goes on to explain how she had struggled to create a spreadsheet and been forced to face the fact that she was no longer coping with aspects of the business that used to come easily.

Mathias watches how she twists her hands nervously, which he's come to recognise as an indication of anxiety or concern. 'That must have been very confronting, Mim,' he says. 'But bear in mind that it could be temporary; caused perhaps by your earlier exhaustion, combined with stress about the shop. So, don't read too much into this single incident. But you're right: you do need to consider stepping back a bit.'

'Doug can do my job,' Mim says. 'He's doing wonderfully well. And it occurred to me today that it would make sense to officially make him the manager, responsible for the day-to-day running of the business. And I would offer him a raise, of course. It's long overdue. But that means spending yet more money . . .'

Mathias leans forward and helps himself to ice cream. 'I have a suggestion,' he says. 'The shop needs an injection of money for those improvements of Doug's and, if you're going to reduce your hours, people power. Well, I would be happy to invest in it.'

'Me too,' Alice says. 'With a bit of extra capital, you could hire some more staff and just pop into the shop when you feel like it. Even if you're not there all the time, it will still always be your shop.'

He and Alice are watching Mim, who is gazing at her strawberry tart, lost in thought. Finally, she looks up.

'Thank you,' she says. 'I was so worried I might have to sell Life Support in order to save it. But this is a wonderful solution and a huge weight off my mind; I can't think of anyone I'd rather share my shop with than my beloved sister and my dearest friend.'

Chapter Thirty-eight

By the end of the month the threat of Coronavirus, known now as COVID-19, is sweeping the world and the global death toll has passed one thousand. In Australia, meanwhile, the federal government has announced a fourteen-day ban on non-citizens arriving from China.

'So, it's not too bad, really, is it?' Alice says as she packs her bag the night before her departure.

'But it's obviously going to get worse,' Mim says, trying not to sound as concerned as she feels. What she wants to say is, *Please don't go*, though she knows Alice really has no choice.

'Can we talk often, Mim?' Alice says. 'This has been so lovely. We found each other again and I don't want us to drift apart.'

'I was going to say the same to you. Once a week minimum. Preferably more.'

They hug each other and Mim tries to hide the fact that she is close to tears. 'Okay, I'm going to check on the food for this evening,' she says. 'Mathias will be here any minute with the champagne, so get a move on.'

She hurries off to the kitchen, where she turns on the oven to heat the mini sausage rolls and quiches. Afterwards, she slips out onto the verandah and leans against the wall, her hand over her mouth to repress her sobs. She has such a bad feeling about this, and she thinks Alice is far too cool about it all.

Mim wipes her eyes, clears her throat and heads for the bathroom to splash her face with water. *Perhaps I'm being ridiculous*, she thinks. *But I so want her to be safe.*

As she comes out of the bathroom, she hears Mathias's car draw up at the back of the house. Reluctant to let him and Alice see how stricken she is, Mim disappears into her room. A few minutes later she can hear him talking with Alice in the kitchen, though she can't make out what they are saying.

'Mathias is here, Mim!' Alice calls.

Mim checks her face in the mirror, decides that the redness around her eyes isn't too noticeable, then goes out to join them.

In the kitchen, Alice and Mathias are putting glasses on a tray and bottles into the fridge, and Mim hears Clare's voice. She and Alice have grown close in the preceding months so Alice was keen to see her and Andrew one last time before she left. And of course, Carla and Jodie would be arriving at any moment. To be honest, Mim would rather have had Alice to herself this evening, but at least the presence of so many people whom she'd grown to love and who loved her would certainly confirm for Alice that she had a family here who will be thinking of her when she is back in England.

So, don't be so damned selfish, Mim tells herself. *Get out there and give your sister a send-off she'll always remember.*

A few days later, when Alice is safely back in Oxford and they have chatted on the phone, Mim starts to feel a little better. Her journey had been uneventful, Alice reassured her, and she was ready to get started on sorting out her affairs ahead of her planned move to Australia.

Alice's reference to sorting reminds Mim that she still hasn't looked through her mother's diaries, which she'd put aside when she and Alice sorted through the contents of the suitcase Alice had brought over. So, on a cool, bright morning, she carries them out to the table on the verandah and with some difficulty – her mother's dating system is somewhat fluid and confusing – arranges them in chrono-logical order. Then she makes herself a cup of coffee, sits down and picks up the first one.

The diary was started soon after Mim was struck down by polio, and as she reads she finds herself being drawn back into her childhood, back to the small red-brick house with its neat garden, to the kitchen with its green lino-leum, the cream-coloured cupboards with matching green handles. The descriptions of the house and the ordinari-ness of their daily lives were, she realised, setting the scene for the day on the beach that would change their lives so dramatically.

John and I weren't all that keen on the beach, her mother wrote, *but Mim loved it so we promised to take her there for her birthday and stay as long as she wanted. That morning, I thought she seemed a bit feverish when she woke up, but it didn't seem to be bothering her. She was so excited, clutching her little blue bucket and spade, walking beside me as I pushed Alice in the pusher. At the beach we spread a blanket over the stones for both the girls to sit on while John and I sat nearby in deckchairs.*

Mim was enjoying herself so much! She started collecting stones and arranging them in patterns on the blanket. We had our picnic, and then John walked Mim down to the water's edge and they splashed about for a while, before John encouraged her to climb onto his back and he swam with her out to the deeper water. I think she felt that wonderful sense of excitement that has just a tiny sliver of fear in it. She was hanging on tight but squealing with delight.

Mim puts down the notebook and closes her eyes against the sun. She has vague memories of the day: the pebbles under her feet; the seagull that swooped and stole her sandwich; the walk with her father up to the pier to buy ice creams.

I got a bit worried about Mim being in the sun, her mother wrote. *She was getting rather red in the face, so we thought perhaps we should leave. John took Mim down to the water's edge one more time. She was so hot and sticky, and we thought it would help her to cool down before we got in the car. They were standing there, hand in hand, looking out to sea, when suddenly I saw Mim drop her bucket. She swayed a bit and then she just fell to the ground. John bent down to help her up, and that's when I realised that something was wrong, because he lifted her up into his arms and then he was running as fast as he could back up the beach to where I was sitting with Alice. Mim was unconscious when John put her in my lap, her little face all red, her hair damp with sweat. John ran up to the promenade to call for an ambulance. By the time we got to the hospital, I was frantic, sure that Mim was dying. All I could think was that they had to do whatever they could to save her, because I couldn't live without my darling girl.*

Mim has to stop reading again for a moment, as her eyes are blinded with tears. She leans back in her chair and stares out to sea until she feels calmer, then turns to her mother's description of the hospital, how Mim had regained consciousness, screaming with pain when the doctor touched her and tried to move her legs. How she tried to tear off the oxygen mask, and her agonising cries of fear as the doctor approached her with his needles.

John took Alice home to his parents, who lived nearby in Hove, then he came back to the hospital and we waited for another, more senior doctor to tell us what was wrong with Mim. I had already guessed what it was, of course, but when he actually said the words – 'Your daughter has poliomyelitis' – I heard myself screaming like a madwoman. I felt my heart was being torn from my chest. My sweet and beautiful Mim. It was a mother's worst fear. Ever since Mim was born I had imagined the different stages of her life, from starting school to her first dance, marrying a nice boy and settling down nearby. But would any of that be possible for her now? Would she have any future beyond agonising pain and disablement? Her lungs might be compromised, I heard the doctor saying, and then he described the treatment at a special hospital for children with polio. I had heard talk about the iron lung before; it sounded like a form of torture, having to lie immobile for months on end.

John and I went in the ambulance with Mim to Harold House and watched as she was wheeled away on a stretcher to the isolation ward, calling to us pitifully. It was the worst moment of my life.

Mim can't bear it. She puts the notebook down again, gets up and walks to the edge of the verandah. Trump is perched on the rail, his beady eyes fixed on her.

'Go away!' she shouts as the tears run down her face. 'Go! Go!' And with an angry squawk, he takes off out towards the sea.

Mim gazes after him, thinking of her mother, the terror she must have felt at the diagnosis, how hopeless and helpless. It strikes her now that she had never given much thought to what her parents must have suffered that day. Perhaps she would have considered it earlier had she had children of her own, but she had thought only of her own fear and trauma. Eventually Mim returns to her chair and picks up the diary with a sigh. Does she really want to read on?

There is so much more. Her mother's despair during those visits to the hospital, never being allowed to see her daughter face to face, to hold her and comfort her. It's hard to read, and Mim finds herself skimming the pages, a reluctant witness to her mother's pain, until her eye is caught by a page with only three words written in capitals in bright red crayon: *MIM'S COMING HOME!*

Mim takes off her reading glasses, polishes them with a tissue, puts them back on and begins to read.

I was so excited the day we went to collect Mim to bring her home. She was a bit standoffish with us at first, as though we were strangers, but as we pushed her around the hospital grounds in a wheelchair while we waited to see the doctor who would be discharging her she seemed to relax. John and I were so excited, but she had been away for such a long time that I suppose it must have been a big upheaval for her. She didn't know what to expect and, as it turned out, neither did we. Finally the doctor and the matron were ready for us, and one of the nurses looked after Mim while we were led into the office.

They told us what a good patient Mim had been and assured us that she had made an excellent recovery.

John and I thanked them, and I said how lovely it would be to have her at home with us; we had missed her so much, I said, that I was afraid we might be in danger of spoiling her a little!

Well, the doctor became very gruff at that. 'It's important to minimise the nature of the disease on the child in the way you treat her and speak to her,' he said. 'She should not be made to feel important or special in any way, and you should not let her get away with anything you would not accept if she were well. The child should not feel special, nor be given any special treatment.' To cut a long story short, the doctor said that if we wanted Mim to recover psychologically as well as physically, we should avoid turning her into a permanent invalid. It sounded terribly hard to me – surely after everything she had been through she deserved a bit of special treatment! But the doctor was adamant, and the matron, too.

'And people can be offended by the disease,' the doctor went on, and wouldn't know how to treat her. To avoid any awkwardness, he recommended that we confine her to her room when we had *visitors in the house so that she was not exposed to people who might be offended by her. Offended by a sick little girl! I was so angry that I just got up and walked out and left John to finish the meeting on his own. Mim was out in the corridor with the nurse. She looked a little anxious and confused, but was clearly happy to be coming home. Apart from those awful braces on her legs, she looked really quite healthy – just like my darling Mim. Finally John emerged from the office and at last – after three long years – we were able to take our daughter home. I was still furious about what the doctor had said – and what made me even more furious was that John agreed with him!*

'The doctor knows best,' he insisted. 'He's got more experience than we do in this matter. All he's saying is that we shouldn't let Mim see other people in case it upsets or worries them.'

I'm afraid I raised my voice at him. 'I will not do that to Mim,' I said. 'I will not behave as though I'm ashamed of her because I'm not. I'm proud of her and I will not have her treated as an outcast.'

She has reached the final page of her mother's first diary. Mim puts the notebook down and wipes her eyes. She had always thought that the polio was hers and hers alone to suffer, but now she is starting to see that it affected her whole family. She looks at the pile of other diaries and notebooks. She is torn between wanting to read them and wanting to pretend they don't exist. *Perhaps I'll wait until Alice comes back and read them with her,* she thinks.

And she gets up and goes back into the house, feeling suddenly exhausted and needing to lie down. She drops onto the bed and closes her eyes, feeling the mattress sag as Brenda jumps up beside her. Mim thinks of her mother, how fiercely she had tried to protect her daughter, the loneliness she must have felt when her husband failed to support her. She wishes she'd known this while her mother was still alive, wishes that they had talked about it and that Mim had been able to tell her how much she loved and appreciated her. How she had made her daughter strong and able to cope with whatever life threw at her.

Chapter Thirty-nine

Mathias and Carla set out to view a house in South Fremantle, but one look at the outside makes them decide against going in.

'It has no character,' Mathias says irritably. 'These modern houses are like boxes. Look – the one next to it is exactly the same.'

'I know, Papa,' Carla says with a sigh. It is a familiar complaint. 'I know you want a place with a special sort of feel to it. We should probably stop bothering with newly built places. Let's go and have a coffee at Gino's.'

As she drives the short distance into town and searches for a parking space, Mathias flicks through the brochures of houses for sale that he had collected from real estate agents and the pages he had clipped from the weekend papers. In the end he throws them all onto the back seat of the car.

'I like old places,' he says, for what Carla thinks must be at least the hundredth time. She rolls her eyes inwardly.

'Has Mim heard from Alice recently?' she asks, to distract him.

'I know they spoke on the weekend, because I was there, and I spoke to Alice myself. She's feeling a bit over-whelmed, I think. Even if she does manage to sort out her visa and the house, if the Australian government closes the borders she won't be able to come. But she said that having made the decision to move has made her feel optimistic about the future, so if she has to wait a little longer than anticipated she will just have to bear it patiently.'

'What a great attitude she has,' Carla says. 'And how is Mim doing? I must pop around and see her.'

'She's been having a rather difficult time herself,' Mathias replies. 'She's been reading her mother's jour-nals from the years when Mim contracted polio and was isolated in hospital. It's been quite eye-opening, I think. She grew up thinking her parents were ashamed of her, that they'd left her in the hospital for such a long time because they didn't want her at home, and that they kept her from meeting visitors to the family home because they were embarrassed by her disability. She was told never to complain and never to ask for help – it certainly explains why she finds it so difficult to accept help now. But it turns out that her parents were acting on the advice of doctors. She has been carrying her private shame for all these years when there was really no reason for it.'

Carla glances over at him. 'So, you two have even more in common than you realised?'

'Indeed,' says Mathias. 'Perhaps Mim and I will be trying to overcome the hurts of the past for some time to come. The relief is enormous, but the wounds we suffered informed the patterns of a lifetime – two long lifetimes; they're ingrained by now and that will be hard to change.' He smiles ruefully. 'It does explain why we became friends so quickly. We seemed to understand things about each other without having to articulate them. And knowing her made it possible for me to finally talk about the past. I'm hoping that I can help her the way she helped me. And I think the task is easier for me now because her mother's notebooks have already unlocked the door.'

Their conversation is interrupted by Mathias's phone. 'Oh, there's Mim now,' he says, looking at the screen. 'Do you mind if I answer it?'

'Of course not,' says Carla.

The conversation is brief, and when Mathias hangs up he says, 'Would you mind dropping me at Mim's house when we've had our coffee? She says she has something to show me.'

'Don't you think it's sad,' Carla says to Jodie when she arrives home, having dropped off Mathias, 'how Papa and Mim had to grow up carrying so much shame, when it could have been avoided if only those around them had been less concerned by what others thought?'

'I do,' Jodie says. 'I guess we all have things that make us feel shame, but we live in a more open and tolerant society than when they were young, and we're more prepared to talk about things that were taboo in our parents' days.'

'Like being two weird dykes,' Carla says, laughing.

'Exactly like that,' Jodie says. 'Now come here and give me a hug.'

*

After waving Carla off at the bottom of Mim's driveway, Mathias walks around to the back door to find it open. There is no answer when he calls out from the threshold, so he walks straight in. There are no signs of life inside either. It's only when he goes out onto the verandah and calls out to her again that Mim responds.

'Down here,' she says from the bottom of the garden. 'Use the side steps.'

Mathias can't actually see Mim, as the garden is very overgrown, but her voice seems to be coming from behind a cluster of trees.

'Are you all right?' he asks, concerned that she may have tripped and fallen.

'I'm fine,' Mim replies. 'Just come and join me.'

He obeys, walking down the steps that curve to a lower level of the garden.

'I've never been down here before,' he says as he approaches. 'It's lovely and rather mysterious.' And as he stops speaking, he sees that the stone wall he'd thought was the property's boundary wall is actually the side of a small building, and Mim is standing in the doorway.

'Come on in,' she says. 'I think you'll like it.'

'Is this yours?' Mathias asks, walking in.

The structure is larger inside than it appears from the outside. It has three solid walls of York stone, and one completely made of glass, with a glass door to a paved terrace.

'Oh, this is beautiful!' he says, feeling the coolness of the stone hidden among the trees. 'That view! It's even better than the one from the verandah. I had no idea there was a little cottage out here. Is it yours?'

'It is mine,' Mim says. 'Though I can't remember when I last came down here. When I first bought the house, I had all sorts of plans for it, but of course they never eventuated. What do you think of it?'

'I love it,' Mathias says. 'It's beautiful. The dappled light from the window, and that beautiful arched window over there. Perfect. And where does this lead?' Mathias asks, indicating a wooden door to his left.

'A small bathroom,' Mim says. 'Basin, toilet and shower. Have a look.'

'What a wonderful place,' he says. 'Have you really never used it? What a waste. You must do something with it. Have you got any ideas?'

'I have actually,' Mim says. 'That's what I wanted to talk to you about.'

'I'd be delighted to help in any way I can,' he says. 'I did quite a lot of renovating of the Monbulk house myself. I can lay bricks, sand floors, paint – whatever you want.'

'What I had in mind involves a bit more than repairs to the studio,' she says as he sits down beside her on the old wooden bench just outside the door.

'So, let me say what I want to say and don't interrupt. Then you might want to take time to think about it before you make a decision.'

'Okay,' he says.

'I want you to consider coming here to live with me.

I think we might be able to share the house without driving each other mad – after all, we're both pretty quiet, and being solitary kind of people, I know we would respect each other's space. You could have the bedroom Alice was staying in; like mine, it has its own bathroom. We could share the living space, and that would leave us with a spare bedroom for visitors. As for this studio, I thought with a bit of work we could make it your writing space. It would belong to you alone, and I would never enter unless invited. It just seemed to me that it might work out well for both of us, and the thing is . . . I feel very close to you.' She turns her head to look at him. 'So, that's what I wanted to say. You can take all the time you need to think about it, of course. And whatever you decide, it won't affect our friendship.'

Mathias's heart seems to be pounding very fast in his chest, and he knows he doesn't need any time at all to make his decision. He moves closer to Mim and puts his arm around her shoulders. She is tense and stiff initially, but then he feels her relax and lean into him.

'Mim,' he says, 'I would love to live here with you and write in this beautiful studio,' he says.

'But don't you need time to think about it?'

Mathias smiles. 'I have been thinking about it. I kept looking at houses, hoping to find a place where I might persuade you to live with me.'

'Really?'

'Really! The trouble was that this house was tough competition. I never saw anywhere that I thought you would consider leaving here for. I love you, Mim, and

I hope that you may come to love me. So yes, again and again . . .'

'Could you stop talking and give me a hug, please,' Mim says. 'I love you too, Mathias, and it's so different from anything I've felt before. It feels comfortable and natural and entirely appropriate. What do you think the girls will say?'

'I think they'll be delighted for us,' he says. 'But what about Alice?'

'Oh, Alice will be happy for us, I'm sure of that. She used to tease me about you, but I made her stop because I would have been mortified if you knew I had feelings for you.'

They sit in silence for a moment, relishing the reality of what is happening.

'What do we do next?' Mim asks. 'How do we start on this?'

'I think we have started already,' Mathias says. And he takes her hand and together they walk back up the path to the house.

*

Much later that night, Mim walks out onto the verandah and sits in her favourite chair. Brenda follows her and flops down onto the blanket where she sometimes chooses to sleep in the warmer weather. It's a perfectly still night, with hardly even a rustle of leaves to disturb the stillness. Beyond the trees, the ocean gleams in the light of an almost full moon.

Mim sighs and rests her head on the back of the chair. In the course of one day, she has taken a radical step, one she had thought she would never make, not since Derek died. There will be adjustments, of course. Both she and Mathias will have to learn to live with another person after being alone so long. She'd thought the prospect of such a big change might make her feel anxious, but in fact she feels peaceful and content.

Earlier they had called Carla and Jodie and suggested they meet for dinner in Fremantle. Mathias had broken their news as the first drinks were poured, and the look of delight on both their faces had brought tears to Mim's eyes.

'About time!' Carla said, kissing her father and then Mim. 'I thought you were never going to get there.'

And Jodie, surprisingly, burst into tears, and hugged Mim so hard she almost couldn't breathe.

Later, they'd called Alice, who said it was long overdue and she was over the moon.

So, there it is, Mim thinks now. So easy. Set in stone practically. She thinks back to her final day in Brighton the year before, when she was about to embark on her journey home. It had been a very hot day and she had stood on the balcony of her hotel room and stared out at the old West Pier. She had known that pier since her early childhood, and had watched as, over the years, it had been battered by storms, burned by fires and eroded by the constant movement of the sea. Now only the skeleton remains, yet it seemed to Mim to have been made more beautiful by the scars of its afflictions and the passage of time. She remembers thinking how good it would be if people could be transformed like that, their hard edges smoothed with age, enriched by their pasts and attaining a measure of dignity and peace. And what about the past? Suppose she and Mathias had met as teenagers all those years ago in Brussels. Suppose they had talked and flirted cautiously, testing the waters of attraction. Where would they be now? Have they missed out on a lifetime together, or would their connection have ended up as ashes decades ago? They will just never know. She had never imagined that it could happen to her, but she knows now that love, trust and forgiveness have brought her the calm and contentment she craved. She had shied away from love because she felt herself unlovable, but now she is whole and peaceful at last.

Acknowledgements

In 1958, when I was fourteen, my mother took me to the Brussels Exhibition. It was an extraordinary experience – a spotlight on the future which I have never forgotten. We travelled to Brussels by boat and train with my mother's friend and her thirteen-year-old daughter who been discharged from hospital where she had spent three years battling polio. Consequently, Expo and polio have always been linked in my mind, and my memories were revived by reading Johnathon Coe's novel, *Expo 58*, which so entertainingly recreates that moment in history. I wanted to learn more about the exhibition and about polio and I am indebted to my dear friend Rev. Dr John Smith for talking with me about his experience of childhood polio and, more recently, post-polio syndrome, and for providing me with access to his PhD thesis, the details of which are listed below.

While writing this book I had a stroke which took its toll on my progress and messed with my brain in very confusing ways. My publisher, Cate Paterson, is a legend, and without her patience and support I would probably have given up on trying to finish the book. Thank you for your faith and patience, Cate. Thank you Georgia Douglas, for a dazzling first edit which made it clear that you knew more about what I was trying to do than I did! Brianne Collins and Ali Lavau, thank you both so much for your contributions which have made this a much better book than it would otherwise have been. As always there are many people who are involved in getting a book out of the claws of the author and into the world. So, my thanks are due to the consistently kind, thoughtful and efficient staff of Pan Macmillan, as well as to my agent Jane Novak.

Finally, a big thank you to my family and friends who have supported me in so many ways – you are simply the best. I am grateful for your love, concern, patience and good humour.

Sources of Information:
Coe, Johnathon, *Expo 58*. Penguin, London, UK, 2013.
Rydell, Robert W., *World of Fairs: The Century-of-Progress Exhibitions*. University of Chicago Press, Chicago, USA, 1993.
Smith, John H, Fear, *Frustration and the Will to Overcome: A Social History of Poliomyelitis in Western Australia*, Doctor of Philosophy by research (History) Edith Cowan University. Unpublished thesis: Call # 378.244 SMI. Edith Cowan University, December 1997, Faculty of Arts, Department of Social and Cultural Studies (Awarded 2000).

MORE BESTSELLING FICTION FROM PAN MACMILLAN

A Month of Sundays
Liz Byrski

For over ten years, Ros, Adele, Judy and Simone have been in an online book club, but they have never met face to face. Until now . . .

Determined to enjoy her imminent retirement, Adele invites her fellow bibliophiles to help her house-sit in the Blue Mountains. Each member has been asked to bring a book which will teach the others more about her. With the women all facing crossroads in their lives, it turns out there's a lot for them to learn, not just about their fellow book-clubbers, but about themselves.

'[Liz Byrski] writes with warmth, insight and gentle humour about ordinary, flawed characters grappling with relevant, real-life issues.' *Courier Mail*

'Byrski . . . is by turns turbulent and tender. Her characters are portrayed as . . . warm, funny, flawed heroes and heroines grappling with the cards destiny has dealt them.' *West Australian*

'[*A Month of Sundays*] demonstrated the capacity of a book to act as a mirror to the soul and an eloquent guide to a more contented future. Executed with wit and affection, the novel delivers exactly what it promises.' *Weekend Australian*

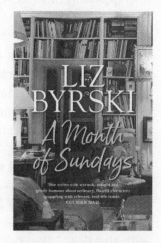

The Woman Next Door
Liz Byrski

Over the years, the residents of Emerald Street have become more than just neighbours, they have built lasting friendships over a drink and chat on their back verandahs.

Now a new chapter begins with the children having left home.

Helen and Dennis have moved from their high maintenance family property to an apartment by the river with all the mod cons. For Joyce and Mac, the empty nest has Joyce craving a new challenge, while Mac fancies retirement on the south coast.

Meanwhile, Polly embarks on a surprising long-distance relationship. But she worries about her friend next door. Stella's erratic behaviour is starting to resemble something much more serious than endearing eccentricity . . .

With her trademark warmth and wisdom, Liz Byrski involves us in the lives and loves of Emerald Street, and reminds us what it is to be truly neighbourly.

'Liz Byrski has a guaranteed cheer squad for her novels which champion . . . women taking charge of their life and growing old creatively.' *Daily Telegraph*

'Byrski . . . is by turns turbulent and tender. Her characters are protrayed as . . . warm, funny, flawed heroes and heroines grappling with the cards destiny has dealt them . . . Byrski here unflinchingly looks age and illness in the face. And what does she see there? Acceptance, yes; but also possibility, continuity and renewal. We all get old. Get over it. And grow with the flow.' *West Australian*

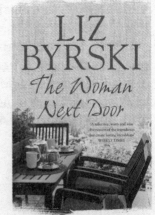